Mor

HIGHWAY TRADE

"In a foggy valley brimming with everything right and wrong about our country, Domini's characters waver between generosity and good old-fashioned American self-interest, between solidity and oblivion. Domini's is an urgent voice, edgy wild, important."

— Tracy Daugherty

"John Domini writes wryly and confidently of a fascinating contemporary counterculture inhabited by a cast of unusual 'outlaws' living in the evocative landscape of the Northwest, fighting to preserve their dignity, sanity, and passion in a world going rapidly mad around them."

—Janice Eidus,
author of *The Celibacy Club*

"*Highway Trade* features compelling stories about ordinary people in Oregon's lush Willamette Valley. As in Bernard Malamud's classic work, many of the characters have sojourned west for 'A New Life'. Here are people readers must recognize—the video store manager, rookie newspaper photographer, paranoid pot grower. John Domini carefully portrays their work and wisdom, dignity and despair."

—Craig Lesley

HIGHWAY TRADE

SHORT STORIES

AND

A NOVELLA

JOHN DOMINI

Red Hen Press

1998

Highway Trade

The stories in this book have first appeared in the following magazines and anthologies: *Agni*, "Senior Transfer"; *Anyone Is Possible*, "Minimum Bid"; *Black Warrior Review*, "The Arno Line"; *Confrontation*, "Eastertime Fogs" and "Second Trimester"; *Indiana Review*, "Hot"; *Southwest Review*, "Highway Trade" and "Three Dreams of Europe"; *Witness*, "Period Sets" and "The Rules of Dancing"; *Threepenny Review*, "Field Burning".

The author wishes to thank the Ingram Merrill Foundation for its generous support during the writing of this book.

Cover art by Giselle Gautreau
Author photo by Godlis
Book design by Mark E. Cull

First Edition
ISBN 1-888996-07-2
Library of Congress Catalog Card Number 97-76241

Red Hen Press

Valentine Publishing Group
P.O. Box 902582
Palmdale, California 93590-2582

This one has to be for Vera

Contents

The incredible postwar American electro-pastel surge into the suburbs! — it was sweeping the Valley. . . .

— Tom Wolfe,
The Electric Kool-Aid Acid Test

The Rules of Dancing

GILLARD'S PLAYING with my daughter on the park swing set. I just got here. Humming my Sunday blues, wagging my horn case in rhythm—and there they are. If the rosebushes hadn't been so ugly, January ugly, I might have walked right into the man. I do like those roses. As it is, the best I can manage is stumbling to a halt. And then my first thought has nothing to do with getting out of there. Instead I'm looking those two over, and I'm thinking: at least he's got the girl in the right swing. Carrie's not two yet. She still has to be fitted as deep as she'll go into the smallest swing, the middle one of the three on the park set. It's made from a tire, this smallest swing, but it's not like your classic down-home tire-swing. This is a tire cut and hung like a crescent moon. Instead of fitting her feet through a center-hole and leaving her back unprotected, Gillard has settled Carrie inside the black rubber U where the inner tube used to be. Her feet stick out the front of the crescent and her back is cradled by the rest. I wouldn't even know it was my daughter in there, if that weren't positively Gillard with her. There's only one cowboy that big with "WILLARD" crimped in tin across the back of his belt.

But give the man credit, he's making it fun. He squats in front of the girl. He's there partly so he can catch her if she gets too crazy of course, but mostly so she can feel as if she's the one running the show. On something like every third forward swing, he'll puff up his chest, she'll stiff out her feet. "Annnnd, *boom!*" Plus Gillard's so wiry. Even back before the sauce had turned me into such a lard-belly, back a year ago or so when I first taught the girl the game— even then I don't think I could have popped up after each kick as fast as old Willy Gilly.

1

Then finally I've got my brains again, I'm backing off. When I go out on a Sunday I've got my horn and my Jack Daniel's, which these days I'll put in a Diet Coke can. That's not too much to keep quiet.

Before making any major move, I hug up the case in both arms, pinning the can to it with both hands. Don't take my eyes from those two at the swing set for more than a look-see left-right. Makes things a little pinchy inside my coat, my old Chesterfield, and with the lapel right in my face I can smell last night's smoke. Of course I also have to get a thumb over the opening at the top of the Diet Coke. Then with everything held up tight like that I break sideways. Backwards and sideways, when earlier all I got was maybe one glance at the bench where I figured it'd be safe. So naturally I end up going straight into one of the damn rosebushes. I clip off a dead New Year's bud or two, break a few soggy thorns with my knuckles. One shoelace catches on something and next thing I know I've got to drag that foot. But Carrie goes on squealing, and Gillard keeps up his patter. I keep on telling myself that it's an honest mistake, coming here, since there aren't that many parks in this part of Eugene anyway and the ones down by the Willamette are nothing but lowlife.

Eventually I make it over to my bench. Clouseau'd my way through things as usual. I'd been planning to set up on the pavilion, off the other side of the swing set. But the afternoon's on the sunny side anyway. The clouds have knuckles, but so far they're holding off from real trouble.

And as soon as I get a decent mouthful from my Diet Coke I can do a little damage control: it's okay, it's okay. Yes this has got to be a mistake. No way I went out looking for my daughter and my wife's new man. On my Sunday blow I try and keep my mind blank to that kind of situation altogether. Of course it's not like word doesn't get around; it's not like either me or my ex has no idea what the other one does on a weekend. Granted. But soon as I get my mouthful and open the case on my knees, I can feel what I'm really out for.

I mean, I've been blowing on Sunday ever since I started doing gigs on Saturday. Going on twenty years now. I've found an opening about one-thirty, two o'clock, when church or brunch is done with and I'm also out of synch with the serious joggers. Everybody's deep into whatever their home thing is. But with me it gets way too intense for home. Like now I've got this couple in the apartment upstairs, all their natter-natter and jumping around. I need it cleaner than that. I need to be sure I'll catch the moment when I should put aside the Diet Coke—though I do love these sassy gold ones, the caffeine-free—and concentrate on my saxophone. There are things you can discover in a more picky and useful way, like knowing when to lift the bridge from one song and take it to another. But you might also get a whole different kind of satisfaction, just making a lot of noise out there. Or then again from time to time you'll understand that all you honestly have to do is oil a few keys till they're quiet again, after which if you hold one of the stoppers open and get the horn up at the right angle you can see some reflections, you can see the trees, or the pavilion itself or some people here and there, and there are moments when you can even find the roses and a couple of the park playthings, all caught and bent a little in that single clean golden stopper's circle not much bigger than a bottle cap. After that of course I'll play.

Except as soon as I start to put the horn together, I can see there's another problem. If I play, Gillard will hear me.

So much for trying to get into my ready groove. I screw the top back on the cork grease. Set the Diet Coke to one side of the bench, the horn (I mean the pieces, halfway there across the velveteen fittings in the case) to the other. Then it's round and up onto my knees so I can check out the situation on the swings. I'm so flabby now that the most comfortable I can get is by resting my gut on the topmost rail of the bench. But through the skeletons of the rosebushes I can make out Gillard's back, Carrie's feet. They're still at it, swingtime boogie. She gets him a good one while I'm watching, bang in the chest hard enough to make him whoop like a smoker. Plus there's the bouncy-animals next to the swing-set, the lion and mustang and dolphin all fixed on springs. Just past them's the slide. Most likely the little girl's planning on staying a while; I used to start on the swings too. And like I say word gets around, I know what my ex is saying about me these days. I know that one way or another I'd come out hurting if Gillard heard me play.

My wife after all was a woman who towards the end would say of my horn: "Let's take it to New York." She'd say: "Let's take the damn fishhook to *L.A.*, why don't we?" Granted, she might have looked angrier than she was. She's got these very fine lines, the kind of tight-knit hips and shoulders I always think of when I think of Western women. She could glare like if you kissed her, you'd cut yourself on her cheekbones. And granted, also, I was no help. How much of my take on the weekends wound up going to the bar tab? But there are rules nonetheless. A person can't go round saying she wants a kid, saying it would be so exciting to have a *kid*, so I'm thinking of like a hokey Christmas card with the whole family in a paper moon or something—and then as soon as the first one's born she turns around and starts talking about L.A.? A person can't do that. The woman was from Cottage Grove, just down the highway here, after all. Very small town, very kids-and-family. She should have known what she was getting into.

So now I'm back facing front, sitting on the bench like a normal person. But my next hit of Diet Coke is much too heavy; it floods the sinuses. After that it's straight to the cork grease and the rest of the horn. I even put the reed in my mouth so I won't be tempted.

I mean it's not like it's never occurred to me, sitting here thinking, that I could just skip it today. Am I no good at all without my Sunday blow? It's not like it's never occurred to me, I could just keep on socking back my sassy golden can of goods till I didn't hear the girl squealing any more. I spent a day like that recently. A Monday not a Sunday, after the last call from my lawyer about custody. Tuesday was just as bad, yeah. And when I showed up at the record store on Wednesday they sent me home. The best I could manage in fact was making my gig for the weekend. Though the people at Lunar Attraction Records & Tapes, some very good people there, they gave me back my stool. They said anybody can fall off it once.

The reed might be soaked enough by now. But I keep it there, taking my time with the chamois. I can see one or two spots that could be a little smoky after last night, but honestly, in this sunshine the horn looks so righteous that I believe I'd polish it even if I didn't want to keep my hands busy. My Selmer Mark VI. And seeing my face reflected in the bend of the hook—my beret's a black rubber band, just barely holding together the fat red bag of beard and mustache—that settles me some more. You know I am the kind of person, the story's been told a thousand times. Just another white boy in love with the blues. From Boston; everybody knows how that one goes.

When I was at the university here (Eugene was the hippie dream, right?) sometimes at gigs I did a goof on that, on the kind of thing everybody knows. I called it the "Rules of Dancing." Strictly a goof. But it worked, it got the crowd in the necessary groove, because everybody recognized exactly the stuff I was talking about. I would say like, do you people remember those dances with names? The Swim or whatever? Well for five years there, any dance with a name was no longer allowed. I'd say like, if you were over sixteen, dancing with members of your own sex was no longer allowed—not in this bar anyway. Or unless you were a gold miner in an old Western movie. Those B-movie miners, right? With the fiddle and the concertina? All they could do was clomp around, clomp and fidget, and they didn't *have* anybody for partners except some other old stinking little wizened clomping miner.

Now I'm chuckling to myself. I've fit the reed into the holder, which means I can have a little more Diet Coke. But while I'm sipping, just sipping, I start to hear some things. Off to my left there's the clatter-rasp of a bike chain running on after a kid hits the brakes. And in the other direction, somebody's mother is giving orders: "*Hurry* dear, we've got to *hurry.*"

Oh. I should have expected this, the sun out so early in the New Year and all. But I'm blinking, surprised. My mouth still mostly dry. That sharp talk to my right turns out to be a Mommy/Daddy/ Baby, the whole unit layered in Gore-Tex and polo shirts. As near as I can tell, the poor kid had to hurry just so they could all stop and look over the park plaque together. I can't be sure, because—when did all this happen? There's a lot more clip-clop out on the sidewalk than I remember, and there's squealing behind me that isn't Carrie. I can't be sure which family I heard, while I was sitting here trying to think how I got here. Only, the baby frowning at the plaque looks hard to budge. And the clatter to my left was definitely a bike. Over that way, four of them have pulled up. Your basic subteen flyboys. They've gathered in front of the dead fountain, the glum civic granite, so their day-glo handlebar grips and the lightning on their chain guards appear even spacier than usual. They're giving me an awfully steady look.

But by now I've caught up to it, I just smile back. Hey brother. I don't mind the turnout, in fact. I might like to start my time outside at an empty hour, but I realize, this isn't Death Valley. In fact I count on drop-ins. I'm after something that isn't just doing another set, sure, but that isn't being alone either. And the crowd in the parks is always so different from the one in the clubs. Love to see those churchgoing clothes, so much clean natural fiber, when I catch a reflection in my raised stopper. Not to mention how it feels to get an entirely new set of faces lined up and bobbing. Talk about an old story, I'm hooked on my Sunday blow. Except today, with Carrie here—

Damage control, damage control. Would I rather not have the girl around? Would I rather not see her at all? Damage control *report*.

The thought sticks, it's got claws. If I hit the Coke I won't stop. The horn goes back down on the case, I go back up on my knees, and then I start looking truly silly. Craning my neck and worrying about whether the bench is going to fall.

It's the people in the way, plus now there are kids to either side of that fishhook swing for the toddlers. And one of those kids, uh-oh. One of them is being pushed by an outstanding blonde number. Such a sweet-face young mom or babysitter, she's got to be the exception to my Sunday-afternoon rule. She's got to be a club type out of her element. I can see her earrings wink from here. I would imagine Gillard's already cooled it on the kick-flop business, judging from how my daughter's changed pitch. But I can't tell for sure. Between us this granny-looking woman keeps whirling back and forth. I mean in a scarf and a shawl and an ankle-length dress, whirling and waving round a bubble wand. A real Eugeney arts-and-craftser. But it's obvious that the two or three youngsters trailing along just love her jive. A couple times now, one little boy's even jumped and tried to catch a bubble in his mouth. So I can't be sure about old Willy Gilly. Of course I hate him, I expect him to do dirty. But then again in this kind of crowd I feel like just as bad a hard case, myself.

Up on my knees this way, I can't see the Mommy/Daddy/Baby sliding past. But I know what I smell like, and those claws in my head haven't let up. I figure Daddy's got his fist clamped tight around his spare change.

On Sundays, if I don't get to have my blow, I feel like the lizard in the flower bed. Gillard, nothing; it started way before that. The worst time—I mean, I felt like I didn't even deserve to be kept around—was just after the baby came. We were renting one of the professor's houses here. No question a heavyweight house. But did that mean that, every time we brought somebody over, we had to drag them through the whole scene from the cellar to the roof-deck? Wow, would you look at that gold-fleck in the dining room. Hey, check out the scrollwork on the fireplace, that's *real brass*. There were times I wanted to scream: This is somebody else's house! I wanted to shake all over and holler: This is a *sabbatical* house! But then I'd notice my wife's smile, or I'd see her lift the baby so the little girl could point out a light fixture. After that there'd be no screaming. I'd just trail behind, yumming and cooing with the others. Feeling like the meanest lizard in the whole green and peaceable Willamette Valley. Like just the most shameful thing that ever tried to get along on two legs.

My feet are getting cold, I'm spending too much time on my knees. And anyway it's looking like my decision will be made for me.

There's something of a crowd by the swings now, and Carrie's in the middle of it. She's got Gillard by the leg, complaining that he's stopped playing. Oh, but he's still at it. He's got some people there grinning just to watch him make his move. I can just see him cock his hips, before that old woman waving her wand drifts by again. That girl could be jailbait, Gillard. Then one way or another he'll take Carrie off, getting coffee or avoiding further embarrassment. And I'll just let the rest of the day go dark.

What did I expect, coming here? Word gets around. Just last night at the club, one of the waitresses was talking about Gillard and my ex.

I should have figured she'd go for the same trouble twice. I mean, what's the difference between Gillard and me, exactly? No question I've been every kind of disappointment to women. In the case of my ex, when she first started showing up at the clubs, I had the nerve to say I *wanted* to be rehabilitated. Where'd I get such nerve? The truth is, when I start to play—like now, I figure I can't just let the keys go cold—I'm following some impulse or line out there that's a lot cleaner than I'll ever be, so that while some woman who's watching me or somebody else standing back from the dance floor might believe I've got the whole crowd blooded up and jumping all for me, the truth is, just the opposite, I'm the most hooked person in the place. The story's been told a thousand times. But it's not like we aren't all of us carried along, carried along helpless except for the damage control. It's not like, if tomorrow I should see my ex give me that gypsy smile, I wouldn't start right in thinking about how I might drop a few pounds and stand up straighter when I play. I'm certainly up straight now, off the park bench. I'm doing "The Moon Got In My Eyes," a little intense but nonetheless a pleasure. And there are some bad feelings in there still. There are some thoughts that don't belong, like a memory of the first time we took Gillard bowling. He hit two strikes, and then after the third he turned to my wife and said, a real nasty deadpan, "You probably have new respect for me now. You probably see me with new eyes." Some joke. But I know that if I keep blowing even the nastiest stuff will clear out for a while. For a while I'll be where I like to be, swinging on a star, only the lamest idea of good or bad or where I fit in there but happy to live with that anyway.

Gillard's trying to think. The others over there too, that arts-and-crafts witch-woman seems to be gone but I can make out some other faces. I'm up by the rosebushes, I can see their looks changing. Of course it's hard to keep up the volume when he grabs Carrie's arm. She'd been pointing, starting to head my way, and it's hard to work with how my lungs clutch. But I can face her now. I can keep on blowing even when one of the day-glo biker boys whips by the bench, impossible to miss, and snatches up my Diet Coke one-handed and whooping.

Senior Transfer

ROBIN COULDN'T stay on her feet. She and her father weren't ten minutes off the hiking trail, and for the third time she was down in the undergrowth. The vines and creepers got under her Gore-Tex. Robin came up with her machete. She laid into the brush around her, whip whip whip, till she wore herself out against her pack-straps.

Her father turned, drawn up to full height for the first time since they'd left the truck. He had the heavier pack. He wore the real camouflage, greasy jungle-issue synthetics, rain gear older than Robin herself. Dale looked every long inch the renegade. Deliberately he tasted his cigarette. Her own coat was burgundy, a catalogue item, and under its sleeves she itched from the wet touch of the plants.

"I know, I know," she said. "We're not supposed to leave tracks."

"Do you want to quit?" her father said. "In two hours we could be back in front of the VCR."

Around her the cut branches dangled by their winter skins, their exposed pulp like new stars sewn into the drizzle. This was a designated Wilderness Area, above the Willamette River valley. The timber here had gone so long unharvested that there were stretches of primary forest, easy travelling. But Robin and Dale had to stick with the ground cover. They had to think about the county sheriff, the men who'd like to find her father's crop. Dale grew high-grade marijuana in these hills. He'd warned Robin, this wouldn't be like one of her senior-class hikes. No trails, no creek beds, and up at the "hole" they'd have to do the planting. So early in the year, putting in the seeds was bound to be ugly. Only after that—only if it was safe—could her father show her where he'd hid the money. The cash was sealed in a coffee can, buried and camouflaged.

"I want to go on," Robin said. "I want to see."

"Well, I'm not insisting." Under his hood he softened, grinning. "I'm not forcing you."

"Dale, I want to." She worked the machete into its sheath. "I mean," Robin went on, "this isn't the kind of thing I do with Mom."

He swung off again through the undergrowth, leaning into his pack-straps. He was carrying the rock phosphates. Dale had that great outlaw stride, almost a swagger. Nonetheless he must be thinking about her mother; one mention was all it took. His walk had some stomp to it. Robin could hear the mulch crackle under him even through the white noise within her hood. And her father began to gab. "Well honey, your mother's still down in the valley. She's down in that mind-set, she's one of the office mice." He knew those office mice. "That's why I keep my ill-gotten gains in the woods, you know. Put it in a bank and those mice can get it."

At a low scrub oak, feisty but webbed with lichen, Dale crouched to stub out his cigarette.

"Robin, listen. Have you ever come up on one of them like, unexpectedly?" Elbows on knees, he made claws of his hands. "Have you ever like, surprised a mouse in its lair? Man, it's a terrible thing to see." He took out the Marlboro box, an eye-catcher, vivid against his camouflage. "They show you their teeth. They show you their claws, oh yeah. They'll fight to the death for the burrow."

Robin allowed herself to laugh, scratching under one cuff.

"They *believe* in the burrow, Robin. They actually think they've got the good life."

She laughed, refastening the Velcro at that wrist.

"Man oh man. The things we let our children see."

"Oh Daddy. Come on. You work in the valley."

Dale tucked his butt into the Marlboro box. He snapped the bright thing back into his pocket. "Okay, I've got a title on my desk. I've got a billboard on the highway. But I'm keeping my dope money in the woods."

He strode off again, in a sudden wash of sunshine. Robin kept her eyes down; she couldn't let him see how he got to her.

In her father's voice Robin picked up echoes of his record collection, half a hundred lowdown singers with baggy black faces and knockabout teeth. Plus he was scamming, talking trash, and that got to her too. In these woods, scamming came as a relief. On Robin's hikes with the senior class, just the opposite, everybody got into that hippy-dippy granola goop. Everybody started waving the flag for "the wilderness" and "the planet." Robin's boyfriend, Anu, didn't like the hippy-dippy stuff either; he said it was a chemical reaction to the landscape. Anu said that anyone who grew up in Oregon had to be permanently stoned on the highway overlooks. Oh Anu. Robin's father was the only other man she knew with such a smart mouth.

Except Anu didn't always come back to the same damn thing.

"Yeah," Dale was saying, "I can just see your mother."

Come on, Dad. Get off it.

"Robin, I mean, your mom has bought the whole fantasy, the office and the good life. Your mom's a believer."

Robin almost wished he'd brought his gun. Dale had some serious iron, a square and colorless .45. Even in her day-dreams, My Father the Outlaw, the gun had always made her nervous. But now Dale was just another grumping old hobo bent under a pack. The sun had gone back behind the clouds, and he was carrying nothing but farm tools and fertilizer.

"I can see her, Robb. As plain as if she's here."

According to Robin's mother—she preferred to be called Roy— the breakup was a done thing as soon as they'd moved West. Back in Philadelphia she and Dale could kid themselves that the trouble was money. Dale had fallen just short of promotion, her mother's people just short of the contract that would make the agency. The scholarship that had carried Robin through sophomore year at the Park School had lost its funding. Meantime out in Tangent, Oregon, a former nobody in Dale's office was doing seven thousand a month designing solar homes. Her father hadn't stopped talking the whole way West. Robin honey, try to understand, people like Dale and Roy aren't that old. People like Dale and Roy still have dreams. Then that same September, her mother had heaved the coffee pot through the glass panels in the alcove.

Tangent is *right*, her mother had screamed.

"I just wish your mother could meet Sharonna or Flo," Dale said now. "One of the younger women I'm seeing."

They were sidling through brambles and hip-high stands of fern. "It would be good for Roy, I think."

Right, Dad. Good for Roy. Dale might as well have been pointing at the sky with one hand and reaching for her purse with the other. Nothing about the divorce got to Robin like that, like she had to cover up and get tricky. Of course there'd been hard places for her. Eating alone had been the worst, jar after jar of Paul Newman Spaghetti Sauce while Roy was on job interviews up in Portland. But she'd talked it all out with Anu, the whole soap opera of the last year and a half, and she'd only started crying once. These days, when she visited Tangent she was happy about it, happy for the change. In the mornings the louvers in her father's skylight lit up in stripes.

What was the problem with the adults? God, the way Roy had carried on when she'd learned about Dale's buried money (Robin's mother had some outlaw contacts of her own, through a coffee shop in downtown Salem). *Thousands of dollars!* Roy had screamed. *Thousands! Enough to move back to Philly!* Robin had taken in the tantrum with hands on hips, concentrating. Likewise last night, when her father had invited her to come see his hole, Robin had nodded, avid, squinting. In both cases, it wasn't just the money that had her hooked.

She could use the money. She'd be eighteen in July, and she and Anu had plans. But more than that, she had to learn this stuff. She had to learn what made these two poor diseased creatures tick. Robin liked to read murder mysteries, the more hard-boiled the better, and in them she always looked forward to the scene in the morgue. She always enjoyed the conversation with the coroner, a doctor with an attitude, a death-pro making wisecracks over the victim. These days, Robin figured, she had to be the coroner. She had to get smart and icy, with the dead marriage on the table before her.

Last night, Dale had kept warning her that the trek to his hole wouldn't be easy. He'd said he would leave behind his .45, but there might be other trouble. Robin at last had fallen back on an old family line, something Dale had picked up from a movie: I don't mind a reasonable amount of trouble. And the fact was, she wanted trouble. Not that she'd told Dale, oh no. If she'd learned one thing about keeping control, it was to let him do the talking.

Since they'd left the trail, he'd been taking her in spirals. Robin couldn't be sure if, overall, they were moving uphill or down. Occasionally there'd be breaks in the forest, but the view left her confused. So early in the year, these woods offered a dishrag beauty, rumpled green and grease. The wrinkles of clear-cut and growth kept shifting, dreamy under the rain. The only clarity in the landscape was either a thousand feet down or a thousand feet up. Above, the sunshine now and again opened a wound in the clouds' beard, exposing red and blue bloodlines in the puffy upper reaches of the cumuli. Below, one time, they saw the fringes of a town.

A town? A mock-up, more like it—the sort of thing her mother did for the Bureau of Tourism. A sprinkling of geometry in the lowlands. Robin tried to pick out a landmark while Dale turned away and squatted. She heard him searching through the small leaves.

"Yep," he said. "Yep. Come and take a look."

His old suit stank, a human mulch. Bent beside him, Robin saw the broken ivy and pine cones, the gravel trod into the ground. Yep. It looked like more than one person, too. Half-legible boot prints lay in a V of aboveground roots.

"It's got to be the sheriff," her father said.

Oh right. It couldn't be anybody except the sheriff. But while he and Robin fell into step again, corkscrewing away from the overlook, Dale kept insisting that the tracks were the worst kind of trouble. The troopers, Robb.

His proof seemed to be based on the cycle of the seasons. "In the woods," Dale said, "you don't measure time by the weather, the way you would back East." He took her into thicker brush, ropy salmonberry. "Here it's just, some days are a little colder and wetter, some are a little warmer and dryer." And so, he explained, a grower measures his year by people and their movements. "Like September first, Robb. That's a key date, that's when hunting season starts."

Or had he said October first? What kind of trash was he talking? "Robin, I'll tell you. You don't want to be in here when there's men walking round carrying guns."

Then: "See, Robb. See there!"

Dale dropped into a squat, his cigarette-arm stiff behind him. "See the cuts?"

Her itching flared up again. Her father gestured across cuts in the greenery, broken branches, plainly the work of a machete. Whoever had done it, Robin couldn't blame them. The way was blocked by a holly tree, a thorny red-speckled miracle. The exposed pulp had already gone dark and sapless, and underfoot the runoff had reduced the prints to a jumble.

"Doesn't look too recent," she said.

"You wish."

She worked her hands under her sleeves, her fingernails cold against the rubbery veins.

"Listen, little girl." Dale was picking through the grass beneath the holly. "In the woods it's easy to see what you want to see. It's like the 'Nam that way."

"Give me a break, Dale. You were at Penn State the whole time."

No response. He fingered something off the ground. "Yep, yep," he said finally. "It's the troopers."

Facing her, he held it up: a black chip about the size of his palm. At first she thought that whoever had come through here had lost a piece of their machete.

"Candy bar," Dale said.

It had to be the cigarette that made him look so fierce. Certainly his find was nothing to get worked up about. Nothing but the little dark cardboard sheet from under a Mars Bar or a Three Musketeers.

"Come on," she said.

His face lengthened. "Okay, okay. I know what you're thinking."

Robin scratched more seriously.

"You're thinking the old man's a little paranoid. Right? You're thinking the old man's seen too many movies."

"Well I mean Dale, even if these were the cops—"

"*If* these were the cops? If? Robin, weren't you listening when I told you about the seasons? The point is, at this time of year nobody else should be around."

Oh Dale. So lost in space that he didn't see it—what could the sheriff do to them? What, even if these were the cops? *Dale didn't have his plants in yet.* Nobody had their plants in yet, it was only February for God's sake, and Robin would never have come out here with him if she'd thought she could go to jail for carrying seeds. As of now, Dale and Robin were just a couple of hikers with an idea.

"Robin, hey. This is the lore of the woods."

She kept her mouth shut. Anu had a name for what her father was into: the Transmit-Only Mode.

"These days, how often does a father get a chance to pass on the lore of the big woods?"

Transmit-Only, software for adults. Dale was back on his haunches, his pack-straps in his elbows. She checked her watch. Past ten-thirty, and it would get dark by four. When would they have time for the money?

"Robin, I know that sheriff." He leveled the cardboard at her; she thought of his .45. "It's not paranoia."

"*Roy's* the one who thinks you're paranoid," she said.

Dale lowered the paper gun. His mouth opened, then shut. He lowered his head and fished out the Marlboro box.

"You know Roy," Robin went on, more quietly. "You know how she talks. She's always saying what a pothead you are."

He got his feet back under him. He showed a lot of knuckle, folding the black thing and tucking it away. And Robin was sorry for him, him and his nic-stained hands, so helpless since she'd learned where to poke him. But Dad—somebody had to carry the iron, on this trip.

Still Dale kept playing the desperado. Every dozen paces or so he would crouch and peer hawk-like around the edges of his hood. When he lit up another Marlboro, he hid the flame. Stalking the wild Butterfinger? Robin, waiting over him, couldn't help but think of Anu. Her boyfriend was Vietnam for real, raised in the canals; he could tell her father something. In fact both her folks should spend a few hours with Anu—*listening*, for once. He could tell her mother how the Communists had impounded his family bank account. They'd taken the luggage, the bicycles, the shoes. Robin would like her mother to hear about that. She'd liked to see if there was any more whining about Dale's stash in the woods, after that.

In the corners of her boyfriend's face (the Asiatics she'd known weren't so sleek, so fine), Robin had found a toughness beyond her parents' wildest dreams. In the bucket seats of her mother's Nissan, where she and Anu had to kiss over the gearshift, there were evenings when they floated free of the knobs and latches by means of eye contact alone. There were long uprushes of staring during which Robin could also somehow look down on this girl in the driver's seat, this tomboy jammed sideways behind the steering wheel. She wouldn't have believed her eyes, her mind's eyes, if Anu hadn't told her he'd seen it himself. And then he'd let her in on his secret plan for getting ahead in this country.

So-o-o tough. Most senior transfers were still trying to learn their way to the cafeteria, and Anu had a plan for getting ahead. In this country, he'd told her, you and I can truly rise above.

Her mother had noticed, because Robin had bought those cowboy boots with the four-inch heels. But Roy had only lectured her on the side effects of the Pill: Honey, I had a hangover every morning. And Robin had gone to Dale, she'd gotten him to rent a video history of the war. But her father too had wound up talking about himself. She doubted if either of her parents knew her boyfriend's full name, Anu Sher Wud. Certainly neither of them realized that now she and Anu had a plan. No fantasy, a real plan. They were going to elope.

Anu had a chance to hook on in Hollywood. A cousin there had steady work as Gaffer and Best Boy. If you're from Vietnam, Anu had told her, the family really looks out for you. If he could take her down the coast—and soon, while the job pipeline was still open—by the end of the year they could both be in the union. She'd seen the letters from his cousin, on studio letterhead, with characters like columns of wigwag pennants. That was why she'd come into the Wilderness Area. She had a gold mine down the road. Once she and her father got into that buried can, Robin shouldn't have any trouble getting him to fork over a couple of thousand at least.

Dale would stop and squat anywhere, once even in a patch of skunk cabbage. Were they actually making headway, between these ticking, faraway stares? They seemed locked into a corkscrew approach, first upslope, then down. Her father's rap took them nowhere new either.

"So your mother calls me a pothead," Dale said. "You know it doesn't surprise me, Robb. That witch sold me out a long time ago."

Robin frowned. Did they have to get nasty in order to move on? They were past the skunk cabbage but the smell had left her dizzy. She fumbled over moguls in the undergrowth.

"Happens all the time," Dale went on. "Every day, Robb, somebody sells out their family for a Macintosh." His voice grew more smoky. "Hey, what do we expect, in this country? It's called career mobility, right? I mean a person goes to college in one city, and then there's grad school somewhere else, and after that they take the best offer they can find. Am I right? For the rest of their lives, they go on taking the best offer. Mobility ever after."

Was he talking or singing? The slashes of her father's camouflage, up ahead, jogged like follow-the-bouncing-ball.

"Career mobility, Robb. It's the great American scramble. And every day, somebody else decides that a family's too big a load to haul."

He dropped again, the cabbage-smell rising off him as he arranged his joints. She had to clear her head. "Every day," Robin tried, "somebody else joins the office mice."

Dale grinned but went on checking the near slope. Beaten down by the drizzle, his smoke drifted across his stare. "Well it's no joke, honey. It's some mean business, we're talking about." Even in the woods, Dale whispered, you found people who'd caught the career disease. "Oh yeah, Robb. I know some guys around here who'll cut their own grandmother if they think she'll hurt the crop." Dale knew growers who set bear traps round their holes. "I mean, a bear trap'll take a man's leg off." Or had she ever heard of punji sticks?

"Daddy, come on."

"It works like this. First you dig a pit—"

"*Daddy.*" She yanked back her hood. "Are you putting dope in your cigarettes again?"

A lame move, a dumb joke. And she'd been way too loud, she'd silenced the winter birds. But the look her father showed her was sheepish.

"Well well, little girl. Is it that obvious?"

His grin was hard to get a fix on, a pointed thing in flight.

"Robb, I'm asking. Is it obvious?"

"You mean you are? You're smoking pot right now?"

"Just a taste. It gives me like an infra-red scope."

"But I thought, I thought . . ."

With her ears bare, the drizzle seemed very cold. Dale remained sideways to her, half an eye on the woods. Robin bit her lips and shook her head.

"It's okay, honey," he said. "If the Man's going to bust you for seeds, he might as well bust you for smoking."

Could they get busted for seeds? Could they, after all? Doping and its complications were still new to Robin. Dale hadn't started growing his own till after she and Roy had moved out, and she'd only occasionally seen him smoking, while firing up a barbecue or watching the Phillies on cable. Cigarettes like these he called "half-and-halfs," pot and tobacco. He'd told her he didn't enjoy them, didn't "appreciate the high." Yet here he sat, who knows how many dark miles into the woods, grinning over a trick Marlboro. He'd never seemed more like a bluesman.

"We could still go back," he growled. "We could turn around right here."

The best answer—the toughest—was to show him her watch. Put it right under his nose.

The next time they stopped, Dale actually hit her. He got her a stiff poke between the breasts, shoving her back. Robin wound up against the trunk of a pine, under the branches. A smell of cinders, a sore spot where he'd jabbed her. If he was this hyper they must be close to the hole. During the last stretch of hiking their spirals had hooked inward more often, and Dale had laid off the smokes.

Around her, the dangling needle clusters were whisk brooms, green and medieval. Beyond that the forest looked harmless. The most dangerous thing out there was her father. Down on the balls of his feet again, he scoped it out, trembling. The dangling tips of his pack-ties shivered. Bitterly Robin thought of her murder mysteries, the coroner's steady hands over the corpse. Dale's hands couldn't stop. He fingered the moss at his feet, the sapling by his shoulder; he reached crookedly behind him, up beneath the pack and under his jacket. Robin glimpsed a bit of black, maybe metal. Or no—no maybe about it. Not after how he'd fooled her with the half-and-halfs. The thing under the back of her father's coat had to be metal. He must be packing a gun after all.

The sun reemerged, brightening the underside of his wrist. The birds kept up their idiocy.

Slowly, Dale's hand withdrew from beneath the rain gear. Robin lost sight of the extra load, the black. And she was talking to herself, when had that started? She was rehearsing the letter for him and Roy, the explanation she'd leave when she took off with Anu.

"I am only seventeen years old," she whispered, "but I know that the Willamette Valley is not the end of the world."

"Oh man," Dale cried. "Oh man man man oh *no*."

He was up, his hands empty. He strode towards another stand of brush.

"What were you thinking?" he wailed. "Oh man. You crazy, heartbroken motherfucker, what were you fucking *thinking?*"

"What?" she said. He usually stayed away from language like that when she was around. "Daddy, what?"

"It's just a hole, you crazy motherfucker. It's just a goddamn fucking *hole*. Were you really thinking it was safer than anybody else's?"

She shouldered out from under the pine. Relieved just to move, aware again of the machete at her hip. Dale stood with his ear on his shoulder, and in the sunshine and drizzle the brush round his legs appeared somehow off. The plants sat too close together for their size, out of kilter. Her father's noise was even stranger. He'd stopped screaming at himself. Instead he choked, he snorted, and it had nothing to do with smoking.

"What is this?" The sore spot in her chest expanded. "Are you . . . Daddy, are you crying?"

He turned his back, kicking aside a fern bush. Talk about out of kilter—Dale kicked the plant over. The stem-bottoms poked up, slashed and pulpy. Someone had laid into the greenery here. What they couldn't chop, they'd trampled. Vines zigzagged across the floor's growth impossibly, and a berry bush had been ripped out by its roots. Humping up beside her father, Robin found mountain-boot tracks, ovals crisp at the edges (Dale's old L.L. Beans left softer indents). The attack had included a spade or hoe. It was five or six square yards of devastation.

"The sheriff did all this?" Robin asked.

Dale turned away again, pulling his hood together over his sobs. Dad . . .

But at least while he was like that she could see his hands. And Robin might have been halfway to tears herself, suffering flash after flash of troopers breaking from the nearby woods, of gunfire erupting. One bad flash after another, brought on by her father's grounds, a manmade pond surrounded by places to hide. The water lay at the center of the ruined brush, a brief deep rectangle alive with scum and insects. Two or three rat-like creatures floated, drowned, at the hole's rim. The rim itself glittered here and there with traces of slick plastic, greeny-black, tent material or a heavyweight garbage bag. A lot of work. It must have taken hours to set in this rain-catch, this buried tarp or whatever. That same day, Dale must have transplanted the ground cover. In the middle of the woods he'd built a self-contained irrigation system, weatherproof and landscaped. And hidden.

"You did all this?" Robin said.

His answer was a mumble, soppy, full of pain. Dad . . .

She tottered around the hole's edges, open-mouthed, tasting the drizzle. She'd had no idea a person could do so much damage just by tearing away the camouflage.

At one corner of the pool, where the stomping and chopping looked worst, someone had driven a stake. A simple garden stake, frail and waist-high. Tacked to the top was a white laminated card:

N.T. Hingham
COUNTY SHERIFF
Please call at your earliest convenience.

She couldn't bring herself to touch it. The thing was an arrow in the ground, with white unnatural feathers.

"Do they . . . boy. Daddy, do they always do this? I mean, I can't believe it. He left his card."

Dale's eyes emerged, eggy above his loosening fists.

"Daddy," she said then, "I can't believe it. I thought all this stuff about the troopers was a fantasy."

What? Robin jammed her thumbs back under her pack-straps. Hey, enough talking for one day. First she gets all fluttery over his smoking, now she gives away another secret—enough. She knew better than to let a few tears throw her off. She'd seen that iron under his waistband. Robin brought her knuckles together, across her breasts, and she wouldn't give in to her itch. Control, control. Anyway her father was coming out of it, yanking back his hood, unbuckling his pack. Once the thing was off his shoulders Dale just let it drop, *ka-wransh-shh*. Rock phosphates.

"It's okay, Robb," he said finally.

She kept her knuckles together, her face composed.

"It's okay, really. Baby, the fact is, you were right. It was a fantasy. Your crazyman father has been walking around in a fantasy."

She frowned. "I don't see any fantasy here. This was some place."

"Oh." Dale flapped a hand. "Robb, the hole is nothing."

Nothing? Then what was he crying about?

"Man," he was saying, "what was I thinking? *What* was I thinking I—"

"Dale." She gave it a beat; this had to sound strong. "You better not have been lying about the money."

He didn't understand. Squinting, he massaged one shoulder.

"The money in the can, Dale," she said. "That better not have been one of your funny stories."

His eyes widened again, differently. "Oh my baby," he said. He raised his face to the half-lit sky and she noticed his height, a head taller than her still.

"I guess I've still got a little mouth to feed," he said.

Robin waved away a bug. Or she waved, anyway; she needed something to do with her hands. If only Dale would act like a man with a gun! But her father wore a Sunday face, unshaven, battered, and his half-and-halfs had taken a toll. When he assured her not to worry, he threw her off that much more. "The money's real," he told her, "eleven hundred and ninety dollars." He lingered over the syllable breaks. "You'll get your cut, don't you worry."

Every slow word threw her off. Eleven hundred and ninety? She was getting a *cut* of eleven hundred and ninety?

"I'll take you to the can," he said. "I realize you didn't come into the woods just to play the pioneer girl."

She dropped one hand to the handle of her machete.

"Dale, I don't get it. What's going on here?"

"Lost in a fantasy, honey. A hand-me-down fantasy."

"Yeah, well, so? So why were you bawling like that?"

"I was lost in a fantasy, and I dragged you along too."

"What are you telling me?"

"I used you," he said.

There was the rain, static in the signal between them. Once more Dale's eyes changed shape. "See," he said, "I heard my hole was in danger. I heard the sheriff might be on to me. I mean, the Man gets his coffee the same place I do."

In the strengthening sun, his renewed tears were bits of aluminum in his stubble. "See, I wanted you for my cover. I have to tell you; if I'm not going to be a rat, I have to. In case we got caught, Robb, I—I wanted you for a scam."

The dead forest rats stank, way too close. Between her and her father, Robin didn't have room to relieve her itch.

"I mean, no way a grower ever brings a kid along. No way, Robb. The job is cut-throat, in here. But see, I was even meaner than the rest of them: I figured out a way to use my own daughter. See, I brought you along and I brought a couple other things, a couple other tricks. I had a way where I—I figured I was covered."

"You were covered."

Chin up, chest up, he nodded. Robin realized she hadn't just repeated his words, she'd echoed his voice. She'd sounded spongy, wobbly. Out of control.

"Robin, that's not the worst. The worst was, I kept kidding myself that the trip was for you."

Then there was the rainbow, the last straw. Robin couldn't look at her father's face any longer, and casting round for better she saw it in an opening between the tallest firs: a double rainbow, breathtaking, beautiful. Bent shafts of red and blue built across cumuli more white than usual for February. She couldn't stand it, such a corny show of good news at a time like this, and the rainbow was all the harder to take for how it unwound from the tatters of the Wilderness Area.

"That was the worst," Dale was saying. "That was where I was totally lost. See, you told me you wanted this, Robb. You said you couldn't do this with Mom. So then I could kid myself, I could say, see, this whole runaround is really for her. Robb, I mean—when a father's acting like a rat, he's got some old, old lines to fall back on . . ."

Robin spun away and ran.

Two minutes later, breathing hard, they were down on their knees together in the forest. Busy with their hands, avoiding each other's eyes. Robin once more fisted together her pack-straps. Dale brought out a floppy leather sack of seeds.

"For the big evergreens," he said. "Seeds."

The bits of pine cone glittered at the bottom of the pouch. It was like he held a mouth in his hand, a worn and thick-lipped maw, and the seeds were yellow fillings at the back. Why hadn't she seen this sack before? Why hadn't she seen, at least, that it wasn't a gun? As soon as Dale had caught up with her—which didn't take long, with this load on her back—she'd screamed at him about the gun. "You can't hide these things from me!" she'd screamed. But when Robin had managed to face him, he'd only looked puzzled. Then she'd dropped. Where was she going to run, anyway? Where? And Dale had knelt beside her, fishing the sloppy black thing from behind his back. It wasn't a gun.

"Seeds," Dale repeated. "It's for that scam I was telling you about."

His plan, he explained, had been to tell the troopers that they were environmentalists. "You know, Robb. Just a father and daughter who care about preserving the splendor of the wilderness." As for the marijuana, he'd kept those seeds separate, in the coat pocket that was easiest to reach. He'd been ready to chuck them at the first sign of trouble.

"Then with these pine seeds, see, the rest of our stuff would all fit. Even the rock phosphates would fit."

Their breathing hadn't settled yet. Robin stumped upslope, bringing her face to his level.

"We'd still be breaking the law," he admitted.

"We'd still be breaking the law?" she said. "Dale, just for *starters*, we'd be breaking the law! I mean, is that your idea of a cover story? Is that your idea of how to get us out? God, an old B movie wouldn't have such a stupid story. I mean, you talk about people trading in their family for a Macintosh, here you are trading in your family for a B movie. A really dumb B movie!

"Dale, man oh man. I mean, if anyone ever deserved to go to jail just for having an idea—Dad, listen to me. Listen like I was Mom, okay? Just listen while I do the talking. I mean, who do you think these troopers are? Do you think they're idiots? People planting trees, I mean, they don't even *use* seeds. People planting trees use seedlings. Seedlings, Dad, seed-lings. Even I know that. They come in with trees that have already started to *grow!*"

There he was with his Sunday face. "Are you through?"

"You must have been stoned when you thought up that one," Robin said. "If the sheriff saw that old sack he'd laugh in your face."

She swatted the thing from his hand. The leather went rippling through the weeds, and for a moment it looked like a mouse, some ragged brown life in a scramble. But then it stopped and collapsed.

"At least I had an idea," Dale said after a minute. "I had a way we might get sprung."

"Oh yeah, a stroke of genius." Oh no—was she starting to laugh? "A legend for wilderness people everywhere."

"Okay, okay, that was wrong. A father should never kid himself that he's a legend."

She was starting to laugh, laughing already. It felt like someone kept plucking a bowstring in her gut. "Seeds," she repeated. "Seeds."

"Well, there's still the can." He tried to get into the spirit, grinning, hopeful.

Oh yeah, the can. The cash. She and her boyfriend would take whatever they could get. Maybe Robin would tell Dale about it, too; yeah, okay, maybe—though no way she could manage it now. Not with this bowstring going *sproing* in her belly. Not while she was hooting, chirping, struggling for a half-decent breath. She was out of it. She was airborne for God's sake. And as for her father trying to work the pack-straps off her shoulders, his clumsy attempts to make her comfortable, that was the funniest thing yet. He was trying to help, and it was hysterical. Hey, was this a father or a feather? *Sproing, sproing.*

Robin tried to swallow, tried to frown, she lifted her face to the cold and wet. But the rainbow was still there. Hey—shouldn't the colors fade?

Eastertime Fogs

THE LAST TWO MIMOSAS have been pretty much straight shots. Nobody's about to get up and mix more orange juice. Yet I have to sit upright, I have to keep an ear cocked for my kids, they're out somewhere near the garage. With that, and with the omelettes and popovers sodden and gurgly under my belt, not to mention Magda here beside me, hinting repeatedly that we should go out to the garage ourselves, we should share some sensamilla with the men— with all that, it starts to feel as if my entire time in Oregon has been one long brunch. Seven months of it now, September into March. Like some local ritual where everyone stuffs bread and wine between a person and the work she's got to get done.

Even the Don, my husband, seems to have the hang of the ritual better than I. He's the one who invited Magda and Sonny. And Magda's with it too, though she's the real out-of-towner. She brought strawberry preserves her parents sent from Cologne.

"Sometimes," she says, "I think that to be healthy in this country, you have to take drugs."

Outside there's a shout, my Angelo. It rings in the tall glasses, the dishware; I can't tell if he and Andrea are staying away from the garage.

Nine o'clock this morning, the Don called these people. Now he's taken Sonny off to "see the workshop." Plus before he went he had the nerve to remind me that I should get him if there's "a call." He didn't say *the* call, the one from Mort, but I know all his codes by now. I mean, he wants me to make brunch-talk and then he reminds me we're waiting on Mort. When the kids asked to be excused, I warned them not to bother Papa. But I can't be sure, not without standing in Magda's face and hollering across the back

27

yard. This when she believes that what we're doing here is making friends. Sharing a few private combinations, the last of the booze and the first close moments: she knows the ritual.

Mist gathers inside the screen door. Magda keeps her elbows together.

"In my country," she says, "in Germany . . . if we see a person like you at the labs, we know they are straight."

Her fascination with getting stoned, I should say, is pretty standard around the labs. Magda and I work in a research park. Over there, when the subject is drugs even our boss, Giptill, can sound like a little boy: In Iran you get penalty of *death!* This is a scientist who's worked with Nobel Prize winners. And Magda's smile today is borderline, she's full of stares. Twenty-three years old.

I take up the last popover. "Oh God, the labs. You know I've still got to get over there today. I've got to check those cultures."

"You see that's what I mean, you are so . . . so good hardworking." Full of stares, and softnecked even in this cold. "And yet you have a husband like Don."

My smile can't be much better than hers.

"I tell you, in my country we would never suspect a woman like you to have him. Or to find such a workshop like his."

"Oh God, the workshop." Shrug. "I shouldn't tell you this, but the Don hasn't made a sale since Christmas."

"But the material things aren't important. We know why the men are really in there."

At least her Sonny is our age, another 'Nam vet. He might be the same kind of pal as Mort, and he wouldn't be so scary. But Don, Don—over at the labs they've got to trust me. It's the only paycheck we have.

The popover tastes like yesterday's gum. I'm at the point of suggesting we clear the table when there's a sudden thump and scuffle, boots on the back stoop. Andrea comes in first, she's better with the latch. The March wet streams from the children's gear. Their coats wrinkle and the Transformers across the plastic start to go through changes. After that of course a couple one-liners occur to me, we mothers must have our one-liners. Got to fortify our better judgment against such rockety blooming. Though I also know enough to wait for the right opportunity.

Andrea brings the news. Wasps are "hatching" from the flowers behind the garage.

"Wasps, baby?" I say. "In this weather?"

But Angelo won't let me fortify. While his sister starts to explain, the boy begins a flailing exercise, squat and jump, squat and jump. At the peak of each leap his arms pop wide, condensation flies. Magda coils on her chair, specks fizz in my champagne. At least he doesn't seem in danger of losing motor control. His neck's firm, and I can see the color of his eyes.

Andrea's spatterproof. "Yeah Mom, just like that." She points at her brother. "Angelo's got it, they hatch and then they fly."

The spray reaches the display case where the Don keeps his Purple Hearts.

"Behind the garage?" Louder. I come out of my chair enough to stop Angelo with a flat hand. "Did you notice if your *father* was still in there?"

"Oh yeah." The girl composes her face, unsure where my disapproval comes from. "We could hear him'n Uncle Sonny laughing in there."

"Laughing?" Magda catches my eye.

Laughing. And "Uncle Sonny" already. Dropping back in my seat, I haul Angelo into me; with my hand at his hot neck I try to check his pulse. Andrea turns away. The Transformer on her back is brick and iron, swollen with color.

The doctors back East told us to find a less stressful environment. They said it would be good for both of them, Angelo as well as Don. And so we found the environment: out here Don can spend all day with his lathe and sandpaper, and I work with people who hardly recognize the world unless it's under a microscope. Still I'm barely hanging on. My knuckles go white and I ask questions like, is Mort actually our *friend?* Back in Boston Mort would have been one of these leftovers from flaming youth. Don and I would have had a certain closemouthed pride about keeping him somewhere in our lives—a last dinosaur from the Ho Bo Woods, a cocaine dealer. The way in the old country our grandparents took pride in calling on an invalid priest. But the man would never have been a friend. Sunday morning back East was time for children, for Angelo especially. We'd never have arranged things just so we could be in the house whenever Mort decided to call.

Of course Don tells me it is for Angelo. He's picked up almost three grand riding shotgun with Mort around the Valley. Nerve disorders cost, Don tells me. Whatever made him think I'm so uptight about money?

A sudden noise, a whine that quickly peaks. The jigsaw out in the garage.

Angelo, freed, staggers into Magda. Andrea turns. She's got Don's features, the long jaw and careful eyes; I shoot up from my chair. How dare he? How dare he use that machine *stoned?*

Now things are back the way they should be: Magda's following my lead. She's getting a tour of the upstairs, or that's what she thinks. Actually I've got a plan for when we reach the bedroom. A little trick to show the Don I can get into the spirit of brunch with the best of them. Magda should be no problem, now that we've been to the workshop and shared a bone. On the way upstairs she missed two steps. In the long bathroom, the echo makes her giggle.

Though I'm not much of a tour guide myself. Don and I were glad to find a rental with such character. We even agreed to have people visit as part of a Historic Homes thing next fall—about the farthest ahead we've managed to plan. But my descriptions keep falling back on words like "swirly" and "crisscross." By the time we reach the bedroom I'm making things up.

"What nice . . . closets," Magda says. There's nothing at all interesting about the shut closet doors.

"Judas closets," I say, and lose my footing just getting one open.

God I'm wasted. Where does the Don get his capacity? Standing again, blinking against the closet dark, I suddenly picture him at his worktable these days. His eyes are hidden by the goggles and most of the rest is lost in his chin beard. All resinous and flecked with warm wood, he chatters Vietnamese, he stiffarms the sweat from the side of his head. Seeing him like that I can understand why he's not frightened of Mort. It's got nothing to do with their history together, the bad black and white days before I Corps defoliated the Ho Bo Woods. It's been almost twenty years. Rather the connection goes deeper: Don too prefers living with a fever. When the doctors told him to find a less stressful environment, they cut him loose from how he's made. When I come up on him over his workbench these days, it's like I haven't seen his face in months.

My sweater catches on an exposed nail. I never expected my first walk-in closet would be so funky. But Magda's patient, she followed without a peep.

We have to sidle along, my clothes hang against the more intact wall. But at the end of the closet there's a delicate touch, a window in its own steep Italianate gable. Magda and I cram in close enough to catch our reflections in the glass. She's such a sweet viny thing, always shooting out one hip or the other. You wonder what Sonny needs with a trip to the workshop. Behind her reflection I can read, reversed, the Beacon Street address on the nearest drycleaning bag. I doubt that dress will ever fit again.

"Okay," I tell her. "We're going to rock their socks."

Magda frowns, murmurs.

"It's a plan," I say. "A surprise."

The window hardly squeaks, going up. The cold is nothing new. Below us, in the drive, the men and kids are playing limply. Angelo's in the Big Wheel, spread-elbowed. He kicks the pedals every once in a while, but mostly Andrea drags him. They move in a rough oval around Don and Sonny, who squat over cigarettes. And there's music, just audible over the thunder of the Big Wheels. Angelo's singing: "*Lit*-tle ones to Him be-long, *we* are weak but He is strong."

Sometimes I think I wouldn't mind the errands for Mort if the money didn't have to go to the Sisters of the Word. Of all the things not to have changed in twenty-five years. . . . But the Sisters are the best in town with s.d. kids. Besides, just relax your guard for a minute and the entire Oregon scene can take on a '50s sweetness. Suddenly it's like Sunday with Mister Rogers. Even the misting is sweetness. We share the drive with a retired couple, the Daleys, and in this weather their groomed stands of spring flowers are Magic Marker hilarity. The house lots out here still look like

Toy Town to me anyway, nothing larger than a quarter-acre. And what is it about kids' faces under hoods?

"Do we have something to bomb them?" Magda is blinking, dopey in the gray light.

"No no no. Just, give me a minute here."

I lay out the plan. Down on the drive Andrea hauls Angelo round behind the Don. The two men are still squatting, conferring over what appears to be one of those humongous G.I. Zippo lighters.

"Right," I say. "One, two, three—"

Magda's scream isn't at all what I expect. She howls like something out of a Nazi rally. I hold my own the best I can, *hey you* or other words just as empty. Certainly not the words that flare in the back of my mind as the noise goes on, *how could you* or *what are we doing here*, none of that ferocity; only the noise, the mist coiling round my overheated head and shoulders, while the group on the drive turn to red shapes against my shut eyelids. When Magda collapses, she catches my hip. The shapes go white with the thought that I'm going to fall.

I brace against the frame, the metal sash-fittings.

Then Magda's giggling at my feet, I'm an adult again. One good look below and I feel like a monster. Don's sprawled back over Angelo's Big Wheel; Angelo's face down and spreadeagle across the driveway concrete.

Sonny stands back, a hand on the Daleys' drainpipe. Andrea's headed for the Daleys' flowers, she can't stand to watch when there's a chance her brother might go into a fit. I'm a monster. I put my own family under the microscope. The boy's neck has a hump and his fingertips poke from his slicker, helpless. His tongue is a germ touched with dye so we can see it under the microscope. I can't move, I can't even look at Don again till he rolls onto his knees.

Magda's underfoot, still fighting the giggles. A coat hanger falls, a racket in this space.

Those shapes against my shut eyes were precisely the collapsed figure-eights we study in the labs. It's as if the very thing that makes me marketable out West has turned me into a freak for pain. I hit the stairs at a run. My ears burn as if I never stopped screaming, and I can see how my little game must have been for Don. The flame from Sonny's Zippo erupting in his face, while machine wheels thundered nearby and all hell broke loose overhead. Of course he and Sonny were reminiscing in the garage. He was the Don again, brimful of himself, the only way to be when you drew perimeter duty in the dying Ho Bo Woods.

When I reach the back stoop he's bent over Angelo. He cradles the boy and stands, too quick and in too tight a bear hug for me to check either of their faces.

Sonny's a big man. He shrugs his fatigues together and the zipper-pull rattles. When he closes in on Don and Angelo, the movement feels like a threat. It's got to be the mist, the run; I can taste sensamilla again. But my husband keeps his back to me, he shows the boy to his new friend. When Magda comes up behind, I fumble off the stoop.

Sideways down the steps, backwards down the drive. Andrea hustles past with a flower for Angelo. She doesn't want to look at me either. In her case it's guilt: when her brother went bad, she couldn't face him. God, maybe she'll grow up associating flowers with guilt. Certainly she's picked a pretty one, a stem willowy as the bone in her arm, a bloom pale as a Petri dish. How should a person in cell biology know their names? But Magda takes the flower, she smiles. The picture's complete. It's children and fathers and a pretty young Mom, their faces that many more flowers in the fog, everyone clumsy with the loving sickness of brunch. My boot steps—moving backwards, heavy on the heels— echo between the two close homes.

It isn't long before I'm yelling again. We're back inside, I'm over the dishwater and yelling. Magda and Sonny haven't been gone ten minutes. The mess in the sink is like my noise made tangible: fingered with grease and vomitous. *Isn't it nice to make friends, isn't it nice. Now maybe our new friends can meet our sweet old pal Mort!*

Really, I don't know why Don stays in the kitchen. The few times I turn his way he's working the long cupboards so stiffly it's as if he wants to fold himself inside. Andrea at least knew enough to get out of the way. Angelo announced that the hearth bricks were warm and she let him lure her off. But the Don just tucks his chin. He works the dishtowel so hard the wine-stained corners fly.

Yelling: *You act like defoliating those woods was the last thing you did in your life!*

It doesn't end, it goes beyond words. Fumbling in the dishwater, I catch a knife the wrong way. I stamp off for my rain gear dripping blood. Never mind a bandaid, I want it to hurt all the way to the labs. Of course he's right behind me, the Don's on the job. He touches my shoulder, my elbow. But at the front closet I have to see the kids on the hearth. Another battlefield scene. Andrea cowers over Angelo, her ear to his chest and her eyes swollen; behind them it's napalm.

I can't face any of them. The man folds his arms in front of me, there are words. ". . . that out of your system?" I put my mouth to the open skin above my thumb, sucking so noisily that it flushes bits of popover from between my teeth.

All the way to the research park I keep after the gears and pedals. That and the oncoming drizzle fill my hood, the seashell hiss of arguments going on ten years now. I mean, out of my system? I need to get something out of my system? Look who's talking. We met at a Veterans' rehab clinic. He'd worked his way up from patient to counselor—though at the time I liked it that he'd been a patient. Usually when I heard the counselors talk, I was glad my talent was in the hard sciences. Their hipness was secondhand; they'd just heard a lot of stories. Health to them was nothing more than keeping the surfaces orderly. The Don was never so smug. We didn't date so much as start reading Thomas Merton together. Then one Friday, instead of the usual Happy Hour, he took me over to the Fenway Motor Inn. I thought, I'm not ready for this. But it turned out that somebody in his old platoon worked as a roadie for Muddy Waters.

The effect would have been impossible any other time, with any other man. Don still can't say "funky" without laying an awful gravity on the word. Granted. Yet as sundown came on I had to keep turning to the motel windows, taking the measure of my ecstasy against the Fenway maples rag-patched with fall. The old musician's obscenities were thick and genial as bread. His boozing was gold in his eyes, but you had to watch every glance to see it.

And from there somehow I wound up here. Working Sundays, the handlebar hell against my wound. More than likely Mort's call has come by now and the kids are with Mrs. Daley.

As I walk the empty corridors to Giptill's labs the doors behind me echo, da-*Don*, da-*Don*.

It would help if my reason for coming in on a weekend weren't so routine. All I do is test the cultures in a medium. The medium itself is just blood serum, your basic human soup. And today even the door to the containment room has that echo. Last thing I need: lately, around here, I've been trying to keep away any thought of Don. I mean, he won't let me say a word about the work at home. Right from the first, the shoptalk got to him. Me: "Well we *want* to keep the cancer cells growing." Don: "Oh sure. On Vulcan we respect all forms of life." The man I married was never so quick with the one-liners.

He doesn't even want to hear about it. And there's no problem keeping him out of the conversation around the lab, I'm the only native-born citizen in the place. Giptill knows the grants. He knows the odder the group, the bigger the funding. Over coffee or lunch, the talk is usually like Magda earlier: in my country, in your country. There's an assistant named Mx'bellah, just incredible, I bet he sees wasps in this weather. But today he's home. Everybody's home, and the work takes half a brain. I'm like the first white man at the Grand Canyon. I reach into the freezer for a vial of serum, and there's another echo. "Don't talk to me about the war, we've all got our . . ." Ducking into my rain gear is no help. The smell is another reminder, all that food and angry pedaling.

Even in the containment room. Actually I should have towelled off before coming in here—the place is a million dollars worth of sterilizer. On the counters along either wall, every board foot has some designated function. Freezer and centrifuge, hypos and dishes, even the water bath where the serum now sits melting. The largest workspace is taken up by the hood, a stainless steel cube of still more sterilizer. When we bring cultures in here, we handle them under the sliding glass that fronts the hood. Our hands are gloved, cleansed with noiseless gas. When we finish we hit the switch for the ultraviolet and kill off everything.

The stool sits so there's no place to rest your back, but I can jimmy it. Rainwater slips from my Gore-Tex and pings the cold baseboard. I watch the serum melt. It's the cheapest kind of plasma, they get it from donors off the street. Yet the melting is almost a miracle: it begins as an Antarctic bristle and ends up winey slow blood. I must have had too much parochial school. Or I must be thinking too much lately about the ones who might pass for Christ in this country, the homeless who line up to donate blood. Lately I have to make an effort not to stare. They stand trembling with God knows what diseases or chemicals, but they're desperate to buy into more. Of course I help, there are drops for food and clothing if you can't give money. I wrote Congress last month when that bill came up. Still, I catch myself staring. Here in the Valley you don't see so many fatigue jackets and paratroop boots as back East. The weather allows skimpier gear, sometimes the very sheets and scrap they slept in.

Is it my nurse's training? Is it Angelo? Most of these homeless have some disability or other.

Don's seen how caught up I get. On our last trip to Portland, I stood in the middle of traffic like I was asking to be hit. But he knows better than to call me on it. He knows he's in no position to talk, the way he gets when I so much as mention the labs. He'll put his back to me. He'll stand and peer between the blinds as if his increased risk of lymphoma and bone cancer were something he could see coming.

You don't want to boil the serum.

The tilted stool makes trouble, I'm off-balance. When I lift the vial from the water, a dollop of the cheap blood splashes over the lip. Before I can focus, the liquorish spill seeps out of sight into my cut, still open from exposure to the rain.

Back home, before the bathwater cools, Don and the kids surprise me. The plastic curtain billows, crackles. I pull the washcloth over my breasts.

"Mama, Mama!" Angelo's face is on the lip of the tub, already beading with condensation. "We saw a lot of money, it was big as a *house!*"

"Gang, hey gang." For all I know, some infection might be living in the steam. "Mama needs some Mama-time." But Andrea wriggles in next to her brother, their coats squeak against the porcelain.

"Oh yeah Mom. You shoulda been with us, we finally got to meet good old Mort. And he showed us his, his *wad*. Boy."

The steam's evaporating, the Don's put his head in.

"The man doesn't like to talk on the phone." He thumbs back his hood and I can see at once that he's sober. "So I told him to meet me at the Road Blossom. *And* I brought along the two little Buttinskys."

He's sober. I sit up, crossing arms over knees; the gauze on my cut blots the clinging water. "The Road Blossom?" When I got home I came straight upstairs, I assumed the kids were next door. But I can smell it now, strawberry ice cream, strong enough even to cut through the lavender bath oil. For a 24-hour place, the Blossom makes an incredible float.

"That's right, Ivy. I wanted somewhere where I could bring the kids."

"Bring . . . the kids? Bring them to meet Mort?"

"Uh huh. That's how I figured it. Find a place where you can bring the kids, and everything changes."

He speaks quietly, there's no echo. My hand slips down my leg, my grip melts in the water. Andrea knows enough to let us alone. She picks at her brother's Transformer, he had some trouble with his float. Still, we're hardly comfortable. Goosebumps prickle my shoulders. I ask about the money, Mort's wad. I know my husband, stubborn as sap stains. He's slow to make friends and once he does, I've never seen him let go entirely.

He explains that old Mort figured the least he could do was spring for the eats.

"Oh, the guy's an angel," I say.

The Don opens his fatigues so slowly the zipper purrs.

"Darling," I say, "he thought he could lure you all the way back over."

"Well." He drops his gaze, the kids have started to fuss. "There was a lot of eye contact."

He whispers to Angelo; his Lincoln beard waggles prettily. His eyes are downcast; there's those long, feminine lashes. The baby's alive in the martyr's bones. It's alive as much as my own hand is alive, though in the panic after my accident I stuck it under the hood and switched on the ultra-violet. And God, this man and I— it's as if we too were part of some larger face or body—we closet ourselves away and rattle every skeleton in there, but give us a minute away from codes and poses and there's still something growing. I know what I saw in his look. Tonight he'll remind me we agreed to have a third. We moved from ocean to ocean, baby; we heard what the doctors had to say and then we made up our minds to recommit.

Andrea's too intent on that spilled ice cream. She's too rough on her brother's ticklish spots.

The boy whoops, unearthly sound. Then there's his tongue, he can't get a breath. He arches and his arms fly out, his eyes roll back, he's lost his footing. Don grabs him round the rib cage and jams a rough carpenter's hand between the boy's teeth. Once Angelo loses motor control there's no telling what'll happen. Andrea backs off, her face huge. "Mama," she starts, "Mama, I didn't . . ." I get an arm round her before she can run. How bad can it be to see her mother naked? The fit knocks tears from the curtain, and I still wonder what that water might mean; but my family tastes it together, we huddle with heads down.

Second Trimester

CORRILLO COULDN'T believe it was just another assignment. They were sending him back to Bennett. According to the memo from his editor, Corrillo actually had to interview the man.

Bennett's new office was a half-hour down I-5. Corrillo headed out muttering. Sending him back to that guy . . . Someone must be thinking, let's put it to the new kid, let's see what he's made of. Farmland snugged the highway on either side, crops just coming to leaf and rangeland freshened by the long spring. In this drizzle it offered no distraction, only green and green again. The Willamette River Valley in the middle of June. And today couldn't be just another assignment. Today had to be a test. After a while Corrillo gave up trying to make sense of it; he fell back on box patterns of words, Anglo words, fitting them to the surges of the old Honda. "Pedal to the metal, pedal to the metal."

Bennett and he had first met at Christmas-time. Corrillo had been at the *News* less than a month then. Bennett's wife had killed herself, asphyxiated herself, in the garage. The *News* had sent the new kid to get a recent photo.

Now *that* had been a test. Corrillo had kept it brisk and polite, avoiding the stare of Bennett's two-year-old. This was news after all. The family had just moved out from back East, and not only was the husband prominent in criminal counseling, but the deceased had held a position at the local rehab clinic. Without a word, Bennett had gone into the back of the house and returned with a studio portrait of his wife. Good stuff: an attractive woman, still young, with a troubled smile. Three papers had picked up the graphic, including Eugene.

And that was six months ago. Corrillo had taken their rookie challenge and come out glittering. Granted, he hadn't done much hard news since. But on a suburban paper, how much hard news was there? Hey, if they wanted a test—wasn't it a test to have a kid on the way? Corrillo's wife was in her second trimester now. He'd felt the baby kick.

At last the penitentiary loomed, a stack of bricks in miles of sheep meadow. Bennett's new office.

But once he got inside, the job was a glide. Bennett had been appointed prison therapist. Since last time he'd even grown a classic analyst's goatee. Eager to please, to conform; apparently losing a wife out in this corner of the country hadn't put down roots enough for him. He had the professional man's vanity about his accessories, adjusting his glasses, tugging his watchband. Strictly a glide. For most of the interview Corrillo couldn't believe that the guy didn't remember him. It had to be some shrink's trick, make you forget you were under observation. Likewise this rope-colored office, with its ordinary window. On the wall opposite, the doctor had mounted one of his daughter's paintings, a knotted scrawl. Make you forget you were in a prison.

Bennett said that he would continue to put in a couple days a week at the Breakthrough House. "The clinic in town," he said, "where my wife used to work." Okay. Corrillo brought up the suicide, doing a few private adjustments of his own. When his mouth was closed he kept his molars apart, he sucked in his baby fat.

All that happened was, Bennett looked that much more determined to stay. The muscles in his head became visible. Corrillo stared so closely that he thought again of the photo, the dead wife. After the *Register-Guard* ran the shot, he'd had the entire page sent up from Eugene over the laser transmitter. Now the husband's face too might have just dropped into the transmitter tray. Nothing but flatness and distance. He hadn't even seen the young reporter who'd come to his house six months ago.

Corrillo sat aching from the drive down, the effort of acting relaxed. This was his chosen work? His notes looked like something from another, dryer dimension. Pay grade, patient load, commuting distance. He left the pad on the chair and went to the window. The unbarred glass was reinforced with thick plastic; it looked down on the exercise yard. Uneasy men moved in clusters, in blue fatigues.

"You don't think it was some kind of test?" he asked his wife. "Some kind of new-kid thing?"

Dora fit the paper plates into woven holders. She continued to sing, humming between snatches of Spanish.

"I mean, the first test is famous. Getting a photo of the deceased, I can understand that. You have to find out what a rookie's made of."

His wife set out the taco makings. The bright stuff was mounded in terra-cotta pots, also primary colors, decorated with birds and fishes. It was as if she was trying to force summer along, setting the table for a picnic. She sang some folksy sunshine thing, a river and butterflies over and over. Corrillo too hated this Oregon excuse for June, this lingering drizzle. Still the scene caught him by surprise. Signs of impatience in Dora? His own wife, and till this moment he would have thought she took every season of the year the same. Dora lifted the shells from the oven. Corn flour: the smell of a hot evening outdoors, baked-blue skies.

She put in a word for his editor. "Mr. Knotts wants you to fit in. This will work out, just be patient."

"I don't know, D. Just because my Dad used to fix his car . . ."

She turned towards the table, he noticed her belly. Another rush of nerves, he forgot what he was going to say. The whole scene was too much like the old country. The breadwinner drinking and bitching, the wife pregnant and docile.

These last few weeks Dora's skin had freckled, thickened, browned. In fact her people were Indian, Quiché, and Corrillo had fallen first for the eyes. That elastic Asian dark. He'd fallen for the old country, computer training or no computer training. But now, so dark? With potions for the weather? Dora might have been one of her own chanting grandmothers. Tonight even Corrillo's drink was Mexican, the spendy stuff after a rough day. He bought his beer in singles—Dora couldn't have alcohol around the house—so he could splurge when he wanted.

She hovered over the tacos, spreading onions and peppers the way she sprinkled food for the angelfish: a flight of skin that wrinkled the tinted water. Corrillo couldn't watch, he studied the fish. The tank took up almost half the table anyway. What were they doing with angelfish in a rental?

"I guess it's Bennett who really makes me wonder," he said finally. "I mean, Bennett himself."

His voice rang off the aquarium, unexpectedly loud. Dora was in her chair now. She folded her hands.

"Think about it, honey." God, he didn't even know if he'd interrupted her. "The man's staying around, he's decided to live out here."

"Hasn't he got a little girl?"

He nodded, taking a bite.

"Well when you're older, and you've got a child—"

"If it was me, I'd be gone." He shouldn't eat so fast, she put in such fierce spices. "I'd be out of here, man."

"Oh, Carlito."

The word came out flat, no accent. She'd been raised in Portland.

"Dora, I'm not kidding around. We'd be out of here tomorrow if you gave me the word."

"Car-lito. You sound like something out of *Viva Zapata!* Do you really think moving would solve anything? In A.A. we have a name for that, we call it doing a geographic."

Okay. Forget the Earth Mother; Dora wore her gossip face. She held her cup of soda by her cheek, a glazed tumbler, jungle red. Just now, it could have been the phone.

"Don't give me that sardonic smile, Carlito. Don't look like such a bright boy. You brought this up."

Bright boy? Corrillo bent to his taco, he fingered in extra lettuce to ease the jalapeño burn. Dora was older, almost twenty-six. Her days on the bottle, whew. There were women in her family who went flat-faced if you so much as mentioned her name.

"Dora, I thought we were talking about Bennett." He sucked his cheeks between his molars.

"I am talking about Bennett," she said. "You said he should move, and I'm telling you you're kidding yourself. Nobody gets anywhere just doing a geographic."

"Well lighten up, okay? I mean, you're the one who said we should be patient."

"I said *you* should be patient. Wherever Mr. Knotts wants you, that's where you should go. You should log in, and you should sit tight."

"Dora—"

"Till the baby comes, man, that's the only income we've got."

She slogged down more Dr. Pepper. Before dinner she'd filled an entire liter jug, careless as she hummed her Baez. Had he misread her, before dinner? Had this tough-guy kick been lurking in the Serenity act? She'd poured so much pop into the jug it fizzed over the earthenware.

"Dora, listen. The man told me he even took over some of his wife's people, at the Breakthrough House. He took over some of his dead wife's old patients."

She ate stiff-backed, carrying the taco tenderly to her mouth. Her smock remained clean. Dora declared that how a person handles major trauma—a death or something on that scale—that was one thing. The day-to-day that followed was the real test. Corrillo left his beer alone, thinking: almost twenty-six. His wife was nearly two years older. He'd fallen for that as much as for the eyes. Dora's grasp of how things worked had been a challenge, a crackle in his nerves as lively as whatever drove him to run up and down I-5 on assignments for the *News*. At first he couldn't get enough of all her buzzwords for hard times; she'd told him about "doing a geographic" before. But tonight it sounded like a lecture. Stiff-backed, telling him what to do. She waved her tumbler around like she was Knotts showing him the office.

He faced away, towards the rain-spotted deck doors. These rentals were laid out in a straight line: dining space, living space, deck space, lawn. Everyone shared the lawn, and everyone observed dinner hour.

"Look, Dora." Never mind if he were interrupting her. "I still can't see how the man can go back to Breakthrough House."

She raised her chin. "I'm working with people at A.A."

"Yeah but, alone in a room with some mush-for-brains? When you know that they know about your wife?"

"A person can't just glide along on the surface, Carlito. That's the big thing you learn in A.A."

"Look, do you *miss* drinking or something?"

He worked his bottle, deliberately. Out of one eye he spotted the angelfish, still and gaping.

"Really, D. A.A., A.A., A.A., A.A.! It's like I'm at a goddamn football game. Plus, how many times do you have to call me Carlito? You said it yourself, I'm the one with the income, I'm carrying the load. Do you realize who you're talking to? Do you *realize* who you're talking to?"

One more swallow. He faced her. After the first moment there was nothing but those swollen eyes, swollen and yet with the darkness in them expanding as well.

"You brought this up . . ."

His hard words went right up his spine. And he'd eaten too fast, drunk too fast, something was stuck above his heart. Corrillo managed. He hitched his chair next to hers, he did what he had to. He put enough into their kisses to draw a smile out of the last. When the baby pressed into his ribs he bent and whispered wisecracks. Listen, *poquito*, I must be crazy about her—that salsa wasn't made for kissing. Her hair smelled of fruit, the conditioner she used for curl. Corrillo came up with apologies.

"I know this is what I wanted," he said. "The suburbs, the life. I know I have to be a big grown-up boy."

Boy? What were these empty phrases? His hands remained cold, the rain, the beer. The lines he spoke had nothing to do with tonight, this spice ball in the gullet. She ran too deep for him. She'd had the extra aging, the worse tragedy; now she contained an additional heartbeat. He found Dora's hand and fit his fingers between hers. In moments the linked fleshy cluster was sopping with tears. But all he could do was fall back on the cosiest role: her sweet little confused Carlito. Really, they were running through role after role here, from folk songs to psychobabble, and he couldn't go deep enough for any of them. This was his chosen partner? Corrillo clasped her dripping hand. They rocked, rocked, between the aquarium and the deck doors.

Coming into the *News* always picked him up. The place was a cutting from a Rubik's cube, made of glass. Round the central courtyard Corrillo could see the whole circuit of the day's production. News, Advertising, Composing, Printing. And the distributors pulled up their vans at the corner farthest from the editor's cubicle. He couldn't wait to bring his kid here, to show the place off. The desks themselves had a new-wave tilt, each one made lopsided by a video terminal on a folding swivel arm. There were mornings when it seemed like one or two turned their calm fly's faces to welcome him.

Corrillo would have preferred a paper that came out Sundays. He'd like to see some think pieces, some deeper probing. He was tired of the promotional copy clamping a limit on everything; even the syndicate stuff got hacked. But the publishers knew where their money came from—the tech firms and the malls. And he'd chosen not to try for the big papers, the *Oregonian* especially. Dora agreed, it would be degrading to start as a gofer. She agreed: before they moved up I-5, he had to make a name for himself.

This morning, the article on Bennett's new appointment hadn't appeared. Of course Corrillo hadn't thought much of the writing. His concentration just hadn't been there. First thing, he called up the file.

No major changes. Yet the piece came up highlighted, glowing electronic blocks against which the letters were rivets. That had to mean Knotts had done a final edit.

After a minute a reflection loomed, a goldfish in the net of copy. Corrillo turned and almost put his nose in the gut of the man who'd come up behind. It was Vic, one of the full-time staff. An absolutely militant jogger. Corrillo had glimpsed the belt buckle, no belly overhang in the way.

Vic wasn't the kind to back off. "Knotts liked how you handled that."

"He did?" Corrillo said. "He didn't run it."

"We needed the space. You remember, we had the promo copy on the new Galleria."

Corrillo turned back to the screen. Promo copy.

"He liked how you handled it, Carlos. You know, since it was Bennett."

Corillo turned again, staring, chin cocked. The older man flexed his fists in his pockets. Corillo couldn't think what to say, and Vic's look gave no clue. Like Dora with an A.A. pledge who'd fallen off the wagon: refusing to make it easy.

"The piece should run tomorrow, Carlos."

Corrillo turned away, trying to clear his head of the man's morning powder, trying to put words to his question. Was Bennett some kind of . . .? Does this mean I . . .? All of a sudden the terminals and cubicles around him lost their tekky thrill; instead they made him think of high school. In school he'd sat in rooms like this, him and a thousand others, filling in SATs. Even then he'd wanted to work in such a place, fluorescents overhead and the noises of paper. White-collar like a *Norteamericano.*

Now all of a sudden the setup was no big deal. His keyboard looked like a kitchen utensil, something his wife might use. Corrillo said nothing.

"You know, Carlos, that Galleria copy is important copy." Vic remained at his elbow. "If that place fills up we might get Sunday circulation."

"Mm-hmm." He set his fingers in typing-class position.

"You'll get a lot more shots at a Pulitzer, you know, if we get Sunday circulation."

"Cut me some slack, Vic." It helped that the guy was aggravated. "I figure we're all going for the same brass ring."

Once more the jogger flexed his pockets; the belt buckle nodded. Then at last Corrillo found out why Vic had stopped by. The man had today's assignment. Mr. Knotts wanted another interview—and this one was *in*, positively. They'd already set aside the inches. Corrillo tried not to grin, he looked too Beaver Cleaver when he grinned. But even Vic seemed to realize he'd passed the test. The man propped his butt on Corrillo's desk.

"You should like this one today," he said. "A real weirdo."

They laughed together. The subject was one of those, what did you call them? An environmental terrorist. The lumber company people caught him red-handed, spiking trees. The judge had ordered psychological testing over at that place, what was its name? Breakthrough House.

The clinic lay on the other side of I-5, the older part of town. The man's name was right there in the foyer. *Randolph Bennett,* the calligraphy softer than you'd expect for a doctor. It was too much of a coincidence. For them to send Corrillo here was almost as hokey as when he used to set up run-ins with Dora.

At the reception desk the radio was tuned to public broadcasting. Roots music, grunt and strum. The woman who came for Corrillo didn't give her name. He followed her into the back and up a flight. The stairway lacked an overhead light, the only window gave onto drizzle. He suffered bad flashes. He saw Bennett and Knotts in one of the near rooms, unsmiling, hardly breathing; they poked a marker back and forth over a map of the suburb.

Cut it out. You'd think Breakthrough House scared him more than the state pen. The building was Alfred Hitchcock material, neo-Gothic, willed to the clinic by one of the pioneer families. More than likely the musty reek never left the halls. The place teemed with '60s types of course. The woman taking him in wore knickers and knee-socks, plus those low-heel sandals with the fairy-tale name he always forgot. Red angels on her gray winter socks. Upstairs, the man he'd come to interview was another one: a huge, limping longhair. His patient's uniform showed some belly. A spook in a spook-house, fraying and hobbled by chains.

The woman stuck them in what must once have been the laundry closet. No door, and built-in cupboards to the ceiling. She had the nerve to smile before she left.

Corrillo even forgot about Bennett. How long had it been since this weirdo'd had a decent shower? The environmentalist didn't answer questions, he followed a private catechism. His gestures widened the V of his shirt, his chest at least wasn't so scary. Some of these big guys caved in after thirty-five.

"Man," the environmentalist kept saying, "if I'm bad and crazy, what does that make *you?*"

Corrillo managed to keep him on track long enough to get a name, Babe. And there were bits of background: "Man, I'm just your basic West Texas badass peyote messiah." But the echo was oppressive. Before long Corrillo had backed his chair against the doorway, he'd stretched a leg into the hall. What kind of notes could he be taking, anyway? *Man, those logging company dudes, they thought this was Star Wars man, they had this laser shit now supposed to home in on the spikes in the trees.* Was Corrillo here to record fantasies? Babe explained what the spiking accomplished. In the woods a fragment could fly back in the logger's face; in the mill a saw could explode. The *News* had all that in its files. Corrillo rested his head against a groove in the molding. He thought of the drive over, the red lights he'd run, the speed traps he'd beaten.

"If I'm bad and crazy . . ." Babe began.

His long arms dropped. After a moment he roughed his beard. The sound was mushy, the guy must be pouring sweat. On the small chair he looked mushy, all hair and hospital fatigues. Abruptly Babe revealed that, this last time out, the spikes had spoken to him.

"They speak dolphin language, man. You know, the squeaks. They squeak when you knock 'em in and they go on squeaking once they're inside."

Corrillo stood and shoved his pad in his pocket.

"Dolphin talk, man. I swear it'll break your heart, you have to listen so close. They tell you they don't want to hurt anybody."

Corrillo faced the hall, craning left-right.

"But man, once those logging guys catch 'em . . ."

The staircase remained dark and empty, the other doors closed. He'd always known these hippie-dippie types were hypocrites. They took you in with their gobbledygook—words like "transition" and "incident," a lot of softcore mumbo-jumbo—but what they had here was dangerous. Babe said that the spikes had told him their *names.* They'd told him about making the big machine saws burst, about flying out the factory windows and living in the millpond. "They can live forever in that millpond, man." Corrillo couldn't look at him. He kept his back to the room till he heard movement, and then he came round with arms cocked.

Babe remained in his chair, sagging, nodding. The noise was from the stairs. And that only proved to be more of the same. A crazy woman was padding down to this level barefoot.

She wore nothing but a long man's t-shirt. Out of the dark stairwell she carried the seaweed smell of too much time in bed. Crazy: she was like an illustration out of an old dictionary. Yet she was lovely, even the slant tangle of neck-length curls, the cloud-color shirt with the rippled heaviness of wear. College age at most. Corrillo heard another sound, fragile. Had he forgotten about Babe? The environmentalist had his fingers pressed to a cupboard door. He was making them squeak against the wood, to show Corrillo how the dolphin-spikes sounded.

He looked in the hall again. The young woman hadn't even seen him. She seemed to float before a door at the far end, then a man answered her knock. Bennett.

It was the doctor, the goatee. He closed his office door without noticing there was anyone else in the hall.

Corrillo had his pad out before he was back in his seat. He could see his interview taking shape as if on his monitor. Question: How could Babe have allowed himself to get caught? Had he really not heard the loggers coming, the trucks, the earth movers? Corrillo rapped his knuckles against the metal folding chair whenever the man started to drift. There'd been enough free association for one day. He himself had acted like a kid, lost in a fantasy about some silly test. This guy had asked for pressure tactics. Question: So you felt remorse? Corrillo broke a sweat, his ribs itched. You began to understand the harm you might do, and you felt remorse?

The motive always came down to pain. It was pain by one name or another, and then the urge to make better. First some bug of conscience, and the rest a dream to provide the creature a home.

By the time the aide returned, the woman in knee-socks, Babe had shrunk into a baggy cartoon question mark. The hair on his underlip trembled.

She didn't smile this time. She might have had words for Corrillo. Can you find your own way out? or something. He didn't catch it. He was trying to figure staff cutbacks. How else could they leave him alone in this narrow place full of secrets? The aide got her arm round Babe, they bent together like an old married couple.

Corrillo had to flatten himself against a door in the hall to let them by. Through the panels he heard sobbing. The woman and the big renegade went out of sight upstairs, up the way the sexy patient had come. Faintly the hallway resonated, sick people in every room.

How could they just *ignore* him? Then Corrillo was at Bennett's door; he was at the keyhole.

He'd had no lunch and he felt the squatting in his stomach. The door was thick, the fitting snug. The laundry closet where he and Babe had talked must have been at the servants' end of the hall. Bennett had the master bedroom. There was a skylight here, a white shine on the hanging dust, hot weather at last. Corrillo knew what he'd tell the editor if he was caught, too. He'd say they should do a story on this guy. Bennett was like Corrillo's old Dad: he'd stuck it out and made a life. He was proof that there was no place better than the Willamette Valley.

But then, no way Corrillo was going to be caught. Not with these old floorboards, not with the kind of laser alertness he had going. He flattened his face against the door. He cupped his hands around his single open eye. The keyhole was old-fashioned, its shape promising, like the raised fist on those posters from the '60s. But the edges of the opening were hemmed in by lock-works, the angle of view was impossible. Corrillo sank to one knee. How could there be so little room? He was as bad off as Dora, the way she had to sling her belly around all the time. The one thing he could be sure of was a window on the opposite wall, a porthole job. He could hear only the rhythms of what was being said, the doctor's clipped calm, the patient's fluttering search. He blinked slowly, trying to focus; there were more bad flashes. There was Dora's hurt look, last night, her stare deepening and darkening. Come *on*. Why should he be saddled with that? She said he'd brought up the nasty stuff—all right, he'd brought it up—"All right," he muttered into the doctor's door, into his own thickening day-smell. But they'd spent the night shadow-dancing through a hundred poses and glances. He'd poured his beer down the drain; he'd presented her with the empty bottle. "You were happy," Corrillo said, "you were smiling." He felt the lock-face in his eyeball.

"Hey, you! Hey. What're you *doing?*"

He didn't hear the voice clearly. He came round expecting the woman again. But these were stocky male legs, old jeans patched at the knee with paisley. The shock emptied Corrillo's face. He dropped onto his butt. The orderly only squared his stance, fists to hips.

"What are you doing? Who are you talking to?"

His editor had a soft face, a touch fisheyed. His looks didn't fit in at the *News*, really. Andy Knotts wasn't much for staying in shape. But that face of his fit in better at the office than it had where he and Corrillo had first met. The man had coached JV soccer. In the locker room they'd called him Candy Nuts; none of the other coaches came to practice in a jacket and tie. Still, Knotts had put Corrillo in at center forward. He'd said many times that he admired Corrillo's father, up by his bootstraps. He'd found a place on the *News*. Today, after Breakthrough House called, Knotts said they should go get a drink.

Corrillo tried the alibi: Bennett's worth a story. . . . The editor's look only softened that much more.

Worse, the man rejected every watering hole they stopped at. On this side of the interstate you got the new places, windows for walls and high-key decor. "Christ," Knotts said after the second one. "Might as well be drinking in a goddamn fishbowl."

Tough talk. Today's case must really be eating him.

"Tell me something, son," the editor said. "Is it just the Valley? Or can't you find a decent bar anywhere, these days?"

Corrillo smiled lamely, head down. This was his own silly fault, him and his imaginary test. And Knotts went on complaining, he didn't have much time. They wound up buying singles at the new Circle-K, across from the new Galleria. "These places are counting on spillover business, right? So why should we be different from anybody else?" They pulled into the Galleria lot. The engine quit, such silence. Corrillo had hoped to get a car like this one day, a gliding Swedish or German job, an instrument panel.

But when the old man spoke, he began with the Bennetts.

"What?" Corrillo asked. "The wife was a what?"

"She was a free spirit. See, she was his patient first, back East."

"Andy, can I just ask—what does that mean, a free spirit?"

"Settle down, Carlos."

"Well am I supposed to know what all these things *mean?*"

"Settle down. If I've heard this story, there's been enough broadcasting it around already."

The doctor had inspired the wife, Knotts explained. She'd gone for her Masters in Counseling, and the only place they'd applied for work was the Valley. "Having the kid was part of it. They were the kind of people, everything's part of a plan." Corrillo wondered what the plan was now, letting him in on this. A last treat before execution? But why would the old man worry about Corrillo spreading the story around, if he wasn't going to be in the office any more?

"Anyway," Knotts said, "it worked out. The Bennetts took their act to Oregon." Then before the wife had been three months on the job—the editor's voice was matter-of-fact, but his hand was busy with the knot of his tie—two of her patients filed harassment charges. Two of the women.

Corrillo recalled his own half-naked visitor, her sweat and madness. A memory like a kick in the spine.

"You're alone with them," the editor was saying. "All alone in that office. And you're hearing about their ghosts and monsters, it must be hard not to come out with your own." The wife locked herself in the garage the night she got the news.

Corrillo couldn't catch the man's eyes. "That's why she killed herself?"

The editor shrugged. "She was his patient, back East."

"That's pretty flimsy. Just two people complained?"

"Flimsy, listen to him. Flimsy. Do you still believe that if somebody's got a degree, they must be hard as nails?"

Corrillo felt a blush rising. He shook his head.

"I didn't have to tell you this story, you know."

His cheeks were hot, his baby fat showed. But who worried about baby fat?

"Andy, I just think, she must have had some motive—"

"*Forget* the motive, Carlos. Look, there's probably some, some wormy little cluster of secrets at the center of every story. It's always the same old shit, isn't it? Guilt, or whatever? There's always some little fistful of worms the person finds it hard to talk about."

"I know that, Andy." He had to grin. "After today, I swear, that's like the only thing I know for sure."

"Yeah, but you can't be charging around looking for that. You can't be a goddamn bull in a china shop."

"Well I'm trying to find out what I can be."

Still the grin, and never mind Beaver Cleaver. A lecture like this must mean he was still alive at the *News*. The old man kept on, he talked about why he'd moved out to the suburbs. He even used the expression "learning experience." Corrillo swigged his beer. He took in the work vans in the parking lot, bright with company logos, and the darker alphabet of the men at work behind the tinted shop windows. He would get another crack at these places after all, he'd find out what they were made of. This was his chosen work.

Rain-spatter clung to the wide Galleria, a glimmering fishnet. Knotts paused, drank. Then he asked, did Corrillo appreciate what had happened here? Did he really, fully appreciate it?

"Hey," Corrillo said, "Andy. You better believe I appreciate it. You could have eliminated my position."

"Well I figured that wouldn't be right. After all, I never expected my little plan would turn out like this."

Plan? *Plan?* Corrillo needed no more than a glance at the man. Those hurting, out-of-kilter eyes. He turned back to the Galleria furious.

"Son—you do realize, I've been testing you?"

Dora, where was Dora?

All Corrillo had to go on was the lounge chair unfolded on the deck. The rubber cross-strips were wormy under the drizzle, and an empty tumbler stood beside the chair. Empty. He stood out on the soaked planks, turning the heavy cup between his hands. Glazed clay, slick and glinting.

His wife had left no note, no word. Her purse hung from the bedroom knob, the wallet inside. Maybe she figured she had enough to lug around these days. The weather was gentle, the development quiet; a person could practically go naked if they didn't use the car. Out on the deck, Corrillo quickly lost the metal-plated ferocity he'd come home with. Five minutes ago he'd come screeching into the driveway, raging into the house. D., we're *out* of here! We're moving! He'd gone straight for the phone—Babe, don't we have the *Oregonian*'s number? And of course he went on talking to Knotts, every word another brittle satisfaction. Well what was I supposed to do at Breakthrough House? Just see the doctor's name and like, shine on? Just like, play along, play the game . . .

Then, these bits and pieces in the rain. Dora's overcoat dangled, dry, on the rack beside the phone.

Corrillo could read nothing off the cup. And there was no one on the lawn, no one in the nearby windows. All the children were at school.

She couldn't have gone far. Even Safeway was only a mile. Any minute now she'd trot in, her brown face bound in a sensible scarf, and he could get back to the table-pounding conviction he'd brought home. The angelfish were still caught up in it. His hard words had them reeling, he could see it from out on the deck. Corrillo cradled the cup at his chest and stepped back inside. He shut the reinforced glass. The heaviness behind his ribs was only beer, a thick wet sack. This tumbler was only an empty container, scrawled with glaze. No way she'd left it out to lose its smell. Here in the living space the smells were reliable, the In-sink-erator and the vacuuming. The tumbler felt like more of the same, squarish, glossy: like all the new-minted American surfaces Corrillo admired. Nonetheless, abruptly, he put his nose to the thing and inhaled—a test.

He didn't notice an odor. What struck him was the sound, the echo; it terrified him. A whistle, a plea, a moan, a wail.

He jerked his head back. Still there was no one in the place except the fish, going crazy in their tank.

Hot

BRO HAD JUST FOUND his good season groove, the groove where you got the big flies and the deep shots, when his brother Sly was kidnapped. The news didn't seem to register. The call came from his mother while the team's equipment manager was in the motel room with him. One minute Bro was arranging to have a video made of his swing, and then without so much as changing his tone of voice: "What'd you say? Where'd he go? Mama who, *who....*" Then while he got the facts straight, the equipment manager standing there brought to mind the old Richard Pryor line, looking stupid was white folks' natural expression. In fact Bro found that what he wanted most was to get off the phone and hurt the man.

He let his mother know he wasn't alone, he roughed his way past the guilt by using the word "ofay." He told her goodbye and then sat more upright between the stiff motel pillows. His younger brother Sly, he told the equipment man. Last seen outside a hardware store in a mall south of Newark. They figured kidnapped because they'd found his Air Jordans, the ones with *Sly-y-y* on the trim. The laces had been cut and the shoes thrown in a dumpster.

It hurt the man, yes. His jawline went through changes and his eyes were too large. But when he shouldered his duffle bag, the manager came up with one of those lame and useless Oregon sweetie pie smiles. Uh-oh. By tomorrow or the next day, everybody on the team would know.

Alone, Bro remained planted. Waiting, waiting, his long spine flat against the wall. Eventually it came to him that he should call his mother back. The receiver felt heavy and the dialing was difficult, the whole instrument just the opposite from ten minutes before.

It helped when he learned, over the next two-three days, that his trouble gave the entire organization the numbs. Of course he expected the team to keep it from people on the outside. But what he got was amazing, some kind of multiplication dance in slo-mo. First the ones in charge here in Salem said they didn't know what Angels policy was, they'd have to call the lawyer up in the majors. Then Bro had to call the lawyer up in the majors himself, and he said he didn't know what Angels policy was either. Plus everybody kept going back to the same word, *personal*. Bro wondered what kind of a *person* they had in mind, putting guys through such a runaround. It took the owner the better part of a week to come and tell him face to face that Salem couldn't pay the airfare. Up with the big club it would be different of course, he said. The big club would assume the expense for this kind of personal matter.

Terrible timing, too. The owner had arrived when the locker room was full, everybody suiting up for b.p.

"Hey, I'm just a guy who sells farm tools. I can't handle round-trip all the way back to New Jersey." He'd hiked one foot up onto the bench next to Bro, one flashy damn boot that somehow he'd found income enough to handle.

"The way you're hitting now," he said, "they'll probably move you up to Sacramento in no time anyway."

Bro went into his Mau-Mau glare. "If you gonna *fly*," he said, "it cost the same from Sa-cra-men-to."

And he didn't take his eyes off the owner till the man had backed into a mop and bucket. Big Guernsey face all stitched up in another of those smiles. It had the effect Bro was after, a couple of the other guys were openly snickering.

The last thing he needed was to have this trouble throw off his rep around here. Especially since every time he called home, every day after his roommate headed for the park, the talk with his mother always left him so out of touch he could hardly say where he'd been between when he'd hung up the phone in the motel and when he'd started to pull on his cleats in the clubhouse. He came to work in a dry-eyed Twilight Zone. He wished this had happened while they were on the road; acting like a zombie was natural on the road. Worse, the woman did it to him with sweetness. Even now, when the guys stopped by his locker after the owner had gone—high five, low five, Bro that was *bad*—he was glad they couldn't hear how soft and easy his mother came on.

Bro believed he knew how her mind was working. He recalled his father, a heavy-handed whiskey beard who'd run off when his mother was pregnant with Sly. He figured she didn't want to make the same mistake twice. All through the week's home-stand, she'd begin the conversation by asking how he'd done the night before. When he finished reeling off the latest she'd say something like: Oh well you got to stay there, then. And she'd remind him that she had his sisters. Even then, all she'd say was, They a godsend. She never told him straight out that Toola had come from Baltimore as soon as she'd heard the news. That kind of thing was up to Bro to figure out for himself.

By Thursday he was asking the local guys if they knew a place where he could work out privately. Somebody with the Fellowship of Christian Athletes offered a church lot, but Bro knew there'd be strings attached. He kept asking, patient with the standard joke— Gee Bro, I'd let you use my *ID*, but. . . . He'd noticed long ago that in Oregon they mostly didn't have black kids. But these locals were walk-ons, your basic marginal talent. He never much liked cutting them down.

Then once he'd found a place and started taking his hacks (at least he'd been able to pry loose a couple pieces of club equipment), it got him nowhere. He set up in the middle field of three empty hundred-yard stretches side by side, some private college layout. Not a Christian in sight, nor some doofus cowboy with the nerve to call himself an owner. Nonetheless it was as if Sly and the rest of Bro's family were still as much in place as the batting tee and the webbing that caught his shots. In fact once he broke a sweat the magic of the groove returned, everything became concentrated in the tension of the grip against his callouses, in the crack as he got hold of the ball and the *thut* as it was snared in the rubberized net. Other than that he had room only for the fantasies, rocking out as usual from just behind his eyes, the announcer's tinny hype and the crowd's vacuum roar and the whole stadium going wild with flags and paper airplanes for 360 degrees round the silent mountain horizon. When Bro spoke there was no echo. Even the weather was vacant, perfect. He'd gone into this streak just as the rain-outs ended, and now the air was so clear that when he finished his workout, all the way across an adjacent field Bro could pick out a man from Building & Grounds.

Another black man, in fact. That as much as his cart and shovel made Bro think Building & Grounds. He hooked his fingers in the cage and squinted. The brother wore a Walkman. He appeared to be laughing and he shuffled his feet viciously; he was dishing lime onto a row of plants, each scoop so heaping and brilliant that Bro was certain it would burn the roots. He realized his own rush, his workout rush, was gone. Still he kept staring till his sweat chilled and he had to start his cleanup just to get the blood circulating.

Sunday, the one day game during the week. Families in the stands and a little more media. Bro was still rocking Godzilla, he could feel it the first time he stepped inside the foul lines. When he got his third hit of the afternoon—a deep, deep fly, way over the Valley Homes sign in right—it became obvious to him that working out alone was only more of the same. It was part of the problem, stonewall stonewall. Just, after the game, how was he supposed to deal with three reporters at once?

Bro made sure the young woman from the radio was there, then ducked into the showers. He had another player bring him his towel and slacks. As soon as the pants were on, he went after the woman and backed her into a corner. He hooked his forearm against her shoulder, so close that when her startled face came round her hair brushed his naked chest. She had that working-blond wave; Bro flashed on a TV commercial when it flared round her face.

Then they were huddled by the doorway. Bro announced that he was dedicating this season to his brother. Just announced it, loud enough to carry through the ghetto blasters and the usual tomcatting.

She punched her recorder, he ran down the facts.

"Whoa," she said the first time he paused. "How long have you been sitting on this?"

He blinked. "Ahh, I'm not sure you're understanding what I'm saying."

"Well you've been awfully strong. You don't even know if he's dead or alive."

"No. No see, this isn't about me. This is about my brother. I want it to be like all the bats and all the balls, everything you see around here . . . plus whatever skills or like, knowledge I may have picked up so far . . ."

He was bent close to her machine, trying to think; deliberately, she wrapped her hand round his bicep. "You want it to be like all that's for him?"

Bro nodded, but already the doubts had set in again. When he straightened up she was slow letting go of his arm, and he started thinking twice about that tickle at his chest earlier. Why come to this white girl? He had something so simple to get off his chest, why complicate it right at the start? When he'd gone after the woman he'd told himself it was the radio thing, getting the exact quote. He had a lot of respect for the men in the bigs who wouldn't talk to the newspapers. Now Bro had to take a moment, resting against the locker-room wall. And though she must have noticed how badly the concrete would soak her sweater, she wedged herself between him and the corner. Of course that was her job, she didn't want the guys hustling past to interrupt. But she was close enough for him to pick up her day smell even with all the cologne and deodorant nearby. And couldn't he at least have buckled his belt? One of the other bad boys on the club ambled past, and he gave Bro that little grin, that little look while he slowed down, rolling easy sideways hip-to-hip going past—and Bro found himself smiling back.

Smiling. How could he have forgotten: this was still so new for them. A woman in their busy, stinking room, all the uptight wisecracks. Hey, check out the new *piece* from the radio. After Bro caught himself smiling he couldn't help glancing sideways, worrying what she thought. But she was busy with her recorder. He noticed instead that she'd dressed down again, granola and jeans even on Sunday. If only she were more like the townies who waited outside the park, the eyeliner, the beaded feather earrings dangling almost to their shoulders. The accessories would have cooled whatever wildcat pump had carried him out of the game.

But he'd cornered her, she'd grabbed him. Now what was she asking?

"How old am I?" he repeated.

He saw that she must have five years on him at least. He wouldn't have been able to tell if she hadn't stood so close; all the rain out here kept the skin elastic.

"Bro?" she said. "I mean are you old enough to come have a drink with me? This is no place to talk."

The other faces were no better. The guys who weren't watching him had their backs squared, shower-drops clinging to their shoulder blades as if they'd turned to chrome.

"Bro? You there?"

The equipment manager swung by, fingering a hefty watch out of the valuables bag. Bro nodded, yeah that's me. When the reporter took it for an okay it seemed like a nitpick, like the kind of thing a wimp would do, to slow down and tell her different.

She drove some kind of soft-shoulder foreign car, looked exotic just sitting in the lot. Not that Bro needed any help. Already he was seeing lingerie. She said her name was Robin, "but I like it when guys call me Rob." She said she had to run an errand before dinner, and when he asked where, she smiled. "It's outside town, Bro— but let me keep it a surprise." All these white girls had *lingerie*.

But the little car's front seat was a hassle. His thinking became more ordinary while he struggled for legroom. A bad sign; for a long time now he'd believed the head-trips had something to do with his success. About the same time as he'd discovered he could hit the long ball, Bro had noticed how quick and beefy the dreams would come. Announcers going hoarse and the whole works. Bro even used them as part of his pre-game, the way other players had superstitions about how to lace their cleats or when to start their run. He thought it gave him an advantage, having an invisible prep. Nobody knew about it, when he stood picturing the shots leaving the park or what the situation would be with men on base. Nobody could mess, and so nobody was ever going to know. Nobody except his brother anyway. Bro had always figured he'd tell Sly sooner or later, the only other man in the family after all. He would have confided in him already if the boy hadn't been so much younger. The boy still clung to their mama more than Bro liked to see.

Bro caught an awful smell, thick machinery rubber. He discovered he had his body curled onto one haunch, away from the woman, his nose buried in the rubber lips of the window. He squared round and tried to look like he was scoping out the view. But Salem of course was nobody's idea of a city. Five minutes beyond the ballpark and you never saw a house bigger than ranch-style, while the cross-streets came out of scrubby open landscape like a line drawn on a map.

"Can we talk now?" Robin asked. "While we're getting there?"

He saw she'd set up the tape recorder on the console between the seats. And the surprise of her prettiness, when she turned and the hair halved her face—that too only made Bro aware of how his head had cooled. If this were a game he'd be off his stroke. He tried to relax, but the seat's headrest barely came up to his neck, and the best he could do for starters were the week-old facts of the kidnapping. Robin appeared to understand. She let the tape run a few moments. When she spoke, she sounded careful.

"Is your family . . . are they working with all the agencies? Will you know as soon as anything happens?"

"They say something like this, you just can't tell."

"They? They who?"

"My mama. I mean my mama tells me what all those agencies or whatever tell her."

Robin nodded, but her eyes were active.

"They all say," he went on, "you can't make no plans on the boy for certain. You could be thinking he's dead and in the ground a long time, and then one night like, his face might all of a sudden flash by on the TV."

Nod again, then silence again. The road was so straight the tape must have picked up nothing but its own hum.

"Was he big, Bro?" she asked suddenly. "Like you?"

"Naw, not like me." The numbness remained, this was more of his mother talking. "He might still shoot up in high school, though."

"High school?"

No hand-me-down lines for that. Bro sat up awkwardly; something under the seat jabbed the tendons in his heels, so hard he winced. Bending, he whacked his head on the glove box. "Gyahh." And then Robin started being nice to him of course. Touching his shoulder, gently repeating his name. His first clear thought was, *The media*. The woman wasn't even saying "Bro," now, but his full, press-guide name. This couldn't have been what he'd wanted. He took a moment, his cheek against the warm dash, and he could pin it down exactly: he'd wanted to get someplace real for the first time in days. Not this—reporter's trick. A stray rocket and then a scene out of a Roadrunner cartoon. A sexy Roadrunner cartoon, to boot. Robin was halfway to giving him a back rub by now.

He felt under the seat and found what had poked him. A record album, that'd do to change the subject.

"Hey Rob, what's this?" He came up holding the LP, and her hand fell away. "Ain't this a little old for you?"

"Oh." She laughed. "That was my boyfriend's—I mean my *ex*-boyfriend's. I'm not seeing anyone now. Wow, that guy was so into the blues."

Bro grinned, setting the album on his lap. The grin was all he could manage.

"That's Howlin' Wolf," she said eventually. "You really don't know?"

"He looks like my father," Bro said. Meantime making up his mind: okay. The media was a tool, they even said so down in Instructional League. Plus anybody on the club could have told him this girl was a newcomer. Okay, so use it like a tool, and pay the price next time her game gets a little clumsy. Talking about the family after all seemed somewhere near what he was after. Except then—couldn't have been more than a couple minutes later—she was pulling off the highway. She was heading up towards what looked like a farmhouse and stables.

Hot

Of course it had to be a farm. Bro could see livestock a field or two away, through the ballgame roar of the driveway gravel. It was just that everything appeared so square and functional. There were none of the nooks and crannies he remembered from field trips in grade school. The satellite dish was planted between a couple naked concrete blocks, the house stood dark and empty. Instead of a garage the owner had nailed pink corrugated plastic to the top of some upright 4 x 4's. The movieola effect when they pulled in under that plastic was wildly out of place, like the once in a while when a pigeon flaps down in the infield.

The woman didn't move after she cut the engine. Bro realized he'd been quiet, checking the place out.

"Your father ten years ago, and now your brother." She exhaled hard and found his eyes.

"Well what it makes me think of, these last couple days anyway, I think of like East Coast, West Coast. I think of the difference between the two, I mean."

She frowned. "What's that got to do with you?"

"Well like, my family would have had it different out here." He raised his eyes to the pink ripples overhead. "We wouldn't have wound up living such a bad life, out here. Because it just isn't bad around here the way it is back East. This is a safe place."

She was silent again, but there seemed an edge on it. He lowered his head in time to see how her frown enriched her eyes, deepened the blue. Then she put in some word just to mark the beat. Bro was left unfolding himself from the car while she headed for the stables.

And inside the building, the brown shadows warmed by the long day's sun, she became that much stranger. Despite a church-like ceiling and a center aisle wide as Bro's arm-span, Robin made the place. Her outfit had a new effect, the boots especially. She knew it too. The woman strutted along crooning. Of course her actual words couldn't be what Bro thought he was hearing, "Yo mama, yo mama." But in fact the whole scene had started to feel impossibly familiar. The hay damp from the loft opposite, getting into the eyes as soon as you came in the door; the snortle and hoof-tread within the deep stalls. Some kind of locker-room flashback? Certainly his head was warming again. Random pink and white

63

craziness fluttered alongside Robin's croon, as it rose and fell through the harsh smoker's cough of the animals. A butterfly in the locker room?

At the next-to-last stall she opened the bolt. "There's the boy," she cooed. "There's my sweet boy."

Her explanations went by in a rush. A gelding on lease, "the fulfillment of an adolescent *dream*." Bro had never liked being lectured at, and Robin's slick work with the reins and bridle made the breathless rap seem like an act. But he could see what all the excitement was about. Robin led the horse out between them— and of course Bro fell back as soon as the first awkward foreleg emerged, it'd been a long time since anything had tightened his nuts like that—but he couldn't stop staring. The face was sharp yet chocolate. Bird-like planes of bone ended in square formal teeth. The shoulders and ribs went by in skinfull ripples, first brown then red, and Bro couldn't tell where the light came from.

Robin was saying, "Yes Mothra, ye-es Mothra." At least he recognized the movie. The New York stations had played those Jap monster things all the time. "You didn't think I'd keep you cooped up all day, did you?"

Actually, getting some fresh air seemed like a great idea. He wouldn't feel so scared out in the fresh air. After all they were under the loft now, in the worst of the settling hay-dirt. Bro set his face. He was past the high, sculpted butt before Robin had finished rolling back the door.

But when she turned and saw him, she stopped him with a stiffarm to the chest. "*Watch* it! You don't ever come up on a horse from behind like that."

Out in the corral, she was apologetic. "Bro, I've wanted to own one of these so long—well I guess I'm overdoing things a little." But Bro, keeping maybe a yard's head start just in case, was still into hyper-awareness. Making a mental note that his head and Mothra's were the same height, doing a Laser Eyes number about the distance to the nearest shelter. On-deck awareness. Whenever he tuned in Robin, it was like she was talking in an echo chamber.

Hot

"It's the same animal," she said, "think of it that way." They'd reached the fence now. She was pulling off the bridle.

"Front or back, he's the same big old Mothra. Just, from one direction he'll be your best friend and from the other, he might kick your head in."

Bro tried to relax, cowboy-posing at the rail.

"But listen to me." She smiled, still apologizing. "Your turn, Bro. Tell me, what do you think of my baby?"

Freed, the horse had moved off, nosing into bulky mounds of grass. When Bro spoke, he discovered the echo was gone.

"Mighty nice," he said. "Someone like you, not that old, and already you got something you always dreamed of. Mighty nice life."

"Oh God. Don't start that again."

Bro cocked his head differently.

"Don't start in again about the peaceable kingdom out here in the Northwest. I swear, people have got their heads in the sand about that." She shook her head, her eyes darkened.

"You know," Bro tried, "maybe if we just stuck to the interview—"

"No no no," she said, "this is part of the interview. Honestly. I think this is why I went into journalism in the first place. I was just so sick of everyone always saying that where I grew up, everything was beautiful. Hasn't anybody heard of the kind of *monsters* we get in these woods? The runaways up in the hills? Listen, I did a piece on one of them, those guys live like savages."

Bro had his tongue between his teeth. All he could think of was another bad-boy putdown—I thought I was the one supposed to be upset.

"Now someone like you, Bro. You've got a real story to tell, *real* trouble." Though she'd lifted her eyes, she was staring past him. "That's what I'm in it for."

He turned away, but the view didn't make things any easier. These last naked hours before sundown. Out here in the farmland, it was as if the mountains east and west were themselves only arbitrary cutoffs, something to give a person a break from the endless air. Bro was in a worse zone than after one of his mother's calls. Someone else was pouring out their soul to *him*: a white girl.

Just to keep himself located, he had to concentrate on the splinters prickling his palms. He frowned at the rattle of a tractor nearby.

"Oh Bro, oh boy," Robin was saying. "*Wow* what a shot."

He turned back, wondering if he'd missed something. She was framing him with squared thumbs and forefingers, a loop of bridle hanging from one fist.

"You glaring across the fields, and Mothra there sort of looming behind you. And when you were like clenching your arms, *great*. I've got to get my camera."

"Camera?" His smile held up decently. "You're radio, ain't you?"

"Give me a break, Bro. You know how it is when you're just starting out."

She was turning on the sweetness again, and her hair and smile were stung nicely by the low sun. But it was the reins and bridle that made him agree to wait. In fact after Robin handed him the tangle of leather and hooks, lighter than he'd expected, Bro was glad to hear her explain that she'd need a few minutes. She'd have to load and choose a lens. Bro smiled more honestly, nodding. He'd decided by then that what he needed was some time with the horse. A few minutes on his own, put an end to this rabbitting around. Horses after all were part of the life. Dick Allen, the original in-your-face badass lumber man, the only player Bro had ever let on was a hero—Dick Allen raised thoroughbreds.

Robin's boot-steps died away through the stables. Mothra stood with head and neck over a far corner of the corral.

The bridle fitted comfortably over one shoulder. Then with that arm Bro clung to the fence top, so stiff as he walked along that he noticed the tractor again. The racket meant business as usual, part of the life. But now the animal faced him, coldly blinking. Bro raised the hand on the fence slowly.

Slo-owly, and with the other hand he held the reins tight across his body so there'd be nothing dangling, nothing clinking. He picked up horse-smell or hay-smell, some rootless lively thickness in the air.

"*Hey* boy!" This was another voice, not Robin's. "What d' y' think you're doing?"

Bro hadn't quite touched the animal yet. He turned awkwardly. Coming through the corral's barn-side gate was a heavyset man with a crowbar over one shoulder.

"*What* d' y' think you're doing? Hey?"

The farmer. He reminded Bro of the Angels' owner, even across the exercise yard you could see him chewing his cud. Overalls tucked into boots. Big enough to throw shut the gate without shifting the crowbar from his shoulder. Plus there was the tractor, the antlike nose of the machine just visible around one corner of the stables.

"Hey, you with me? Hey boy?"

He'd focussed past the man. His eyes burned from the fat lick of sun that kept the hills and cropland skeletal. What *was* this numb-fuzz all the time? Bro didn't even lower his hand till he noticed it hanging there, and as he backed off along the fence he was trying consciously to think. He was making himself recall when this kind of thing had happened before. That time in the elevator after one of the high school playoffs, and waiting for the subway once in Philadelphia. Plus the street types in Newark were always saying they were going to kill you. But then those street types were *brothers*, what'd they have to do with this?

Bro caught his foot on a hoofprint and lost his balance. He sat a moment on the bottom rail.

The horse swung its face away. The farmer grinned, or half-grinned. Really it was hardly more than a tic, something extra in the grimace as the man shrugged the crowbar into his hands. But that was enough to set off fantasies so rough and adrenalized that Bro stumbled again as soon as he got to his feet. "Aww, don't worry," the farmer said. "Nobody's going to do anything too nasty here." But the guy didn't know: Bro had a headful of it. The most intense flashes concerned the man's tool. The crowbar would be terrifically warm from the tractor and the sun, almost scorching. It'd have such perfect heft, the peak of the swing would just *click* in.

Bro counted off a couple seconds in his squat, and when he pulled himself back upright against the fence he went hand over hand. In his head he panned backwards, deliberately, getting some distance from the head-cracking and murder. For the first time, Bro discovered that he himself wasn't any part of the picture. Bro himself was just a blur in his mind's eye. He was triumph: the soundtrack was *The Good, the Bad, and the Ugly*. But he was smoke, colorless smoke, nowhere near as vivid as the iron.

"You all set now? You with me now?"

The man had spread his stance, just beyond arm's reach. Bro wasn't going anywhere, the bridle pinched his collarbone. And then Robin was trotting back through the barn. The farmer made out like it didn't faze him—"What say we start with just, you tell me who you are?" But he was getting in slant glances towards the door, and when Robin appeared he lowered the crowbar a notch. She came out head-down, over a vertically-arranged camera such as Bro had never seen. She must have first spotted them through the viewfinder.

"Oh! Mr. Rutgrove!" She snatched the camera up in front of her neck. "What are you *doing?*"

"Caught this boy trying to make off with your beauty there."

"This what? Who are you talking about?"

Mothra had sensed something. The animal moved off slow-haunched, away from them all, more or less into the center of the yard. Meantime Robin yanked Rutgrove back towards the barn. As soon as she started whispering at him the man pulled up straight, tucking the bar behind his back as if it were a cane. Bro found himself following the horse. Never mind which end he might be coming at this time. Never mind the head games about Philly or his high school playoffs, either. All he could ever think of when he recalled those mean places were comebacks he wished he'd made at the time: more superstar fever, long since worn out and rutted. Bro just tracked the horse—no. Actually now he was veering towards the far side of the horse, the side away from the stables. He had some idea that he needed Mothra between him and the other two.

"*Look,*" Robin suddenly shouted, "that's Marvell Gunne, the designated hitter for the Angels."

With that he was lifted into grief, choking and weeping as he tried to get away. For a moment the echo was back, way too loud, though he hid his face in his elbows and tried to swallow, swallow. But a step or two farther, stumbling blind, and what difference did it make if anyone noticed? No one could reach him anyway. No one could be there. Things happened: he almost went flying when he hit the fence again. At some point he ripped the bridle off his arm. And he had thoughts: useless explanatory tags like outsider, man of the house, bad nigger. Finally however the time careened along unmarked, just the opposite of any workspace with plans or breaks good and bad. Bro was nothing but the heat in his face, the occasional mercury sound when he whispered *Sly*. Even then he flubbed the name.

When Robin took his arm, Bro hadn't quite gotten under control. Nonetheless his first swollen glance at her was all he needed to know that not only had she seen everything, but also she'd told the farmer why. His head cleared and he turned to face the man. But Rutgrove was gone. The crowbar stood by the stable door. And though Mothra was in the way—the fan-like shoulder muscles were lovely through his last tears—Bro could see that the tractor hadn't moved. Robin meantime was making her explanations.

"I mean when he saw you were crying—" she slid her hand down his arm, squeezed his hand. "Well he started grinning like he'd just robbed you of your manhood or something. So I just went, think fast, sucker! When I told him about your brother, let me tell you, it *scored*."

With his free hand, Bro swabbed his face. All right, this woman now. Her conversational swagger was a reporter's thing, sure. Nonetheless he enjoyed it. Plus with her elbows on the fence top and her camera hanging, Robin's sweater hugged her breasts nicely.

"We can talk about it more at dinner," she said.

"Dinner? Oh yeah. Yeah, listen, Rob. I don't think I can make it."

"What?" She let go of his hand. "What do you mean you can't? What about our interview?"

"Got to get home, Rob. Got to do some serious talking with the folks at home. Sunday's the only day I can call without a damn game hanging over my head."

But though his mind was made up, Bro was glad to hear Rutgrove returning. The ride back to town would be hard enough. The farmer's boots were heavier than Robin's of course; even Mothra looked toward the door. At that Bro moved away from the fence and, with a final clearing of his throat that turned into a murmur, he slipped a hand up the neck to scratch the back of the horse's ears. It surprised the animal. The tiny muscles under Bro's hand were agitated, the dark eye hawk-like. But Bro kept smiling till the farmer emerged. Rutgrove carried a bat over his shoulder this time, and a ball in the other hand. Bro could see right away that the bat was wrong for him, a whip-handled Aaron model. Way too light.

Then the man was in his face. "I wanted to show you these, Mr. Gunne." A real cracker; coming from him, the name sounded like "gone." And of course—his son used to play for the Angels. "These were his, his bat and his ball. I wanted you to see them."

"That's okay, Mr. Rutgrove. You worked hard, you got yourself a nice farm here. I understand."

"I'm not a bad man. I'm a good man."

Bro nodded soberly. "Something happen to your boy?"

"Happen?" The guy must have ransacked the house to find the stuff, his lower lip was soaked. "Well, he's in concrete products now . . ."

Enough. Bro took the tools from Rutgrove and asked if he'd like an autograph. Too rough about it, yeah, and he sounded too high and mighty. Couldn't help himself. The farmer was left with dumb open hands, and Mothra shied away. Plus the horse rumbling past triggered yet another of Bro's flashes. He saw himself swinging up onto the animal's bare back and jumping the fence like in a Western, tearing off against a landscape of poster board mountains and prefab sets, this one wild isolated blur dark with speed bringing all the rest to life.

He let it go. Nothing to pay serious attention to, but no call to stomp it flat either. Especially now, when all of a sudden Robin and the farmer had started playing hardball. Rutgrove was ticked, his face was heavy again. He said he didn't want a damn autograph. And Robin came round from where Mothra had stood. She shoved her camera at Bro, a flash of color off the lens making him notice that sundown had come at last. Did Bro *object*, she asked, if she got her picture now?

Bro smiled. He said no problem, he'd give her a beaut of a shot in fact. But she had to be quick. Then he stepped back and went into his stance. Adjusting for the bat, he found enough of his sweet groove to take the ball deep.

Field Burning

I COULD STAND the Video World if we didn't get the professionals. It's my first time working behind a counter since high school, so I notice. Ordinarily shopping is blue-collar. Even the cotton candy the teenagers are wearing this summer, those drapey tops and the pants that show a lot of ankle. Pastel, but blue-collar. The stuff's in the outlet stores by the time it reaches the valley. Still, here at the Video World, somehow we're the class of the Miracle Mile. We get women wearing career clothes. I mean women, my own age. My first impulse when I see them is to hide in the back. And tonight it's Lilah and Valerie, the worst, since the two of them worked with my husband Josh before he was fired.

A coupon night to boot. It's hardly like Oregon at all in here, a couple people have actually gotten surly.

A break's out of the question. Makes no difference that I'm the weekend manager. I've spent the last fifteen minutes tying up the store's phone with a call to the babysitter. Love you, Denise; Daddy soon, Denise. For fifteen minutes—Josh stays out so late on Fridays. Worst of all, we're the corner slot in this turnoff. Clear lines of sight from exit to register. If I'd prefer something else, I'd have to burn down the entire lot and remodel.

Professionals. When I'm a *worker*; I might as well be wearing coveralls. All I can hope is that Lilah and Valerie get lost in here.

It happens all the time. When a person's out front, you're talking Welcome to Fantasyland. The widest selection this side of Portland. Six double-sided racks and the long walls jammed. A person might not even see the security mirrors, because below the mirrors, in both front corners, we've got a TV dinning the promo trailers simultaneously with the widescreen. The voiceover lying a blue streak, insisting it's life and death. I swear it makes the display boxes buzz. Plus the things are all lathery colors, lightning titles, cardboard neon. They're almost weightless too. We've had to replace the actual cassettes with wood blocks; some mighty toney citizens turn out to be shoplifters. Senssurround, Panavision, rooty-toot-toot. The one time I brought Denise in here, I figured that was the way I must have looked back when she had the colic, when the lack of sleep started me hallucinating.

Still it looks as if Lilah and Valerie spotted me. In fact it shakes me, how quick they cut round behind one of the racks.

It always shakes me to see women like that do something hustly. They're both so rangy and correct, former sorority queens. Also they haven't even had a minute to stop home and change. Where did this rule get started, that if a family makes enough money it's the women's job to pick up the flicks for the weekend? Josh says it's another ripple effect, like the way fashions come up the coast from L.A.. Except in this case the ripple's just getting started. The Western managerial class is barely off the farm. Forget about *Dallas*, forget about DeLorean—I swear this speech is like some kind of ritual dance, for Josh. The culture's projecting *way* ahead there, and you notice DeLorean wound up getting his ass *torched* anyway.

Thinking of his talk, I'm frowning. I crane up on my toes to track the women from mirror to mirror, I cock my hands against the rippling hive of weekend girls.

"Mrs. um, Boweroff? Should we hit the alarm?"

"No no, don't panic. I know what I'm doing, don't panic."

Julie. I would have known her from her voice if it hadn't been a coupon night. And flumping onto my heels again, more aggravation. How am I supposed to be angry at Julie? Julie's the one girl here that doesn't fit in. Always the stray bangs in her eyes, when you shouldn't even wear bangs with hair so fiery, so rich. Always the uneasy zigzag posture, as if she were trying to scrunch down into something like my own curly shape. She's the one girl here who was obviously raised on a ranch.

The way I deal with it for the moment is to ask for her returns, a double-armload, and duck into the back to do a nice slow job of re-shelving. The soundtrack's muted, back there. Between the high, subdivided stacks there's no color, only the fluorescents overhead. But Julie returns before I've reached *Night of the Living Dead*. She's empty-handed, and God that ranchy awkwardness is easy to read. Don't tell me. There are two friends of mine out front who need some help.

"Um, they say they don't know about some of the choices."

"Oh God. Hasn't anyone else in this town ever seen a foreign film?"

Her chin drops. What am I doing, trying to impress sixteen-year-olds now?

"Mrs. Boweroff, um. There's something I'd like to talk to you about sometime. Like, a special project. When you're not busy on the phone or anything."

"Busy on the phone? Have my little scouts been spying on their den mother again?"

But no, that kind of smarting off, no that's not right here either. That's Josh talking again. I hand over the returns with a lot of extra contact, shoulder and fingers, and I tell her to call me Dolly, Dolly please. She manages an un-flustered smile. I figure that's as decent a pickup as I'm going to get before I have to go face my—friends.

"Val, Lilah."

"Delores. We *thought* we spotted you earlier."

The women and I stand facing each other at the slower end of the counter, down by the popcorn and candy. The machine takes vegetable oil instead of butter, it reeks of grease. But of course I know what movie I'm going to suggest already. These two can come flaunt their bow-tie blouses all they want, their tinted contacts and Kappa Delta cool, it isn't going to rattle me. And Julie peeking round the base of the widescreen won't make any difference either.

The owner, Orr, said he hired me for this. You people from back East, he said. It's like you remember all the movies you ever saw and you got 'em stashed away in categories. But the fact is I recommend by rote. I have exactly two choices that I suggest for people who ask, and I couldn't tell you a line from either of them. I don't want to spend any more time on this than I have to. I don't want to hear another word about parties that I'm not invited to. It's like I'm a diabetic working in the candy factory, and the worst is when I start to blame it on how happy I felt six months ago. Oh I was just thrillingly happy, six months or a year ago. I could swear that when I slipped in a nursing pad, the tickle would dart through me till at last it curled up again inside the shrinking space under my belly. But while I went humming around, playing snuggle and coo, Josh was flailing away as the new Director of Downtown Development—the king of the three-color resume, flailing away while it all went up in smoke. He was supposed to get people to come out of their holes. And I was as bad as anyone else, I wouldn't even try walking the streets.

The upshot is that nowadays I feel as if I'm going on with my life behind some kind of papier-maché husk. I'm always at a tremendous internal distance. I can tell these women what to get while by far the larger part of me's sitting back and giving them a onceover. *Well listen, something came in last month, you two really ought to have a look at it.* Must have been a rough week for them too, Lilah's makeup looks cadaverish. *Ten Oscar-winning animated shorts, really they're slick.* Valerie's eyelids tic at the words "Oscar-winning." But after that her gaze levels, grows calculating, and I can guess the real selling point: showing shorts will help break the ice. *You won't believe the claymation. You know all it is is play-dough.* I can see also the resemblance between Julie and these two. Josh is right when he says that families like Valerie's and Lilah's are just off the farm.

"But with the claymation, it's like magic." If I hadn't tasted Chapstick, I wouldn't have known I was smiling. "It looks they're hardly giving it a touch, but then the doll or whatever keeps changing shape and changing shape."

When they agree, I send Julie off to get the cassette. Just to get that one cassette, which is bad management, no question. Likewise I don't interfere when she takes the time to read the women's choices out loud; on the Fellini she practically squeals. All this while the other girls are schlepping round with double orders and VCRs. Ah, but it pains me to see Julie schlep. Trying so hard to leave the ranch behind, ruining that perfect t-square of neck and shoulders. Julie, another five or six years and you're going to be so lovely—will you have enough left of yourself to know it?

So I'm talking to the girl when Lilah and Valerie leave. Power suits, who cares? Just another summer fashion. Julie reminds me that there's something we should talk about, there's that project she mentioned earlier, and I avoid the other girls' stares by studying one of the corner mirrors. Then, sure. I guess it is time for another break.

Lately I haven't been coming straight home on weekend nights. I'm not meeting anybody, nothing so earth-shattering. And I'm certainly not all fired up from work. The way I poke around, it's as if I'd never heard that there'd been complaints. Still I'll open the windows on the Toyota, and I'll drive a while.

This time of year, even in the middle of the best subdivisions, the air's dusty with field burning. The smell's the same no matter where it comes from, no matter what the crop was, but I want to see. I park away from any trees. There: over the alfalfa highlands, to the east. A heap of smoke the color of a lost nickel, spreading its shoulders and shadowing the low full moon.

I jam her back into gear, so rough she lurches and dies.

Josh has the stereo on. I can hear it while I'm still fishing for keys at the door. In fact these new duplexes have such a styrofoam excuse for walls that I can tell he's playing talk, not music. Not TV talk either. You only get static like that when you record an interview off the radio. And he wouldn't be playing back an interview just for himself, he must have brought Jesse and Willie over.

"Hardest thing to play is the blues." Do I have to hear this the minute I get in the door?

"All the rest of it, you can just throw on some technique. But the blues is the blues is the blues."

Then, click. "That's Mr. Oscar Peterson," Josh announces. His voice is a letdown. Your standard Long Island honk, after the musician's honeyed gravel.

I've come in so sensitive to sound because Josh hasn't got a light on in the place. There he is on his knees in front of the stereo, trying to read his own notes on the cassette's label by the green glow of the tuner. Frowning, obviously drunk. Obviously everything. I come home wanting a little honest family feeling, and every time what I get is Entertainment Tonight. Jesse and Willie. The one who works for a living, most likely he's racked out on the sofa. And that *brrek-brrek* across the room somewhere, that's got to be Willie in the rocker. A condo "living area" like this, there's nowhere else those guys could be. It holds the stink too, the beer and cigarettes like some dank indoor pollen. We hadn't lived here a week before Josh had dubbed it Cliffdweller Estates. Now my eyes are adjusting, he forgot the curtains, and I can make out Willie's agitation against the waxen blear of the windows. I'm reminded of a grasshopper whirring up in the middle of some smudgy farm acreage.

"Dollbaby! Hey, at last. You remember that tape I asked you for?"

"Awh." Forgetful Me, all five fingertips to forehead.

"Forgot *again*, honey?"

"We just get so *busy*, honey. It's a consumer paradise around here, I swear."

Josh settles his weight back onto his hands. Deliberate, unruffled: we listen to his slacks flap as he extends and crosses his long legs. Not that it fools me. Oh yes I'm in the mood now, I want it to stay dark in here now, and none of his junior-exec smoothy is going to fool me. But before I can move in Jesse stumbles up out of nowhere. Okay Josh, Jesse says, or brays. You promised. You said if she didn't't' bring home *Wild Bunch* we could watch *Magnifcen' Seven*. The mood I'm in—yes keep it dark, and don't anybody get up to kiss me or anything—I have to laugh. This is a guy with a million stories about when he was captain of his Ultimate Frisbee team. Josh however plays to the distraction, laughing differently. He puts out a hand, give me five. I yank off my shoes and start in about Denise.

But the drunken shadow beside him keeps fumbling through the cassettes; Josh keeps up a steady protective buzz. He prefers Sony. The collection must be twice the size it was when we moved west. I get louder: when did you pick her *up*, Josh? And what did Denise, our *daughter*, have for dinner? I'm way past worrying about whatever Jesse or Willie might hear. They've never held anything back around us. Josh calls them Martyrs of the Revolution. Jesse's wife has spent most of last year on an internship in Boston, working towards an MBA; Willie's was studying dance down in L.A., then wrote at the beginning of the summer to say she intended to stay there. Willie even read us the letter. I laughed at one line, where she referred to the valley as "a hive full of drones." The guys all got upset with me that time, too.

"Oregon's been fantastic for us that way, man." Except Josh of course, he never gets upset. He just goes on playing to Jesse. "I think the collection's three times the size it was when we came out here."

"Josh, I am *not* talking about Clint Eastwood. I'm asking about dinner, what did you—"

"Didn't cost us a dime, babe." The light from the tuner pools greenly a moment in the top of his beer can. "We had the free tacos at the Lost Mine, don't worry about it."

At the Downtown Development office, they couldn't handle these moves. Josh's favorite was to come on like a party boy at a meeting, then go back to the office and work some angle off the very information the people had given away while they were dazzled by the scotch and one-liners. But I'm circling closer. He has to give me a straight answer, and I don't miss how angrily he shoots his beer back in among the music tapes, either. Shadow boxing. I'm almost between him and Jesse now.

"You didn't pick her up till eight? She had to sleep on Honey's *sofa?*"

"It was better for her there. Really. The TV going, it's soothing."

"Oh Josh, I can't believe you. No wonder Lilah and Val told everyone you made a pass at them. I mean you are capable of doing some of the *stupidest* things, Josh, there's just no end to it. You're like a goddamn black hole of—"

But Willie interrupts. Willie this time, and not with his rocking. The chair's quiet, the outlines in it have shrunk. Still even after turning to look it takes a moment to realize that the sound that stopped me is sobs. First reaction—sag back a step. One of the sofa-arms catches my leg. The pain's surprising, though I must have known how tightly my muscles were clenched.

"I can't stand it," Willie's saying. "It's like no matter where I go, it ends up the same old scene."

What shakes me most is seeing how good these guys are for each other. I get a glimpse of Willie's hands, bent back, shoving his tears into his beard; then the other two are there to help. Josh starts his patter while he's still stumping across the rug. Oh that's just 'cause we're from New York, man, don't pay any attention. That's just the way couples talk in New York. Slick stuff, typical, but Willie jams his face into my husband's chest as soon as he gets close. Which means I also have to notice again how big my husband is. Even kneeling, Josh can fit his arm comfortably around Willie's shoulders, and with Jesse at the crying man's feet I'm reminded of one of his old rugby scrums. Bagels Boweroff, the only boy from the Five Towns I'd ever heard of who could really play preppy games. I used to want to snuggle forever in that wraparound bulk. I used to think—God we're helpless—that his drinking made him exotic.

Willie's sounding better. "I know you're nice people," gulping and nodding. "That's what makes it so hard, all these nice people turning into monsters."

God we're helpless. My legs have gone slack, my ears have cooled. "You know you guys," I say, "I had something interesting come up at the Video World tonight."

"Oh Christ," Josh says. "Did those assholes from Downtown Development come in again?"

But I'm caught up in Willie's look, his eyes mica. Josh was too smart for me, bringing these two home to run interference. He's got me hating myself for my viciousness when I came in. And I'll probably be asleep again by the time he comes upstairs. This must be what they mean by that word "estranged", a word I've never quite grasped: this shrinking back inside my husk, like an insect dying inside its skeleton, all while sinking into the sofa with an itchy smile and telling these men, for no good reason, about what Julie's asked me to do.

"It's called the Shadow Project. They've set it up for the anniversary of Hiroshima."

Willie won't give me a break. He's as bad as Julie, staring while I babble on about claymation. But I meet his look. "You guys remember the victims near Ground Zero. They left nothing but a shadow, a permanent shadow, like on a wall or a sidewalk." This coming August 6th, while people were still asleep, the Project would paint the same kind of shadows around town.

"We want them to be exposed to it." I've dropped my smile. "We want them to feel that flash, for once in their lives."

Apparently that does it. Everybody gets enthusiastic, Josh especially. Hey I've heard of this thing, Dollbabe, it's like a big nationwide *group* thing. Willie gets the rocker going again, Jesse seems to cross in front of me more than once. In any case somehow they find their movie. While Josh keeps up his happytalk—you'll get to show off your *skills*, too—the room starts to brighten at last as the FBI warning comes on. Toothy low shadows are cast across the ruts Willie's made in the shag wall-to-wall.

"The only problem I see with the whole project," Josh goes on, "is downtown. I mean like what you were saying earlier, about the consumer paradise, that's only out towards I-5 you know. That's only the Miracle Mile."

His back's against the farther sofa-arm, his eyes are on the screen. You notice he's not coming after me about anything else I said.

"Really babe. Trying some kind of downtown outreach in a community like this, it's a fantasy."

But when the titles come on, the music, it makes Josh look so the opposite of what I feel for him. He has the color of some Romantic hero. Tubercular, with blue lips.

Valerie, you know, had a daughter who was kidnapped. A four-year-old just erased from the planet one afternoon, in a mall west of Portland. The woman says she's still young; she can start again. And I once saw Lilah get wonderfully excited about some wildflowers she'd spotted on a hike through the Cascades. She squatted right in front of Josh's desk, sweeping her arms to demonstrate how the Oregon Bleeding Hearts had clustered at the base of the fir. Tragedy and passion—not the exclusive property of a woman who used to do mockups for a couple agencies in mid-Manhattan.

It's the stairs that give me such long thoughts. The climb back into the dark, with a finger of wine remaining.

Denise. Maybe she'll free me up for a good long cry, my little Denizen, my pouchfull of dreams. Her crib is warm. Her cheek is an absolute pliancy. It makes me think again of tapes and films, their trembling surfaces in motion, and then the touch seems to take over my nerves. I don't feel so nasty and withered anymore, but what happens next isn't anything like a nice glowy crying jag either. Instead my hand goes numb. It's magic; she got me while my shell was down. And though I figure it must be only the soreness from hauling videotapes, nonetheless when my arm begins to dissolve I know for certain that in another minute I'll be helpless: helpless dust, crunched and helpless before every chance break of time or place or sweet talk or fashion or mood that might happen to blow through. I pull away gasping. The wine glass drops and shatters, splashing my naked toes.

After a while, standing riveted, I become aware of the soundtrack underfoot. Shrieks and gunshots right underfoot. And even here there's the smell of smoke.

Three Dreams of Europe

SHE WAS IN A CAFÉ, a hashish café, and she was smoking the hashish, sitting and smoking steadily, because as she smoked she at last found the distance she'd been looking for. A strange way to find it, without logic, with eyes closed. A strange kind of distance.

Distance, difference—you would think she'd found that already, Mrs. Mooney. Already she'd put thousands of miles between herself and the Circle K where her husband and son had been killed. You would think she'd have been sprung free of her former life forever, the first moment the addict in the Circle K had panicked and started to shoot. Yet she knew him, the addict. So much had her former life followed her here, she could see him now in the bowl of her pipe. The young man who'd murdered her family had a stare she knew all too well, a rabitty stare, desperate. Trapped.

She couldn't look at him. She lifted her eyes from the glowing bowl. Yet still she had to smoke, Mrs. Mooney, she had to stay in her chair and smoke, because until she'd begun to smoke she'd gotten nowhere. She hadn't found distance; she'd only become smaller. She hadn't put distance between herself and the graveyard over the Pacific, as she'd dragged herself first to the East Coast and then on across the Atlantic. She'd only shriveled up and blown away. A child's lost balloon, driven by a speaking wind. And the words the wind was speaking were nothing special either, words she'd memorized long ago. She was only doing what a woman in her position was expected to do.

Until today. Today, sitting, smoking—what exactly had changed? The stuff made her choke, but since her last stop at the grave site she'd been forever about to choke. She'd been forever caving in over shriveled balloon lungs. The stuff was grown here across the Atlantic, but even across the Atlantic she'd continued to drift according to what was expected. She'd crawled along the garden paths of Lutheran meeting houses. She seemed to remember crawling through this city, actually down on all fours, over cobblestones and canal banks. With her spirit so helpless, she'd huddled down where no one could see. Must have been a dream.

And yet it *is* strange, now. It *is* different. Now, right now—with every ragged intake of breath the balloon is refilling. Or those low mounds of earth over the Pacific—they're bulging, they're ready to burst. A strange refilling, a wind within, wordless but irresistible. She's never been so frightened.

The porcelain bowl in her grip, the ember there, shows her faces no longer familiar. Maybe a murderer's, maybe a child's, maybe her own. The heat threatens her hand, the hand balloons till the lines there disappear—and she needs to stop, to speak, to move. If she's at last found distance, shouldn't she be able to move? But she's weak as a baby and her legs look awful, her hose hangs torn and filthy and her knees are caked with blood. From behind the register someone rushes to her, maybe the man who put her here, and anyway what did her mother teach her? *Never trust a stranger.*

"Loss is always the subject," said the leader of the dream circle. "To grow older is to accumulate loss."

Mary's face went flat. "I thought this group was supposed to do better than that," she said.

The other women chuckled supportively. A low, easeful sound, it suited the space, a domed circular home on the coast. The chuckling suited the colors, earth tones that were either timeless or, Mary was thinking, utterly chic. '70s retro was all the rage.

The leader was making some reply, unoffended.

"But what I noticed," one of the other women said, "was how it was so very male. Did people pick up on that?" She shifted on her floor pillow, an otherwise gray-haired woman with a lavender forelock. "A man sold you the hash, a man was the murderer. I mean, you even gave yourself a son."

Mary shook her head. Shook it twice, still needing to clear her thinking, to bring herself back out of an Old World alley and into this airy, raftery space. During her turn she'd stood and moved to the oceanside window.

"Yah," said the leader of the circle. "You have no son, is that correct?"

Koh-wrecked? Perhaps it was only the woman's accent that had Mary so bristly, so demanding. It wasn't the leader's fault that the Dutch sounded so much like the Hollywood notion of the Gestapo. She reminded herself of the woman's Anglicized name, Inksa. She found a warmer tone of voice and admitted she'd never had a son. "And I'm sure you remember I prefer my maiden name now."

"Ach, yah. Correct."

Mary turned away again. At the bottom of the cliffs beneath the window, the Pacific heaved under late-afternoon brightening.

"That's just what I'm saying." The lavender woman again. "Mary, I mean, what was your ex doing in there? It's your *mother* who died."

That brought her around. Mama's death was no secret—the retreat had begun, last night, with a two-hour "sharing session." Nonetheless: "Excuse me?"

"Mary, this is avoidance behavior."

"Avoidance, oh. I'll tell you about avoidance. Right now, I'm *avoiding* scratching your eyes out."

Again the domed space got noisy. Women bristled back, startled, loud. They tugged at their bulky socks or at the drawstrings on their hooded sweatshirts. Yet Mary also sensed a relief in their carrying on, a letting go that surged up in her as well—this was the very blowup that she'd been pushing for all day. All day, the eight women seated around her had been reining themselves in. They'd been acting ladylike since the opening Call to the Demiurge. Mary would've thought they'd sworn off that kind of thing years ago, now that the kids were out of the house, now that they'd bulled themselves to management level and permanent fitness. These were hikers with certification in accounting, devotees of yoga with a staff of half a dozen. Years ago, Mary would've thought, they'd left the old roles behind.

And she'd put off her own turn till last, today. She'd had enough of spilling her guts last night. Now, standing and catching flak, hearing the others too get pushy at last, Mary found herself grinning, couldn't help it, and maybe she was even grinning at the one with the lavender hair. That woke 'em up, sister.

But Mary couldn't remember the woman's name.

Eventually a single voice emerged, under the echoing dome. Not the leader's: Inksa sat watchful, neutral. She was a born head-of-tribe, tall with strong features. The opposite of Mary, a former bosomy catch whose hourglass now had thickened into a chianti bottle. Meantime the woman whose voice prevailed was the oldest, the one who had dibs on the lone rocking chair. A grandmother named Teri.

"Mary, you just said you wanted to do something more."

Mary shook her head.

"Hello? Mary, hello? We all heard what you told Inksa. You thought this group could do more."

"I said I thought we could do *better*."

"Well this is better. I believe it's called honesty."

"Honesty, oh. Flinging my mother in my face like that?"

"Well what are we supposed to do, speak in riddles? I think it's high time we let our hair down, here."

One or two others murmured assent while Mary exhaled slowly, bringing the older woman into focus. Aging had shaped Teri for confrontation. Her hair in a white helmet, her nose dented but swollen, she belonged on a shield somewhere. Or inside a smoking pipe, staring from an ember.

"Teri, tell me. What do you think of my dream?"

"What do *I* think?" The woman spoke as if there'd been no change in Mary's tone—exactly as Mary had hoped she would. "I think you don't want to scratch out somebody else's eyes, you want to scratch out your own."

"Ach, yah." Inksa nodded. "The guilt of the survivor."

"Guilt and anger, sure." This was Lavender. "Think of it that way and all the men fit right in."

85

Teri kept talking. She said Mary was only human, and there must have been hard moments while her mother was dying. "Aren't there always? And yet you wanted to be, you know, the perfect, supportive saint of a dutiful daughter."

"You did your best, Mary," another woman said. "Last night, you told us, you held her hand."

But again Mary was shaking her head. "I've been all through that. I mean, all the steps. Anger, all the steps."

"I can see that." Lavender. "You've clearly been empowered, Mary. Empowered in a major way. But everybody breaks down sometimes."

Mary found herself glaring up at the skylight, the sweet blue heaven behind it. September was too kind, too warm, and someone here was still murmuring nicey-nice.

"I mean it." She set her knuckles on her hips. "I know all about guilt."

"Tough girl?" Teri asked. "You're a tough girl? That chill on your neck, Mary, that's eternity."

"I'm not denying that. But, guilt, oh. Listen, after the last couple years of my marriage, when it comes to guilt I'm a connoisseur."

More chuckling. Two or three of the women relaxed, creaking back into the good brown leather of the mammoth sofa. But Mary caught herself glaring at that, too, and she couldn't think why. Why the aggravation over Inksa's taste in furniture? The circle leader wasn't just chasing a fad, bringing them together here—and she wasn't cashing in on one either. What Mary and the others were paying couldn't cover a single month's mortgage on this place. And Inksa was too much the long-faced watcher, the immigrant not in on the homegirls' jokes, not to be making a genuine effort.

Then too, she was taking Mary's side. "Remember the directive of our circle," she was saying, sweeping an extended finger around the room. "We have joined here in a dream *circle*. Not to psychoanalyze any one member."

More women sat back.

"The night images must by their nature remain a mystery in *one*," Inksa said. "It is in the congregation that the unconscious takes on its greatest meaning."

Her gaze shifted from face to face. But when she got to Mary, Mary had to turn once more towards the window, the heaving surf. Guilt, oh. But not the guilt of the survivor—the guilt of the skeptic.

Hadn't she had choices, for dealing with Mama's passing? In the month since the funeral, how many times had her daughter mentioned the Grief Workshop at St. Peter's Central? Mary had turned instead to the sort of books she'd always sneered at, even to radio call-in programs; she wasted whole Sunday afternoons gabbing into the phone about the end of the century, the looming new millennium. And last night she'd agreed to have her loss serve as the "group focus." Yet here she stood, still holding these notions at arm's length, with clenched fists. In fact giving the circle its assignment had wound up working against her. She'd wriggled and shifted in her sleeping bag, feeling alternately anxious and silly, long after the other two women in the room had drifted off.

Maybe Mary was just tired. Maybe all she needed was a walk on the beach.

"It's interesting that Mary dreamed of travel." This was a woman with a Brooklyn accent. "That makes three of us, doesn't it? Doesn't that make a motif?"

Mary always heard accents like this as the voice of the real world. When she'd first been introduced to the circle, it had made all the difference that one of the women sounded like a neighbor from Bensonhurst.

"It makes four," Lavender said. "Remember I was in outer space, the Ursula LeGuin planet."

"Okay, sure. Plus I was in Vietnam where my boyfriend died and Inksa—" the New Yorker pointed with her head— "was touring those Egyptian ruins."

"Ach," Inksa said, "we don't know they were Egyptian." But the circle had already begun nodding, gesturing, bringing up other possible connections. Only Mary fell still, unable to escape the heat of the bay window. Blearily she looked over the talkers at her feet, thinking in an accent. *Gimme a break. "Motif," my eye.* For women like these to dream of travel was no clue to the universe. Nothing emergent or millennial, nothing nearer to wherever Mary's mother had gone. It wasn't a dream at all, travel—it was a daydream. Even Teri's antique shield of a face stretched into a faint but easy to understand smile. One windfall contract, and Teri too would be on the first plane to Paris.

"To establish a motif," Inksa was saying now, "generally requires three."

Three? Mary was thinking. Try all nine of them. There wasn't a woman in the room, Inksa included, who didn't eye the bargain fares in the Sunday Travel section. And it had to be Europe. The Old World was key to the daydream, the Sunday dream. The vineyards around Aetna, the ruins of Agrigento—yes, Mary knew what everyone was thinking. Sleepy as she was, she knew. They had in mind a Hollywood Mediterranean: fat-free breads, painless kisses, and singsong cathedral services without smoke, cold, or a cadaver.

"Now what we begin to see is ourselves," Inksa was saying. "Our wholes emerge as archetypes."

Archetypes? Mary was thinking. Try stereotypes.

But then recognizing the thought—hearing the accent—she had to include herself in it. Herself and her anger. It was a garden variety women's anger, a kind Mary knew all too well: another stereotype. And her dream, her damned still-terrifying dream had been just the opposite. She'd dreamed of being different.

Neutral. The feeling's everywhere: in the crossroads that defines the brown and stony village, in the oboe-easy call of the native horns—horns bodylength and buttress-like, played while standing up. A horn chorus stands at the edge of the meadow (edelweiss blooms low, no presumptuous flower); the players' lederhosen calls attention to their legs, a reliable musculature right up calf and knee and thigh. Strong, these people. Hikers, forever going up or down the mountainside. Strong, flexible—and neutral, grown-up and neutral, very real world even in the measured echo of the horns. Then why is she scrabbling around so desperately, Maria? What is she searching for?

But don't the villagers realize—they need it too. What Maria needs to find, it's vital, it's as much a part of the local life-flow as all their stolid marching. Just visible at the seams of the local restraint, in the shadows—there, there! Don't the villagers see them? Elves perhaps. Fairy folk. How's she supposed to know the species? They're smaller-scale creatures, that's all she can say: the sort of faces one sees in a fire. *There!*

And these faces, wayward and shrunken as lost balloons—somehow their creeping and peeking sustains the clockwork of the rest. Somehow it provides essential backup. Yes, they're key to the dream, the workday-dream: these bird-bright imps who, at intervals in the clockworks, pop with a raucous squeal out of one neat brown cubbyhole or other. That's when she'll sometimes spot one.

But she needs to do better than that. Hard as it is to pick out these small faces in the brown grid of flowers and muscle (the men so handsomely preserved!), Maria has to do better. She has to protect them. For they're disappearing, these fragile mites; she can feel them fading out, as if her back were to the sun and the sun was going down. How could they not be fading? They're the little people.

Over one shoulder she spies one she knows, one that surely even the villagers would remember. A girl in a red cap and cloak, carrying a basket. Just visible as she ducks into the forest. Maria can't let this one get away, she's off at a run, hollering for help from her college roommate. For isn't this junior year abroad? And isn't there someone else who can help, a friend of her roommate, a pretty Irish boy? She hollers for him too, making wild promises if only he'll come. But then, oh. Then, running, she sees them both—her roommate and the Irish boy. Oh! They've shrunk to something even smaller and easier to lose, they're no more than fireflies in the forest dusk. She had a friend for life and a boy who loved her and yet now she can only catch a last flickering glimpse of them before she comes up against the wolf. The wolf, its breath stinking of bugs, its legs terrifying. Legs so tough and powerful that the chorus at the crossroads is suddenly nothing by comparison; they're a sham; there can be no other, standing at the crossroads.

"This is growth," Inksa said. "The fairy tale, the old magic. This always indicates greater maturity."

"Rich stuff, Mary," Teri said. Her voice too was soft.

"Rich, yah."

"Mary? This makes your last one look like one of those anti-drug comics for children."

One or two others chuckled, but not Mary. She was still swallowing wetly, blinking in spasms.

"And in this one again we see the subject of loss." Inksa sounded warmer than Mary would have thought possible. "Insofar as we may psychoanalyze, here, I would say that this is what I see. Your loss."

The last word was almost a whisper, a caress. Still Mary couldn't look at her. Once more she stood at the bay window, actually propped against the window, her hot forehead working against the glass. She knuckled her face. Midway through her turn someone had touched her, tried to put an arm around her, and at that Mary had erupted from her seat.

The next to break the silence was Lavender. "I can't leave it at that. Not after all we've been through."

Mary felt the response in the windowpane, a rowdy vibration. Today the circle had passed on acting ladylike.

"I mean you know I love Mary," Lavender went on. "We all love Mary. But that dream, it's a manifesto."

What? Bouts of grief like these still left Mary empty, thoughtless. That was the wolf, or that was one of them—a sadness that devoured her brains first.

"Haven't we been asking where we go from here? Haven't we? Mary, you're *so* evolved. That dream is a manifesto."

It took Mary a long shut-eyed moment just to recall that today too she'd asked to speak last. And till now the talk had concentrated more and more on a single issue. They'd wondered whether their circle were truly something formal and dedicated—truly a church. One of the others had dreamed of a Ukrainian Christmas egg, and that was how the women shared the idea, today: like something fragile, made by hand, and covered with cryptic designs. Mary in fact had taken the lead (she had? really? this sopping wreck?).

She had. She'd argued that Inksa hadn't come all the way from The Hague just to arrange a little girl-talk. Mary had even opened up about her anger the day before. She'd warned everyone that she'd had another dream about Europe, then joked, *Now don't set me off again. Don't start talking about bargain rates.*

But what was this dyke behind her saying?

Mary jerked upright, stiffening. The anger. The anger again, bang on top of the grief. Behind her the other women chimed in after Lavender, before her the big windowpane shivered once more with the echo, and all Mary could think was a nasty pun: *Good vibrations. Oh, wow.* She shook her head. The Brooklyn woman was saying Mary's dream felt like proof they had a church, a real church, because it connected them to ancient stories and patterns.

"Isn't that a true faith?" she was asking. "One that encompasses both past and future?"

Mary thought: How about one that encompasses both weeping and insults? In the same minute? Oh, she was whirling. On top of everything else, she stood there as sleep-deprived as yesterday; last night she'd lain awake again. Now the ocean's rise and fall, at the foot of her view, triggered a jaw-cracking yawn. Whirling.

Last night she'd even started worrying about work. She was stretching an already-extended leave from one of the State Senate offices. Then her thoughts had gone the opposite direction, back to the haunts of childhood insomnia: terrors about the size of the universe.

Teri was speaking now. "I think Mary's dream reminds us that in order to go forward, first we have to go back."

"There's something I need to tell you about my mother," Mary said. "Something about her dying."

The only one she could look at was Teri.

"Your mother, Mary?" someone else asked. "Something personal? Aren't you the one who's been saying we have to get beyond the personal?"

"Hello?" Teri said.

"I was jealous of her," Mary said. "Jealous of her dying."

She kept her eyes on Teri. The old, heavy face hung low, halfway down in the well of the rocking chair. "Working with Mama day after day, working through all those stages. I started to think, now this is truly getting somewhere. This is truly—spiritual communion."

"Ach, yah. The greatest challenge of the Demiurge."

"The chill of eternity," Teri said. "I'm with you."

Mary was shaking her head, turning back towards the sun-flecked ocean. "No. No, I don't think you're with me. I think we're all still only talking about ourselves." The window held a faint reflection of the group. "We're still just finding out about ourselves, the kind of women we are."

"Oh now, Mary," one of them said. "You're not going to chide us again for making money?"

"All we've ever done," Mary said, "is find out about ourselves. For us, our generation, even when a mother dies it's only another book from the library. It's only another set of steps to read about. It's really about ourselves." The surf's noise, a static beneath her, had Mary thinking of the radio shows she'd called in to; she was on hold again, wondering what she'd say. "So many steps, so many movements. Once upon a time, we came clear across the country."

"Hey, speak for yourself," someone put in. "I was born in the Valley. Right in Four Corners."

"We left everything," Mary went on. "We crossed the country. As if all that mattered out there was ourselves."

Teri: "Are we supposed to be virgins, Mary?"

She frowned. "I'm just saying, I think I'm saying—we aren't the heros of this story. Not losers like us."

After a long moment Inksa spoke up. At her coolest, her most Aryan, she pointed out that previous movements in fact provided a useful structural model. "The circle expands in this way too, via intrapersonal pyramiding. I must thank you, Mary, for the suggestion."

"What? Thank me?" Mary couldn't stop talking, she couldn't let go of the floor, and she found herself apologizing, an old reflex. Sorry, guys. Teri came back with reassurances: It's always good to hear what you think. Then somewhere in this old-shoe give and take, as if she and the others were ten years into a difficult marriage—in there, somewhere, Mary grew hot with the discovery of what she needed to say.

"Mama," she said, "what Mama went through, she *was* a virgin." She whipped round, scowling at lineup on the sofa. "At that we're all virgins. Every time, we're a virgin."

The women before her retreated, sliding deeper into the noisy old leather.

"I held her hand. I *felt* her go."

"Mary?" This might have been Teri. "Mary, maybe this is all a little too soon for you . . ."

Mary stamped her foot, a huge noise in that space. "I felt it, like that. Gone! Nobody understands, nobody."

"And," Lavender said, "you were jealous?"

"I was *jealous!*"

"But that just shows you're evolved. You're right on the verge, so close to some greater—"

"Close? I was close when I was in the terminal ward."

Lavender fitted the sleeve-ends of her sweatshirt together, hiding her hands.

"The millennium," Mary said. "We need a new spirit, a new connection to the spirit, for the new millennium."

"The millennium? The end of the world?"

"The end of our miserable empty lives. When Mama went, I had *nothing left!*"

"Oh."

Mary had no idea who spoke. She had her head down, suddenly, and when she again stamped her foot it wasn't nearly so loud. Massaging her forehead, her dry old forehead, she felt murky contradictions behind the bone. It felt almost as if all her kicking and screaming had been about opening up to the others, about asking their help. Coming away from the window had put her in the center of the circle. But still she didn't care for how Teri and Inksa sat poised behind her, like two pincers ready to close in. She didn't care for the room's silence, alert, breathless. The clogs and Birkenstocks before her, along the front of the sofa, were up on the balls of their feet.

"Oh, Mary."

She couldn't tell who spoke, but she heard the sympathy. The good vibrations. At the first touch—someone creaking forward on the sofa—she bolted for the door. She ran for the sea air, the cliff steps.

Where was she going? Why didn't she head to her bedroom to pack? The anger didn't allow her an answer, the anger or the pain (was there a difference, really?). If she heard a shout as she crossed the scrap of lawn under Inksa's window, she couldn't think about it. She couldn't say why she slowed down so soon, either; she slowed to a stagger just minutes after coming out on the beach.

She stopped, leg-sore already on the soft sand. She kept yawning, tasting rare oceanside heat. Inksa's window must have been treated, photo-sensitive. Out here the sun seemed stuck in place, some organ too fat and slow for its gauze-like blue body.

In a nook between fingers of cliff, protected from what little breeze there was, she found a hump carpeted with soft grass. It wasn't sea grass; it didn't crackle. And she was through with running.

At last a place she knows: a church. She knows the church and she knows the country: the mild, homey sun that catches the designs on the cathedral floor, the ancient Imperial tile recycled to make those designs—mosaic circles and whorls, such designs—and she knows the worshippers too. Everyone's dipping down on one knee, down into a three-point genuflection, and she herself dips down, with knee and toe and knuckle to the mosaic floor before the Resurrection. She knows well that dip and touch, as natural as surf, and yet personal, intensely personal. Mary knows the whole stony arena so well that at first even the film director carrying on behind her doesn't disturb the stodgy warmth with which she waits, almost asleep in her pew, for the Host to come around.

But he's impossible to ignore, the director. He's nothing like a man at mass, shuttling people around with the full vocabulary of gestures this country is famous for, with meaty thoughtful pouts and eloquent shrugs. The director does so much of this—too much, really, for someone in such a good silk suit—that Mary's eyes open again and stay that way. She understands that the national instinct for gestures is bound up in the rituals of the church: in that brief stagger as a worshipper enters the sanctuary. She understands, as she watches the director taking bearings through a lens that dangles around his neck (at first glance you might mistake it for an icon), that the cathedral is missing its fourth wall. The tile underfoot is plastic. The sun in the stained glass is halogen.

How long has she been in a movie? *When*, she demands, *did I ever say I'd play the hero?*

The director is nothing but compassion, kneeling beside her with a lippy expressive face almost a mother's, a sister's. He speaks apologetically, though with something in his tone that makes clear he's explained this all before. He must have her face, he says. He simply must have her face.

What's this, she asks, *a fairy tale? The old magic?*

Looks like it: now through the cathedral ceiling—no, through boom mikes and track lighting—descends the oldest magic of all, the Great Mother herself. The Great Mother in her famed watchful pose, down on one knee so that she may spy on the latest indiscretion of the Great Father: on his latest "epiphany" before her pretty young votives. Slung on a rig beneath an ear-shattering helicopter, the Mother drops hugely into place before the Resurrection. And she's not marble, not white, but honest brown.

Hides-the-dirt brown—hashish brown, cuckoo-clock brown— all these and other browns spin through Mary's head (the color's basic after all, she reminds herself: as basic as dirt) because now she's spinning literally, or her face is at least; the director has taken her face and flung it towards the low-hanging head of the goddess. In the wash of the rotors Mary spins, she crosses vast distances— crosses oceans and continents, tossing and turning—but there's no denying gravity. She ends up the face of the Mother. It's what's best for the movie.

Then too, the set's ungainly mannequin doesn't feel so bad, against the inner lining of her eyes and mouth and ears. It's a snug fit, natural as dirt, and it's not nearly as scary as Mary had thought it would be to hang exposed up here—exposed just as she is, alone and no longer pretty, in the vibration and echo of the domed machine over her head. Behind Mary's face, now, the jerry-rigged deity speaks. Hello, it says. I've got a riddle.

What, it asks, walks on four legs in the morning, two legs at noon, and three legs at night?

Mary chuckles supportively. She's heard this one before. And they do more of this, riddle and answer, she and the blind, unfinished creature within.

Yes, she's at ease at last, Mary, settling into the role. But she needs to ask the director one final question. *Is this all it takes?* she needs to ask. *Another dream?* The man is hard to find, however, in the confusing, wide-open church. She sees only extras, a thickening circle, uncertain but eager foreign folk struggling for something that will come across as grace, faith, communion.

Period Sets

STANLEY WAS OFF draping towels over all the mirrors in the house. Nonie waited by the coffee. She studied the strip of newsprint between the steaming mugs, an inch-long cutting, curled at the ends like a tiny boat. Stanley's doubts were so obvious—this last-minute delaying tactic with the mirrors—that Nonie made a point of keeping her own face formal, unafraid. Studying the newsprint. The stain on the paper at least was interesting, a mazy rainbow stipple. It was a shrunken slice of the Grand Canyon wall, a flat patch of cartoon coyote once the Roadrunner was through with him.

When Stanley returned Nonie allowed herself a short smile, watching him work. He used his X-acto blade to halve the paper, splitting the stain precisely in half. He used tweezers to lift each half into their cups. Careful as a spider. He buttoned both the blade and the tweezers back into his kit before he touched his coffee. At such times Stanley reminded her of her father, switching off between a twenty-pound maul and a bottle of Rainier. If only the man could always be at this busy distance, handling his tools. Then there'd never be any question about loving him.

But as he stirred in the stain, the drug, Stanley started to talk about the old days again. He said the business with the mirrors had made him think of it. Today would be so different from back in the old days, back at NYU, when he and old Ollie used to do acid all the time.

A lie: Alden had told her Stanley never tried hallucinogens. Nonie lifted her cup and drained it.

And choked; you weren't supposed to gulp such a rank brew. They'd picked up some Nicaraguan blend in Eugene yesterday. It meant a special trip, one more hassle before they'd headed up here to Brownsville. But Stanley had insisted: a little extra kick, man, a little taste of the Sandanista Revolution to help us get off. Likewise by the time Nonie caught her breath he'd already started to embroider the lies about his acid trips with "Ollie"—with Alden. He'd started to work in details he knew she would have picked up from her younger professors, or from MTV. Guys like Timothy Leary or Allen Ginsberg, he said, they were in control right from the start. Guys like Ginsberg didn't have to play it straight in front of their parents. But now Stanley was older himself, and a glimpse in the mirror wouldn't make him freak the way it used to. It wouldn't make him go jump off the roof or anything.

Today, Stanley said, he'd covered the mirrors for Nonie's sake. He didn't want Nonie to freak.

She kept her face formal. He was lying, and at the same time he was putting her in her place. He had a mean streak, certainly. But strange mean, indirect like just now: she'd been with Stanley two years now, and only in the last month or so had she begun to pick it up. Who *was* he, anyway? Even his clothes were a lie. That biker's jacket and cap, that Italian undershirt, and always the light gauge on a chain round his neck. Granted, Stanley had the face to go with it. A rough-knuckle handsomeness, the eyes aging soft but the cheeks aging mean. His heavy mustache centered the vivid wrinkles and lines. And he had the energy, he was up clearing the table. Last night he'd hauled the table out from the kitchen, out here by the windows. There were still times she couldn't keep her eyes off him.

He withdrew to the sink, still making explanations. More new trouble, he never used to complain so much. But now it was Nonie, my life is crazy, this wasn't what I wanted. What kind of an artist works as a professional photographer? Stanley shook water off the coffee mugs and set them in the dry rack. He arranged them, really, propping each so the handles faced together from opposite sides of the rack. Meantime still griping, what kind of an artist has a contract with *Sunset* magazine? Man, all this western good-life stuff just isn't *me*. He returned to the table with two hefty slices of the bread he'd baked this morning. Each slice was paired on its dish with a folded cloth napkin, the dish a bumblebee-colored earthenware that Nonie hadn't even known her family owned. The bread was warm with butter and honey.

"I just have to remake my whole life," Stanley announced. "I have to strip it down and see what it looks like naked."

He sat and spread his napkin across his lap. Then he said it was time they got started, it was time they looked at Alden's letter.

Nonie turned to the window. Brownsville, and another foul September sky. Her face was slack, ashamed. It wasn't just that Stanley had finally brought up Alden's letter; it was Stanley himself. There were still times. It was that Stanley lied to himself, as natural as lying to her, and when had their life together become this long-undusted houseful of lies? Everything knotted with dirt and smothering.

When Nonie had first seen the letter, yesterday, the effect was just the opposite. As soon as she'd spotted it in Stanley's hand she'd withdrawn to an icy private sanctuary. She'd withdrawn to safety even as she stood there answering questions and knotting her thumbs. A mental holding pattern, she'd discovered the place when she started taking dance classes. Though yesterday, Stanley too had acted remotely. He'd made no move to open the letter. He'd smoothed the envelope against his drafting board, watching the paper emerge from his hand, and he'd asked about her folks' place up in Brownsville. Still empty, babe? You still got the key? He'd asked—zoning off even further—if she'd heard the news: some outfit from Hollywood was using Brownsville as the set for a movie. A horror movie, babe. You heard?

Of course the house was still unsold, of course she'd heard about the movie. The answers were blips across a screen unreachably deep in her head. Only then had Stanley begun to come to the point: Think of it, Nones . . . just up the road, an actual movie.

Talking around a thick chaw of bread, Stanley pointed out the letter's return address. Managua, babe. But in the other corner of the envelope, the postmark said Mexico City. "Alden must have had someone hand-carry it over the border," he said. "Makes you wonder what he had to hide."

He went back into his bag, getting his X-acto. Nonie hugged her knees. One instep jigged hotly at the edge of her chair, she couldn't get back into her holding pattern.

She wished the drug would take over. God yes, *take over*. Better that than Stanley's pick-pick-pick, so many delays that she wondered if he knew. Out the window, the landscape kept turning briefly to quartz. But it wasn't enough. Nonie blinked and the stony interior folds were gone. Indeed the glimpse only made her think of herself: of how exposed and foreign she looked on Stanley's contact sheets. Today's shot had particularly harsh angles. Dancer's shoulders and strong cheekbones, Indian hair and the long straight fall of her Peruvian skirt.

And Stanley read the letter in a normal adult voice, without the usual tics and twitches intended to sound streetwise. She had to stay with him; she had to keep thinking. He'd always played the straight man around Alden. His goodboyness after his friend arrived in Eugene had prompted her first suspicions about the stories. Alden proved so much more than the amphetamine-heated liner notes scrawled across a few bootleg Dylans. He was sloppy with red meat and scotch. He was marriage and a child and the separation which had brought him out West. Till then they'd both ridden the same legend, MacDougal and Bleeker and Stanley and Ollie. The first two into everything. But come June, Alden had actually shared the house. Commencement was past and Nonie had nothing going but her workshop sessions. Now the letter described his divorce. Alden was the first to try that too.

Stanley read this part with terrific feeling. Alden was saying goodbye to his daughter, the shape of the sentence was itself soft from bruising. Nonie faced him again at last. Such a voice, such a stare—Stanley couldn't have known what had gone on. He couldn't have known the letter was from the man with whom she'd cheated. Instead the job of reading well was for Stanley another dip into the tool kit: it was his own above-it-all sanctuary.

Good God, why didn't the damn drug take *over*? Out the window, she noticed only the bits of hard color visible between the trees. The film company's color, the fakery down on Main Street.

She waited to see what Alden would reveal.

He claimed that Nicaragua wasn't enough for him. He belonged in another time, Alden said, a time when a man could take an honest leap off the edge of the world. These days it was nothing but meanness any way you went. You blundered into old lives, you stirred up old pain. Beg, borrow, steal. Nonie was still sorting out the emotions when Stanley began to refold the letter.

He pinched the folds, the paper squeaked.

The out-of-place table, the autumn cold.

Of course Stanley began to talk. Old Ollie, man, so many ideas. He even used to take *acid* for the ideas, when the rest of us just took it for the thrills. Nonie let him go. She was goofy with relief. Some clottage inside had burst and set free a thousand skittery creatures, every one of them made of relief, every touch of their feet another tickle. She had to laugh. She sprawled in her chair. Every time she caught her breath she saw more of the whacky outdoors invade the house, visual overlaps flip-flopping from Stanley to the kitchen and back. His mustache blipped across the fridge and linoleum; the mugs and dry rack settled web-like over his head. His noise was a chatter on the edge of sleep. The chair itself made more sense, creaking *Alden didn't tell, he didn't tell* as she tried not to fall. Certainly she was too busy with laughing to finish the new questions coming to mind: Were they already . . .? Was it all going to be like . . .? Certainly she couldn't be bothered trying to read Stanley's gestures, or what it meant when he hiked his chair closer. At least the dry rack's grid had left his face. She could see the strain in his grin. Finally she caught what he was saying, enough to understand. Easy babe. Stay within. . . .

Soon as he touched her, she tackled him. Just erupted from her chair and tackled him. Her ankle clipped a table-leg, and the clatter of furniture behind them was pain as well, but she put it all into her bolt and grab, into a squeal of delicious need and power. She intended to kick over a lot more than tables and chairs. She'd had enough of everything boxed up and subtle: same old, same old. By the time the trip peaked she wanted a free fall. She wanted a revolution. No more lies forcing her into formal talk, strict posture, aching feet. Alden didn't tell; she'd get to tell. She'd get to tell; nothing else was going to take over for her after all. That was her relief. If Stanley couldn't handle the freedom, she'd find some place where no one so weak and ordinary could ever touch her again.

They were halfway across the living room before they fell. Nonie's nose was full of rug as she hauled herself upright. She straddled his tummy, she wanted him pinned, she needed a moment. The grating on the space heater loomed at her side like a tin net, while the trip lifted off in rushes that carried her awareness higher each time.

Stanley looked stunned but grateful. His cap was gone, his hair so wild it covered his bald spots.

"Stuntzie," she began, "Stuntzie . . ."

No good, the love name sounded mean. Past the giddiness, this new level was trouble.

Stanley . . . she thought through the words, she said some of them at least. Always remember, I was in love with you. Honestly I was—

"Hello? Are we in the right place?"

Was that him? She blinked but couldn't ask; unexpectedly she was almost crying.

"Hello? Oh! Oh, *sorry*. We were told the place was empty."

The front door was open. The chill proved this was real. In the brief entryway, bordering the living room, stood a man about Stanley's age. Other than that his looks were dark. Nonie let her face shrink again. She fisted her skirt together behind one leg and lifted herself off Stanley. But this man had a whole army with him. A woman as dark and striking as himself, and a boy and a girl. They all were burdened with soft, bright luggage. Though the children still fiddled with their grips and shoulder straps, their looks were even worse than their father's, honestly frightened. Nonie butted against the space heater and fell into a squat. Too close, the grate buckled against her spine. But she couldn't let on how the tin thunder shook her, and she could only cross her arms against the wind ripe with the coming of rain.

The man's name was Anthony Marcella. He'd arranged the rental with a realtor. Stanley got to his feet grinning, apologizing: Man, we never thought we had to check first with the *realtor*. Not in this market. The father didn't smile. He said he and his wife were with the movie, they needed a quiet place to unwind. The movie! Stanley did a big chinny take, he slung his thumbs in the scoops of his undershirt, he was onto a party wavelength already. Did you hear that, Nonie—the movie! Anthony Marcella interrupted before she had to answer. His look was the opposite of Stanley's, his voice ragged with smoke: So who are you guys?

"Tonight's the only night we need the crib," Stanley began. "And we'll be cool, we'll be just fine."

He had to fish out Nonie's license. See man, Winona Burnslides. But her father, man, get this: he was Joshua Burns Old Hides. Nonie couldn't believe Stanley's willpower. He'd made an instant commitment to ride out the complications. But she'd gone into this thinking it would be simple. Buying the acid had been less trouble than buying liquor. Nobody'd asked for ID; there'd been no whispering. Now however the mother pulled the father back into the doorway. And Stanley was making another offer, something about dinner. They wouldn't need to haul the kids around, they'd have a couple slaves for the night.

The parents' gestures at the children left fleshy trails that turned brown after the first second or so. When Anthony Marcella frowned, Nonie thought of a Disney stevedore. His whole family was that way, dark on dark. The mother, Lucy, might have had Indian blood herself. The boy was named Tonto, the girl Posey. Except their mouths didn't look Indian. They pouted somberly, their lips were twitchless staring tropical fish. Then it appeared an agreement had been reached. The parents handed Stanley the plastic card with her name.

He hefted a pair of suitcases. He led them past Nonie towards the stairs. A ripple of smiles and satiny backpacks: she suffered another surge of giddiness. She cupped her mouth and nose, she choked.

God, how had she ever handled living here? The stairs were so narrow that the troop had to go up single file, clomp-clomp right over the open snout of her giddiness. The place was a shoe box with gables. And when she'd lived here, there'd been family all the time. Clomp-clomp a lot louder and more regular. She'd been one of those girls who could spend forever perched on the bedroom window sill. In the spring she'd actually sit out on the brief gable downslope, she'd watch for the ghostly night visitors: the baby spiders that rode their webs on the breezes. But it was autumn now. Autumn, and upstairs they were dragging round furniture.

Nonie scooted away from the space heater and stood. The blood-rush triggered another kind of openness, a terror spasm. The time remaining till her trip peaked yawned ahead out of control. A chatter from the edge of sleep rotated the living room clockwise round the treetops and scrap of sky visible out the front door. Nobody had thought to close it.

She had more important things to do, herself. While the room settled she got her face in line. Forget the stretching: she went into her workshop program.

She went for the holding pattern. Nonie wanted to be up there again, up where she could judge distances and keep count, while the movement and noise around her were no more than radar. And the withdrawal seemed speeded by the drug. It started to come over her even as she finished her first brief jeté. Yes brief; too long a jump would carry her right out of the house. The space was better suited to the sauté. Nonie turned, she skipped back and forth between the fallen kitchen chairs and the facing sofa. She slipped further onto her safety level each time she repeated the chorus she and Stanley had sung in the car on the way up. Another of his favorite blues: *You got to move, you got to move.*

By the time she began her fouettés she'd broken a sweat. The chill from the open door was a useful control. Kept her from getting giddy again, because she'd always been best at fouettés, her body snapping round prettily, prettily, while one leg remained locked and extended as if the foot were netted in mid-air. Her body was a perfect match for the line-drawing across the walls of keeping count. There . . . there. The inward tuck she was after.

Upstairs the noise got worse. They must have been moving the beds, oh Stanley. Up in her holding pattern she could see him so clearly. Him and all the men in her life: they didn't dominate her, they didn't tie her in knots. Just her being here proved she wouldn't be pushed around. She'd had a session scheduled for this afternoon, and the director had warned her last time, if she skipped again she was out.

But Stanley now, he was pushed around. When he went on staff at *Sunset* for instance, all he could talk about was the money, how it would help with her tuition. And even after she graduated he remained a slave to the dollar. Sometimes he took assignments that meant he had to be gone all weekend. When she'd begun to work with the company from New York, there'd been no one to pick her up but Alden. She'd come out freshly complimented and ready for a drink, and there would be Alden. Even then she might have been able to handle it if *Sunset* hadn't run only the most routine and soulless shots. Stanley would go through four rolls of film over a weekend, and the one shot they'd print would be of a kid leaping after a butterfly. Caption, *The Never-Ending Joys of Childhood*. How could a grown man allow himself to be used like that? She still had a hard time understanding, she couldn't stop thinking about him. If it had been her, she'd have kept more of what mattered untouched.

"Babe? You straightening up in here?"

Stanley stood in the hallway door. A speckle of hallucination fled across his jacket as she came out of her last pirouette. She tasted hair at the corner of her mouth, she realized how she must look. At least Stanley had kept the others from coming through the hallway door, they hadn't seen. Now his jacket was mere gray planes of reflection. Keeping her feet in fifth position, her sanctuary snug, Nonie bent and brought up one of the chairs.

"No no, babe. Don't bother." The Marcellas were in when she came up. "The father's got a little program in mind."

Fifth position, tight but comfortable. She fingered the hair off her face, she nodded when Stanley explained that the parents wanted to look at some slides. Something to do with the movie, babe; nod nod. Still she almost lost her balance as the kids darted round finding the curtain pulls, turning the room dark. The sweat from her workout became oppressive when the father banged shut the door.

The kitchen was normal again, Stanley had moved the table back. Kitchen chores were better still. Holding patterns older than Elements of Dance. But instead of Mom, today she had Lucy. Lucy had insisted on helping, and as they chopped up the vegetables and cheeses the woman talked about Hollywood. The gossip threaded the surface tension with dangerous color. Apparently Anthony had a lot riding on this movie. He was the primary editor, his first shot at that kind of responsibility. The slide show now was something the director had insisted on; the director had a particular kind of horror movie in mind.

The wife paused, Nonie tried to pitch in. She told the story she knew best, about the day when Stanley had come in to photograph her dance troupe. You should have seen him, this slinky old *guy* in a biker's jacket and cap, getting off all these East-Coasty one-liners. Nonie managed to giggle without losing control. When Stanley found out she had Indian blood, she said, he'd called her Princess Summerfallwinterspring.

But Lucy didn't follow up. In here she didn't look nearly so old as she had standing next to her husband. She was hardly older than Nonie. And yet with these kids, this fast-track position—Nonie turned from her stare. She took the mugs from the dry rack and held them under the faucet.

"Well." Lucy fell in beside her, took the nearer mug. "I'm sure in Stanley's business, there are times when he's under a lot of pressure."

Nod nod. She started on the spoons.

"I'm sure you know what that's like, when a man's under pressure—say, where are your dishtowels?"

"I think there's one in the bathroom," Nonie said.

God, how had that popped out? When Lucy returned from the downstairs can, towel in hand, her stare had deepened. Then the light went out in the living room; Lucy's face turned to stark makeup, geisha makeup. The idea took over, too fast for Nonie's inner radar. Both of them might as well be geishas. They could have been doing this kind of thing anywhere on the globe. They'd fallen into the scutwork shoulder to shoulder, and yet at the same time they'd avoided anything more intimate. When the stories ran out, they could only stare. Girls from the escort service. Their men were waiting for them to finish.

Stanley called, Lucy moved. Still Nonie went into the living room carefully. She couldn't trust what she could see of how they'd rearranged the furniture.

Anthony Marcella at least was grateful for the guacamole, she'd figured that right. He was drinking tequila, he'd commented on the Inca design in her skirt. But she chose to sit on the floor. Stanley perched against the sofa arm like a daddy long-legs. He'd lent the boy his jacket, but he looked worse than cold. He looked as if he'd been giving away pieces of himself forever, as if that were his own geisha-vision, his own global nightmare. Even on the floor Nonie found the paranoia hard to shake. The children were two more ruptures in the safety place. They played at the edge of the projector's funnel of light, quick as puppets. The boy was huge in Stanley's coat and the girl was squeally. Nonie tried to stay with the father's explanations.

"That's Pompeii," he was saying. "That sort of burnt, smudged look, that's what he wants for this picture."

"Sure," Stanley said. "A horror flick, everything should be smudged."

The father dolloped more liquor into his glass. How could he drink so much? Nonie's one sip had tasted like she was licking a match-head.

"And those props on Main Street, man, those looked nice." Stanley was desperate; the chatter had to make up for what he'd given away. "It looked like the '50s out there."

Nonie didn't want to hear it. She put her head against the heater and closed her eyes. But with that another landscape appeared, its colors secure, its weather simple. She pictured the mockups Stanley was talking about, the props and trimmings just a few short blocks away. Out there—she didn't want to think about it. But the slides kept changing, the click and whir kept her mind from wandering: out on Main Street, she could have gotten into some truly freeform craziness. What was she *doing* in here? Why hadn't she gotten out when she had the chance?

Click, regret, click, regret. The two kids appeared to be dancing in time, their carefree hops and tumbles mocked her. A romp out on Main Street would have been perfect craziness. Those period sets were made for a trip like this. When she and Stanley had come through town yesterday, the Datsun itself had seemed nuts, a foreign car in Mayberry RFD. Storefronts dark for years were decorated with awnings bright as a clown-face. In one window there'd been a poster, Christmas-colored: *Try the latest rage— WHAM-O FRISBEE!* The barber pole was spiffed and revolving again. The bench in front of the pharmacy was spiffed, and the man sitting there wore a bow-tie and the gap-toothed smile of a lunatic. Well how did Nonie look herself, now, huddled and uptight on a strip of fake-brick sheeting? How many opportunities to get out was she going to fumble? On the set, she would've been able to stay in her holding pattern forever. On the set it was only natural for a person to go crazy.

"Will you *stop* it about the set?" The father was loud, his voice rang inside the tin heater like an alarm. "You know that isn't a playground out there, that's a movie!"

When had this happened? All she could see of Stanley was his shirt, aglow in this dark.

"They're eating people alive out there," the father said.

Tonto came motoring between her and the others. The boy had zipped up the jacket and scrunched down inside; his feet were out of sight and only his eyes showed over the collar.

"You think the '50s are fun? To me, when you talk about the '50s, it's mean, mean talk. You don't know how those bastards keep us stuck on the '50s."

Lucy laughed. The noise was worse than the father's carrying on, totally irrelevant, a dent in the atmosphere.

"I swear to God, every goddamn movie they make, it's got to be the '50s. Never mind if you had some ideas of your own for the picture. Never mind how all the little girls have their *tits* hanging out."

Lucy again, like a lawn mower catching and dying. And Stanley laughed too: hey, what a party. Nonie squinted against the projector beam. When had this *happened?* When had they started . . . covering up, or whatever this was? It wasn't funny, certainly. But the couch presented a solid front, three adults. The mother was the least visible, and already her laughter changed shape in Nonie's memory, it started to sound sincere. Nonetheless the nerves and raw talk were getting to the kids. Tonto's engine had stopped, he sagged at the beam's edge. Posey sat cross-legged beside Nonie, and somewhere the girl had found a set of rubber stamps. Now as Nonie watched she began to print one repeatedly, mechanically across her face.

Anthony Marcella was pouring himself another. Stanley, chuckling, admitted he didn't know anything about Hollywood. "Down there, man, I wouldn't know how to get anything done."

"You eat people alive," the father said. "You just wait for them to get stuck, all it takes is a minute. And then you eat them alive."

More laughter. Nonie became aware of her goosebumps. They snagged her leotard, the talk shredded what was left of her sanctuary. Stanley was saying exactly, man, exactly: he didn't know about Hollywood, but he knew the feeling.

"Take myself, I moved out here because this is supposed to be just the opposite kind of place. And okay, it is. The Willamette Valley, man, it's the nicest, most laid-back place you could want. And I've got my gig, I mean, I'm a professional photographer. I've got my love of my life here, Princess Summerfallwinterspring."

"Stuntzie—" Nonie said.

"But then, man, then . . . suddenly I'm stuck." He was a shadow back there, a ghost. He needed to get out of here even worse than she did. "I mean it, I'm stuck. You know before this girl graduated, last June, I had to carry her whole tuition? Yeah. And then she wanted to take some workshops this summer, I had to pay for that too."

"Stanley!"

But there was a tug at her arm. Posey. Turned towards the projector, the little girl's face was garish. The stamps wove insanely across her nose and smile, Nonie thought she saw blood. Meantime Anthony Marcella was giving Stanley more rope: I hear you, man. "Ancient history, man. You start out the strong man and you end up the clown."

"Exactly, man, exactly. And I mean, I'm not somebody's father. I'm not somebody's bankroll. I'm a *rebel*, man. Or at least I was a rebel when I came out here. But then somehow I wound up holding the bankroll. Somehow in this wonderful laid-back place I wound up with like a bankroll in my teeth and, and claws instead of hands. I don't even know who I am."

"You know who I wish was here?" Nonie said. "I wish *Alden* was here."

She'd had to shout. Tonto's motor was going again. The boy rumbled into the projector beam, the leather was seared with yellow and brown; the mother ordered him out. But they weren't going to stop Nonie this time. If Stanley didn't realize how much he was losing here—talking mean was the next thing to going crazy—well she'd get him out herself. She'd get them all out herself.

"I *wish* Alden were here." Who cared that she'd always been careful to use the nickname with Stanley? The way she'd felt when the drug first hit, the giddy surge to freedom, she had to get back to that. "Alden wouldn't just sit around, he wouldn't just sit around and glide around. He'd burn through the surfaces and he'd pull us all through with him."

"Nonie, baby . . ."

"He *would*." Waves of isolation spiraled from the faceless shapes on the couch. But she'd had it with their bullying, she faced the screen.

"Look at this slide here now, is this still Pompeii? Alden could, he could really take you out of this world once he started on a slide like that. I mean with all those naked dancers on the wall, my God, the men even have *erections*, God!" She had to get the kids out of here at least. These people were corrupt. "And those, those two things down in the front, in the cages. What are they, some kind of ancient Roman monster?"

"A husband and wife," Anthony Marcella said.

"What? Those two like, mummy-things, in the cages?"

"A husband and *wife*," the father barked. "What's the matter, don't they look like a husband and wife?"

Nonie flexed her feet. The draft along the floor sustained her energy.

"This was their bedroom, kid."

"Tony, honey—"

"No Luce, no. We can all learn something here. Lots of Romans had porno murals in their bedrooms, kid. And these two, that's where they went to hide when the lava came."

The children had started squabbling too. Tonto rumbled into his sister, Posey hugged her stamp box to her knees. It was a tank going after a fortified bunker. Unquestionably this family needed what Nonie could give them. They needed her to convert their energy. Even the naked grotesques on the screen shouldn't hold them up once she got them to feel the power of the drug's remaining unused space, the vacuum rush to both freedom and safety at once.

Stanley kept trying. He said Nonie was right about one thing: old Ollie could really do a riff on a slide like that.

"Stanley, no, no what I'm saying is—"

"Old Ollie could probably do a *dance* on a slide like that. One look and he'd see all the things he was into. He'd see LSD in there. He'd, he'd see self-destruction."

"No no, Stanley. The slide's beside the point."

"Christ, the guy had an idea for every weird thing he ever did in his life."

"The slide is *nothing*. Listen to me, everybody, a picture like that doesn't shock me. Not at all, not after the kind of things Alden taught me."

Stanley made some small sound, a drink going down the wrong way, an obscenity.

"*Listen.* Earlier this summer I worked with a real dance company, I mean a big famous one from New York. And compared to what Alden found out about that company from New York, a picture like that is nothing." She had the truth on her side. If she kept talking it wouldn't be long: they'd all get to say anything they wanted. "I mean, Stanley, you were off doing all those weekend assignments, you never knew the half of it. Alden—I couldn't believe the things he found out."

"You guys," Stanley said, "you should know something. Nonie here didn't start dancing till it was almost too late."

"Alden just went out with those people a few times, they hung out at the Hilton and had a few drinks. But I couldn't believe it. He found out *everything*."

"Coming from a hick town like Brownsville, see. Nonie didn't start till college. She's kind of bitter."

"Alden found out everything about these people, Stanley, you never even knew. There were, there were eleven women in the company and Alden found out five of them were gay."

"Christ," Anthony Marcella said, "the guy sounds like a genius."

"But listen, listen!" The laughter wasn't the only distraction. Beside her, Tonto had backed his sister into the heater's grating, and their squabble was getting nasty. *You're the dummy here. No, you are.*

"Listen. Here I'd been slaving along, dreaming that this workshop might finally get me free of all the dumb bad luck of my life. I mean a company from New York, they should be in control, right? Like what you were saying earlier Stanley, about those old Leary Ginsberg people—dancers from New York should be in control all the time too, just like Leary Ginsberg. Right? So I was *dreaming* of this workshop. And then the people show up, the real thing, and Alden finds out they're even worse off than me. I mean Alden tells me they're crazy. They're nasty, and they're crazy."

Lucy had started something with her husband. First whispering, now louder: C'mon, big boy, lighten up. At least change the slide.

"But listen, listen. When I really learned something was when Alden told me about the suicide. I was shocked. Everyone in the company was whispering about this poor man back in New York who'd jumped off a roof."

"Nones," Stanley said, "could we talk a minute?"

"The suicide guy, he was one of the gay ones, of course. Gay and anorexic. I mean, I've had some problems but not like that, not like an IV right through the chest."

"Nonie, hey, please. Let's like, get away for a minute and talk."
On the screen, the wall paintings appeared to tremble. Behind
her the wife's talk took on an edge, c'mon honey, the slide. Nonie
got hold of her skirt, pinching the Inca trim.

"This poor man. When Alden told me about him, all I could
think was, the whole *thing's* corrupt. It's like some unstoppable
force in history, every time you think you've got a nice setup, that's
exactly what kills you. Alden told me that first, the man's marriage
fell apart. And then he tried to lose himself in his work, like your
work is supposed to be a nice setup, right? Your work is supposedly
something you can fall back on. But everybody at work was
whispering—"

The screen burst white, then black. Something crashed,
someone shouted. "Stop! Just please *stop!*"

Nonie took a poke, one of the kids. She humped round the
space heater, the grate scratched her goosebumps. And when she
caught her breath her nose was full of dust. In the sudden dark the
floor draft seemed colder. Still Nonie was happy, she was
delirious, she choked but had to laugh. There were shoots of fresh
nerve up through her temples, too alive to be kept down any
longer. This time Stanley wouldn't be the only one to tumble. Also
she'd take down this troop who'd forced her to play the
handmaiden. Sick family, sick house. First they had to fall, then
they would fly. Already the scene appeared all flakes and trails,
coated with smoke—she was blinking, fighting for air while her
eyes adjusted. The kids tussled, the little girl crying and flailing
away with her open stamp box. The projector had been knocked
off the coffee table and the table itself had gone over. Lucy was on
hands and knees, going after the white blots of spilled slides. The
father stumbled past the fallen furniture. He came for Nonie.

"Are you crazy?" he said. "Stop! Just *stop!*"

Her skirt in her fist, she braced herself for what she had to say
next. She'd scream if she had to. It was the word that would set off
the permanent upsuck, the truth that would liberate them all at
last: her and Alden in the Model Motel on 99W. They called *Sunset*
to make sure they had a free hour. They fed quarters to the TV so
they could find a soundtrack.

But—"Easy babe, easy." Stanley was the first one to her. The cold had gotten to his hands, but his breath was still sour with coffee.

"Nonie, baby, please. We really have to talk. It isn't like you think."

What was he doing here? Stanley should be fading from her life by now. He should be cringing before the truth, pulling together a raft of tough-guy dressup and getting set to ride off on the shock waves. Nonie felt something under her haunch, one of Posey's stamps, and she pinched it against the floor deliberately. The pain would help her concentrate. Plus Anthony Marcella stood over her. His liquor glass was iron in this light, and he was still trying to push them around: Tell her I didn't come out to the damn *woods* to hear this shit.

"I want my Mommy! I want my *Mommy!*"

Posey. The screams were so loud they echoed up the heater's chimney-pipe. The girl had broken free of her brother and sat bawling in the middle of the floor. Lucy was coming for her, crawling, murmuring. But Posey shot to her feet and backed into the entryway.

"Not you, not *you*. I want my real Mommy."

"Now, darling—"

"Don't you call me darling! Only my real, true Mommy can call me darling!"

The loudest yet. The girl swayed in the entryway with arms bent up for a hug, her lips huge and strange again. Over her empty hands the street lights fluttered in the door's ornamental window, twisted brown butterflies. Her hoarse outcry was too much for a body so small.

"Only my real true Mommy! My *real true* Mommy!"

The father went down on his knees. He left his glass behind, it rolled weightless into Nonie's toes. Poor little lost princess baby . . . Nonie didn't catch the rest. She dropped her chin, her face was burning.

"Your Papa hasn't seen his babies in three months, Posey princess girl. Your Papa was just so *nervous* about seeing his babies again."

"Now darling," Lucy said. "Don't make yourself crazy."

The father didn't respond. The good father: in his arms the girl was shrinking already. Alcohol, what a freakish mix. It roughed up the man's talk but warmed his embrace. Lucy kept trying: it was good for the kids to see the whole story, they should know about the rough stuff. Anthony wasn't even looking. He waved for the boy to join him and Posey, big elbow-and-shoulder gestures across the entryway. Tonto had gone for cover behind the screen. Nonie's face was burning, it was singing.

"Nonie, Stanley." Lucy got a light beside the couch. "Guys, I mean—you two have seen worse, right? Like Nonie said, you've seen a lot worse. It's just you didn't know how that gossip can get to Anthony."

Stanley let go of Nonie's hand. She hid it in her lap.

"I mean, that gossip." Lucy shook her head. "You guys picked up on how nervous we were, right? Every time I laughed, I about made *myself* crazy."

Stanley. The way he hooked his elbows round his knees left his shoulders perfectly level. Whatever Lucy and Anthony were doing here, he said, it was cool with him. Nonie frowned and kept blinking, she was red-faced. She squirmed against the toy under her butt. But the table that faced her—it wasn't going anywhere. The same false oak she'd known since childhood, same dull crisscross of notches and scars. The projector's tinker-toy engine still whirred. Somebody had saved the guacamole and set it in the corner of the sofa. Only the slides had gone far.

She had a toy under her *brains*, that was the problem. She'd actually believed in the game.

Lucy was still smiling, though her tone had changed. "Well hold on, we're not just having some fling in the woods. Anthony left his wife for me."

Nonie stood. In the blood-rush the people at her feet turned to sketches and dust, the fallen slides multiplied like infection. Nothing she couldn't handle: she'd been high for centuries. She focussed on the doorway. The huddle there was too big to get around, the father had both kids now. She tried to muster some excuse: I'm sorry . . .

"Oh, don't be too hard on yourself," Lucy said.

There was something complicated in the woman's shrug, something like pulling rank. But Nonie couldn't get caught up in the geisha thing again. Stanley clambered to his feet beside her. Saying yeah, Nonie. Yeah, I think I need a breather too. And he tottered once he was up. It shook the floor, he was still in his biker boots. Judging from his eyes, he couldn't even make it to Main Street. But then what had the man ever had to give away except lies? He served up such stories you didn't notice the meal had grown cold; he designed holding patterns for two. She'd mistaken that skill for strength; he was fifteen years older.

God, God—what was Nonie doing feeling *sorry?* Feeling sympathy for the man, feeling warmth. It couldn't be real. All the worst of today's tricks had come from within.

"Nones, a little talk. Please." He was whispering now. "It's not like you think."

"Oh you don't have to go," Lucy said. "Honestly, we'll all be fine if you just stay away from the gossip."

Nonie was backing off, nudging round the space heater. She spread her other hand against Stanley's ribs. A little talk would only be more of the same. She'd been bouncing off the walls of his talk for centuries. Stanley bent his head closer, his pretty furred head. The spider again.

"I know about Alden," Stanley said.

She broke for the back door. What he'd said set off a terrible head-chatter. A garble lurching into fast forward, the words like surf and the surf the renewed heat in her face. Yet there was a doomy rightness to him knowing, the perfect final ruin of any hope for secrets and sanctuary. It was what you expected of the drug. At its peak you were past any fall-back. The hallway had no rug, her knees hurt from the first long step. But there didn't seem to be anyone coming after her, another minute and she'd be out in the soft grass. Except at the end of the hall was the downstairs can—its door open, its mirror exposed.

All Nonie could see were the eyes. They had such mania in them still. Such black desire: an absolute hunger for more and higher. There were tears, her tears, and yet they didn't seem like hers. Nonie skidded, stopped. Positively not her own tears. Her sadness was distant, the breakup with Stanley would be sorted into parts and extensively rehashed. But the thing in the mirror was bug-eyed, ferocious. It was more than she should have had room for, neverending surges after God knows what. And the Indian in her made it worse. She had no eyelids to speak of; the want, want, want in the mirror came flame-shaped and unshaded. She thought of fire arrows, of the tracer phosphorus in Stanley's books on Vietnam.

She was at the stairwell. She turned and headed up, she took three at a time. The eyes were out of sight, but she still had to get free of the voices. Lucy was calling after her. Hey Nonie, really, it's just the *gossip*. Every day at the studio Anthony has to go in and face the same mean talk.

She remembered when Alden had told her he loved her. Nonie was in her old bedroom now, huddled under the gable. Her breathing was heavy, very loud in this space. Coming in, she'd fluttered the silky remembrances pinned to the walls; a girlish thread or two still floated. But she could hear him. Alden, he'd told her he loved her. He said he'd fallen hard. The memory was the only thing real enough to matter, after the glimpse at the foot of the stairs.

Winona . . . it's either love, or we're both nothing but mean, mean, mean . . .

But she was starting to pick up her reflection in the gable window. The curtains' ribbon tie was too difficult, she put her back to the glass. Then she realized someone was actually saying the words out loud. Stanley was the one talking about love or meanness, not Alden. Stanley was coming up the stairs.

Nonie turned again and fought the window open. She wriggled out onto the roof.

Not nearly so easy as it used to be. With her heels in the gutter, her head didn't fit under the gable's peak. The brick porch steps below circled swoozily. Plus the rain had started, a tattered cloth coldly sponging her down. When Stanley found her, she couldn't catch every word. The confusion with Alden persisted: Nonie, please . . . Too many voices, the place was haunted. Her father too had left a piece of himself in these woods. She could feel his hands on her now, stony and dry with millwork . . .

Stanley. He was trying to get Nonie by the waist.

"Nonie, I know this looks like a mean trick. Like I wanted the acid to do it for me. . . . But I love you, baby. I took it too."

She lurched free, the gutter bit her instep.

"Look Nonie, just . . . once I came home at the wrong time, and suddenly I was history. Suddenly I was a clown . . ."

Yet while she couldn't catch every word, her attention seemed total. She could see the work crews pulling tarps over the homey props down on Main Street. She could read the initials at the edge of the walk beneath her. And under the grime that filled those initials she could make out the radium-trace of her father's last disease, the glue and nicotine that had ruined his fingers first. Every man's home is his castle; every old tract house in the Valley was haunted. Meantime, in a holding pattern above the sky, the insatiable sun waited. It rode the tattered cloth of the first serious rain, poised to trap and smother, patient on its winter web. Her attention burned through every surface. This had to be it, then: the furthest reach of her trip.

Stanley tried for her again. Nonie hadn't much room. The takeoff was helpless, a slapstick jeté. Her noise was a "*No!*" that had nothing to do with time and place. Nonetheless while the brown woods turned over and melted she still strained for an echo.

The Arno Line

WHO WAS THIS GUY? Sitnell knew that the publicist came from back East. But he hadn't expected a—what *would* you call a person in that getup? Even the guy's baldness was hard to take. It was like another accessory, a khaki-colored slip-on skull. The publicist was a good twenty-five years younger than Sitnell after all. Though no way Kroh was young enough for that tie, either. The thing was an inch wide at most and flecked with what looked like war paint. Plus when the man toed round on his barstool to say hello, Sitnell couldn't miss the bulge of Kroh's camel's humps, especially ugly under his red leather jacket. A Michael Jackson jacket, in this case zippered shut around a sack of dirt. Drew more than a couple of stares from along the bar.

"I was beginning to wonder," Kroh said.

Was that supposed to be funny? Granted, once Sitnell broke off the handshake he discovered that the Happy Hour nachos had gone cold, the cheese gummy. But the publicist was the rude one here. Kroh had called, that first time, after ten at night. Sitnell had found himself sitting through this entire breakneck publicity hard sell while watching his wife get undressed for bed. After the call, the old girl had propped herself upright against the headboard and told Sitnell the stories she'd heard about this guy. She'd said that, if he met with Jimmy Kroh, he might as well sit down with their youngest and teach the boy to smoke pot.

Sitnell ordered a martini. "Very dry," he said, "and never mind what you've got in the well. I want real liquor."

Kroh's smile became triangular. As soon as Sitnell came up with a brand, Beefeater, the guy started to make a fuss.

"It's so great," he kept saying, "to be with a man who likes real liquor." They found a longer table, by the window. "Most guys my age, you know? They drink nothing." Sitnell hoped that at this distance the stares from the bar would stop. "I want to tell them, hey. *Forget* about being sleek and pretty for a minute. Just forget about being pretty."

Nor was there the usual breather after they sat. Kroh went straight from the booze talk to saying how excited he was about working with Sitnell. "Really want to do your book up right, Walter," he said. "The dust jacket too." The dust jacket? When had Sitnell mentioned that? He tried to keep a distance, starting on his drink, eyeing Mt. Hood. He'd chosen this place because of how much he remembered liking the view. The view was worth the kind of lumber-mill workers and four-wheel-drive cowboys you got in a lounge this far outside the city. But what with the sketchy November rain, Hood itself didn't cap the landscape the way Sitnell had expected. What he could see of Portland from up here had a null smogged color and too many moving lights. Beyond that, the mountain's hefty poke appeared more gray than white. And then Kroh was butting in again.

"Oh yeah, isn't it beautiful? Isn't it something?" Though he had his back to the mountain. He was jerking a thumb over one shoulder and at the same time clearing the candle jar and the menu teepee off to the side of the table with a stiffarm sweep. "Sometimes when I'm downtown, I swear—" he slapped his portfolio onto the tabletop— "it seems like old Hood's up there *nodding* at us. Saying like, 'Come on, come on.' Beautiful."

Sitnell wondered how many Kroh'd had. But then he must be feeling his gin already himself, the portfolio seemed to have the most raucous zipper he'd ever heard. Of course he hadn't gone out drinking like this in, what, two-three years now.

"I mean Walter, just your sitting here tells me what I want to know. Just your sitting and looking at Hood. That tells me you're a man who knows what he likes."

Sitnell took a swallow that lifted his chin.

"I mean most guys, when they retire, they don't go write a book."

Sitnell undid his reversible, fitted on his bifocals, and frowned. Kroh never broke stride. Bent over the half-open portfolio, doing some preliminary fiddle and sort, he moved on to Sitnell's taste in bars. "Those cowboys over by the TV, I love it. And the basketball sneakers nailed to the *wall?* Exciting. Tiger stripes even. And I'm not even talking about the posters with the prices, those great old Peter Arno champagne glasses. I mean when I saw those, I knew you and me could set this up."

Peter Arno champagne glasses? But just a few days ago Sitnell's editor, another New York type, had pulled the same stunt. He'd thrown around a lot of names Sitnell had never heard of, when what they'd been talking about after all was the title of Sitnell's book. New York preferred catchy vagueness like *Underbelly*. Finally Sitnell had put his foot down. He'd said he hadn't written the book in order to go on TV. It didn't matter how they'd gussied up the jacket photograph, Sitnell had said: he was no Lorne Greene. The editor's silence after that felt almost as good as the letter of acceptance. Except then Sitnell's wife had used the same argument against him when he'd told her he was thinking of getting together with Kroh. First she'd repeated the awful stories about the man's marriage. But when that had failed to change Sitnell's mind, she'd asked him straight out: if he didn't want any TV sort of publicity—if the truth of the book was what mattered— why was he meeting this guy?

Kroh slipped a couple samples of his work across the table. Sitnell raised his eyebrows, pouted approvingly. Talent had never been a question. At the hardware store where Sitnell shopped, over the cash register, they'd even glued a couple of Kroh's cartoons together and hung them on fishing line from the ceiling. Nonetheless the publicist's third sample took him by surprise. Sitnell had to cup his drink to his belly with one hand, pick at his hair with the other. Kroh had drawn a map of the U.S. in the form of hundreds of naked babies. The infants were crammed together coast to coast, often with just a part of the torso showing. Florida hung upside down, a bawling head and shoulders only, its hands trapped by the crush above it. New England was mostly a pair of kicking legs. And Cape Cod—Sitnell needed another long swallow—was the boy's exposed genitals. He thought of the propaganda flyers dropped over his positions during the war. The piece was in black and white, but the wall of babies appeared to have all its natural suddenness and pudge.

"It's for pro-choice." Kroh threw back the last of his drink. "You know that—"

"I *know* the abortion people, yes, thank you. I live in the same century you do."

And then the barmaid stood over them, awful timing. Worse, now that he'd got his glasses on, Sitnell could see that the girl was pregnant. Her belly rose almost to her pigtails. It was all Sitnell could do to keep from slapping his arms across the publicist's latest piece, and he wound up taking a refill.

Kroh busily made peace. More one-liners, more of that eyewash about "most guys these days." Sitnell wondered if back East this kind of shake-and-shimmy actually worked. Now the man was insisting that Sitnell call him Jimmy, making it into yet another nervous joke. "Out here Walter, whenever I call people, like trying for an assignment? They think I'm an Indian." A very nervous joke: the guy patted his lips with a flat hand, woo-woo. "And then they think I'm *dreaming*, right? They think I'm trying to *hide* the fact that I'm an Indian by spelling it the way I do."

But Sitnell cracked a grin at that, and Kroh followed up well. "I'm telling you, Walter. These days I'm death on the phone."

And the second drink helped. The pricklier edges on the give and take got lost more easily in the country-and-western out of the speaker overhead. Sitnell even began to see the pattern in Kroh's talk: first something pushy, then something apologetic. Even the gestures changed: first all knuckles, then a loose wrist. So after another one of those—while the younger man was still saying he was sorry and tugging at the tip of his jacket's single lapel—Sitnell thought he understood why he'd come tonight.

He believed he'd pitied the man. It wasn't only those renegade looks that made Sitnell think so. There were mill workers at the bar almost as dark as Kroh. Though they kept their caps pulled low (red Budweiser or white Cat), every time the cowboys looked this way you could see that a couple had Kroh's Mongol eyes. No, it wasn't just Kroh's appearance. Also the man seemed to insist on putting something disagreeable in every piece he drew. And how was that supposed to help him do dust jackets? How was that supposed to help him do publicity at all? The poor misguided clod. Sitnell could even identify what the pity felt like, a booze-tinged seepage down the back of his neck. Interesting to pick it out so clearly. Sitnell began to fuss with his hair again, rotating his head shoulder to shoulder, in order to isolate the sensation better. Kroh was only whining anyway. He'd started to badmouth the *Oregon Journal*, which had folded under him after he'd moved "all the way out here" to take the job. Sitnell's wife had told him as much already.

Besides, while turning his head he'd discovered there was another couple in the lounge. They had a table over by the restrooms. A businessman in a three-piece suit, almost Sitnell's age, sat across from a redheaded girl in a full-length dress. Rather nightclubby for this place, though they weren't getting the stares that Kroh had. Sitnell however peered over his bifocals. The couple had some brightly decorated box between them, a present perhaps.

"Yeah," Kroh said. "Now she's my idea of *publicity*."

Sitnell returned to the cartoon on the table. This one featured a torture victim beaten into a human triangle, all backside and broken joints. He tapped the face of a guard in the corner.

"A lot of your men, Jimmy. They all have the same . . ."

"The moon faces? Wingtip mustaches?"

"Yes, yes. I'm sure you have ah, a whole vocabulary for this sort of thing. But to me, they look almost like the man on the Monopoly board."

Kroh's hands quieted a moment, clasped index-finger-up in front of his smile. "Well that's the Peter Arno touch, Walter," he said. "The guy who did the Monopoly board, huh. He got it from Peter Arno. Just like those champagne glasses in the poster there, you remember when I said—"

"The champagne glass, yes. I remember."

At least Kroh didn't apologize. He frowned at his fingernails, shredded along the cuticle, and seeing that, Sitnell suffered a flashback to his own last couple years at Timberline Printing. Union rules wouldn't allow them to let him go, so they'd kicked him upstairs. By the time he'd asked out Sitnell had started talking to the walls.

"Peter Arno," Kroh repeated. "Well I'm not sure that's what we should be talking about, but." He shrugged with his eyebrows and explained that Arno was a cartoonist and poster artist of the '20s and '30s. "Say like, your father's generation, Walter." The man had done very different work from Kroh's. "His show posters especially, the Broadway stuff. You oughta see them. Always very ritz-and-glitz, very—a champagne-type lifestyle, Walter. Lots of old Manhattan aristocrats chasing after these gorgeous young showgirls." Kroh had taken to the style early on.

"I was attracted to it, Walter. What can I say? It was so the opposite of what I'm into in terms of content."

But he'd been attracted to it. And Sitnell thought he understood, in fact with getting to know the man, with the second drink helping—Sitnell remembered that he himself had seen a spread by Arno once. Just a shadow in his mind's eye by now, but he knew what Kroh was getting at. Seen it in the old *LIFE*? In one of the magazines that had circulated at the Allied hospital anyway. In those days, after Sitnell's last action, it had been the name and not the work that got to him. In Italy, the Arno River had been where the Nazis set up their northernmost line of defense.

Sitnell ran his fingertips down and up one side of his reversible zipper. "You know," he began—and then didn't want to finish.

He didn't want to share the war with a guy like this. The Arno action had almost killed him. Sitnell clenched his teeth till he could feel the booze in his gums, and he tried Mt. Hood again. The peak was afloat, a disintegrating arrowhead above the twilight fog. He looked around the lounge, but so stiffly this time that the barmaid headed back their way. Nachos/Men's Room/Date of delivery? But then Sitnell had decided to get a third, and to tell Kroh about where the names connected. The need to say it had come over him like pain catching up to a wound. And once he'd started to talk, he felt good about it, excited; it was more than gin fever. It felt like he'd been working up to this since he'd come in. Though he could keep what he said in line. He'd worked the last two and a half years on the story of his time in Italy, after all. While the next round arrived, Sitnell played it tough. He took off his bifocals, gestured with them in one fist. He made sure to start with "You know."

"I wonder if you can imagine," he was saying after a minute, "what that last Kraut line looked like. The last, worst bastard of them all." He swept his bifocals left-right across the tabletop. "The land stripped naked for a hundred yards in front of the river. Not a tree left standing, no cover anywhere this side of the Kraut emplacements." Left-right, this time more noisily. "I'll tell you the truth, I've never been so frightened. Nothing but you and them and—"

Kroh took hold of the hand with the bifocals. He pinched the wrist a bit, lifting it aside.

"Watch it on the samples, Walter," he said.

Sitnell wound up concentrating on the lyrics in the latest tune from the speaker overhead. Something last chance, last chance. By the time he got his next swallow he was trying to think of the quickest way out of here. Though Kroh wasn't long in sensing the change, give him credit. He'd been talking about studying design in Florence one summer. But then his rhythm slowed, his hands dropped.

"Walter, hey. Lemme just say, I'm coming at this from a different angle, I realize." He even finger-doodled on the topmost drawing: no big deal, buddy. "See now a man like myself, my age. I've been trained as an artist really, and—"

"Oh stop that. We don't live in sod huts out here anymore, you know. My own son you know, my youngest, he may be an artist." Sitnell went through a finger-by-finger rundown of all the work the boy was putting in on the senior-class play, the sets and costumes and lighting.

"Wait a minute Walter, wait a minute. Senior-class play? You mean you've got a kid still in high school?"

Sitnell shrugged, his fingers still extended.

"Boy, Walter, you don't slow down much, do you?"

"Well that's my point, you ought to see what I have to contend with. My own son, sometimes he comes home from that play just lost in a dream. Singing and dancing and acting out all the parts, it's goddamned amazing. The boy fills the house."

"I can imagine, Walter."

Oh sure. According to Sitnell's wife, this guy didn't have the first clue about children. "So don't try to trick me, Jimmy. Don't hand me any more of this talk about how different you are, how much younger you are."

"Oh well, Walter, then—hey. I'm *sorry*, Walter." He tugged the red tip of his lapel. "Honestly man, if it sounded like I wasn't giving you credit, hey. I *apologize*."

Sitnell thumbed the rim of his drink, frowned and pouted. That hadn't gone right. He was still in the meeting, Kroh was still getting round him. Now the guy was buying time with his portfolio. He fit the samples back inside busily, counting and taking the occasional unnecessary peek. Sitnell thought of how his wife had started fussing with his hair. From time to time these last couple years, she'd stood over Sitnell while he was at his desk, picking and stroking and talking about his "wild mane." It had got in the way of his work so much that finally he'd had to speak to her about it.

And remembering that, Sitnell had his plan. He waited till Kroh redid his bratty zipper.

"Jimmy, I don't believe we can get together on this." He kept it throaty and regretful. "Not on my book, anyway."

"Walter, hey! Gimme a *chance* here."

"No, it's nothing to do with you, Jimmy." Sitnell figured he could ignore how his pity for the man had changed, how leaden and achy it had started to feel. "Your work really, really brings people up short, I can see that. I can see you're special. It's just that my book, well." Another mouthful of booze should see him through. He'd made the speech twice after all, first getting his editor to back off, and then his wife. "You haven't got the picture yet, about my book.

"It's just the story of a guy, he went to war. Like a million other guys who went to war. And then he went after those square-headed bastards the best he could, first in Sicily and then moving north up the boot. Just another Joe." For some reason he couldn't keep up eye contact. He found the basketball sneakers on the wall. "Some of the men this guy fought with, well, they were some of the bravest men he'd ever known." But at this distance the tiger stripes were too blurred, they upset him somehow. He wound up scowling into space. "He'd never realized that the world had so many incredible men in it, before he went to war. He'd never realized there were so many of these incredible, brave, wonderful guys out there, and that so many of them had to die."

Again the booze? Sitnell surprised himself, he went for his martini as if he wanted to hide his face. And once Kroh started talking—took the publicist a moment to realize the speech was over—Sitnell slurped up his olive and winced.

"Oh Walter, oh wow," Kroh was saying. "That was *beautiful*."

"Nnn." The pulp was so fat and sour that Sitnell couldn't straighten his tongue. "Gw, gw."

"I mean, you say *I'm* a special talent. Hey. I'd say there's room for two at this table."

Didn't this guy ever stop? Sitnell knew that he'd blown the speech, after all. He'd cut it in half and taped on the end. Forcing down the olive, he shook his head.

"No Walter, don't be coy. Don't be modest. When you talk like that, man, I can see 'em starting to pack the halls already."

"What's this?" Never; Kroh never stopped. Sitnell found himself grinning. "What're we talking about now?"

"We're talking about getting out and selling your book. We're talking about *speaking* engagements, Walter." And when the guy nodded, he even made the candlelight interesting. A yellow V, inverted, flared up and down his naked dome. "And I'll say it again, you're going to pack the house, Walter. I mean, I'll make it a promise. Because this kind of thing, this kind of thing, really. It brings people *together*."

Sitnell felt the roots of his hair tug, he realized he was at it again. Yet the small pain made him grin that much more. He even started to nod. It was the astonishment of finding himself still here—and knowing for certain, at last, that he could never have pitied Jimmy Kroh. No, not even at the guy's whiniest, over the phone. You didn't pity a sharpie like this, so much body English all the time that the lighting here left a black outline around him. So loud and handsy that the lugs along the bar still gave a look every now and then. It'd been fun, Sitnell had to admit. Fun enough to set him aching. In fact between the tug at his scalp and the olive sting in his gums, Sitnell had rarely felt so aware of his skull. A bony oval jigsaw so close to the skin. But this guy, this cartoonist. You could almost imagine Kroh twirling the narrow tip of a long mustache. "Walter," he was saying now, "compared to most men these days? You're going to be like the last of the gunslingers." Sitnell had to laugh. He dropped his chin, looked over his bifocals.

"You got the picture, Walter? You see how it can happen?"

"Oh God, Jimmy. You are a con man."

"Hell sure. How do you think I made it this far?"

"A con man and a liar."

"And I'm working for *you*." Kroh kept grinning, his face a booze-bright moon. "So tell me. Where'd you like to have the first performance? In town?"

Sitnell shook his head. "Come on, Jimmy. We understand each other better than that by now."

The publicist of course still tried to slick around. He talked about "smaller gigs, Corvallis maybe." Sitnell had to say no four or five different ways. He flattened his bifocals and got them back in his pocket, hulked up with his elbows on the table so he could use his height advantage. He pointed out that he'd tried to tell Kroh nicely, he'd tried to explain how he felt. "You're the performer here." Sitnell said. "In fact I should never have let things get this far, I should have known that a faker like you would want me to put my own face on the line." The publicist didn't so much give in as run out of room to maneuver. Sitnell once or twice allowed himself to sweep one stiff hand across the tabletop, out from the crook of his elbow and back. Otherwise he stonewalled it. Nonetheless he may have said more than necessary—made a couple more wisecracks about con artists than necessary—before he realized that Kroh had gone silent.

At once he was sorry he'd taken off his bifocals. Something had changed, Kroh had gone still. Squinting, Sitnell saw that only the man's mouth was moving. Kroh sat gnawing a cuticle, so wet and active about it that Sitnell checked the man's drink. Surprise: still almost full. But then he should have known the man wasn't drunk. A drunk couldn't have kept his look so flat and simple.

"What about that fine *speech* you just gave, Walter?"

Sitnell straightened his back.

"What about it, hey? All that fine talk about brave men dying. Didn't you mean it when you said that?"

"Now, Jimmy, I just admitted that I let things go too far . . ."

"Call me a liar. Walter, the way it looks to me, *you're* the liar. Your whole pretty little speech was a lie. It was probably just something you plug in whenever anyone crowds you. I mean, what'd you write the *book* for?"

Sitnell leaned closer, making fists in his lap. "How dare you. How dare you talk to me about lying. That book's more honest than anything you've done in your entire fast-talking life."

"Oh yeah? Then what're we even doing here if you don't want to get out and sell it?"

Sitnell wished the zipper on his reversible were as loud and final as the one on Kroh's portfolio. He regretted how the liquor had slowed his hands.

"Oh, would you answer a goddamn *question* for once? Jesus, I swear I've never seen a man pansy around as much as you do. Staring at the girls, staring at the wall. Would you for once show some *balls* and give a person a straight answer?"

Sitnell had been taking a squint at the rain. But after that last shot—well what did Kroh expect? Plus now the publicist had worked up a glare that seemed to pull his whole upper body into it. The gleamy forehead, that fist still at his teeth, those flattop padded shoulders. Sitnell felt his own chest and arms fluttering, tightening. He figured it'd be best to begin with a lie.

"I came here," he said, "because I pitied you."

Not bad. Kroh started working his thumbnail against an incisor.

"You see this isn't New York, Jimmy. You should have realized."

"Realized what, Walter? What are these chickenshit—"

"You should have realized that when anyone behaves as wildly as you did, out here it's news. It's news all over town." He made sure of the noise level, cocking an ear to the overhead speaker: something cheating something hurting. "New York is big, Jimmy. Big and crowded and nasty, and that's why people have always moved out here. They've always wanted to get away from all that and build a new life, a respectable life. Respectable and solid. So when someone starts crashing around like a bear in the woods, the way you did—well as I say, it's news."

"You mean my marriage, right?"

"No Jimmy, I mean you." Kroh was keeping up a good front, fist and shoulders holding steady. But the folds round his eyes had softened. "I mean the way you ran off when your wife was pregnant. You ran off a couple of times, once for more than a month, and I do believe there are people in town who could give you the specific dates. Oh, and there doesn't seem to have been any particular woman involved, not just then at least. You simply couldn't take it and ran."

Definitely softened. Kroh's fist had started to open.

"Though after the baby was born, auspiciously soon afterwards in fact, you did start to shack up with someone else. But the most revealing part of the story, the punch-line I'd say, is what comes next. The punch-line is, as soon as your wife went back to New York with the baby, you up and left the other woman as well."

"That one," Kroh said, "was more like we both saw the light."

What? The guy was making *jokes?* But the publicist had spoken more quietly than Sitnell had expected, as well. Kroh had almost whispered. And his look had wobbled off, the hand at his lapel appeared to tremble. Sitnell told himself it was all another trick. He kept frowning, hard enough to feel it in his ears. After all, how long had they spent telling the truth? A minute and a half? A minute and a half, and now Kroh looked so slapped and gut-shot, how was Sitnell supposed to take that? Too many tricks and switches, crowding him, crowding him.

He was back at the bar before he could think why he'd gone there. But even with his boot on the rail and his fists on the naugahyde, the rack of liquor behind the bar was no more than a colorful dim array. Battle ribbons or totem poles. When the pig-tailed young mother stepped in front of him, Sitnell had to look somewhere else. Again, somewhere else. But up on the soundless TV they had a city in ruins, the mill-worker nearest him reeked of sweat and machine oil, the girl repeated "Sir?" with such insistence: he was back in the war again. The barmaid had brought it on. Sitnell used to picture his wife that way, pregnant and with her hair too long, just before going into combat. He'd chase that picture across the enemy line, so blindly sometimes that later he didn't know where the nightmares had come from. But tonight, in a lounge like this—it was the last thing Sitnell needed. It had to be the gin flashes. Even the businessman and his pin-up seemed to be part of the action. The couple was bent together over the present she'd given him, as if huddling for protection against the bursts of crumpled bright wrapping paper on the tabletop. Sitnell asked where the Men's Room was. Of course he didn't have to use it, he wound up reading the walls. "Kill the faggots," "Kill the niggers," all with the glare pinching his eyes. It was something he'd always hated about Oregon, how fast neighborliness and the good life gave way to prejudice and a quick trigger.

As soon as Sitnell came out, Kroh had his elbow.

"*Look* man." Kroh was right in his face, too close for Sitnell's height to matter. "Perfect concerned family man, everything's so set and clear for you. Shit. Did I ask you to judge me? Did I *ask* for any of this?"

He waved his free hand at the rest of the lounge. Sitnell didn't even want to look.

"Did I ask to come out West and have, have all you assholes out here hang my *guts* on a line? Did I? None of you know what it was like. Not when I was really up against it, none of you assholes know! You don't know the *loneliness*."

Sitnell didn't know whether he'd pulled his arm free himself or Kroh had let go of it. In any case now the publicist stood waving both hands as if the air itself in here had to be clawed out of the way. And was he about to start crying? Somebody else might have said something but the words didn't register, it was all Sitnell could do just to keep up with this man in front of him. Kroh had moved on to some story about trying to get his baby to sleep. "I just couldn't get it to close its eyes. And then I'd think of Eunice, when I kissed Eunice these days—I couldn't get *her* to close her eyes either!" Which one was Eunice? Pointless gossip. Yet even as Sitnell realized that much—how pointless talking was, compared to this man's pain—he suffered crazier thoughts. A tune came to mind: *Gotta sing. Gotta dance.* Wicked gin flashes. What was Sitnell turning into, here? It was that Motown jacket, and the way the fat little man had started to stamp his feet, paw his eyes.

Sitnell tried to clear his head. He spread his hands to get a better sense of how much room the two of them had. Close enough so his bifocals didn't matter, he tried to keep track of the whole man for the first time tonight.

"I know what loneliness is," he said. "Listen Jimmy, please. My wife and I were separated for two years during the war."

"Do you two *mind?*" This time he couldn't ignore the other voice; Sitnell himself had been speaking so much more gently. "The lady and I would like a little quiet."

The businessman. And somehow it stung Sitnell worse to see the girl, her neck bent and her face out of sight behind one hand.

"I'm so sorry." The words were a reflex. "Honestly sir, I apologize." Blind reflex, and Sitnell was practically standing at attention. "I don't know how we've—"

"Oh, hey. Are we disturbing you? Are we really *disturbing* you?" Kroh had already spread his hands on the couple's table. "Do you find us two rather disagreeable types?"

That fast, Kroh and this other guy were on their way. Sitnell hadn't seen two men so determined to start a fight in years. And he didn't want to look anywhere else either, he knew everyone in the place was lined up against him by now. Sitnell shuffled a step closer. Already the businessman seemed nothing but knuckles and an upthrust chin. Kroh's muscling in had knocked the girl's gift out where it could be seen, it was some art book with a fleshy triangular design on the cover. But Sitnell looked past it and tried to catch the younger man's eye.

His smile felt awful, the limpest kind of fake. The shouting didn't seem to leave room for him.

"What's your problem?" the businessman was saying. "Are you two from New York?"

"Do you have a job for me, sir? Do you have some *money* for me, sir? Because if none of you laid-back West Coast pricks has any way I can get some money *right now*, you can just get out of my *life!*"

Almost crying again. Though nobody else noticed that of course, in fact Kroh's belligerence kept jacking up so fast that Sitnell himself was frozen a step or two away, his hands folding towards his jacket.

"Because one thing you should all know, I'm no goddamn *publicist!*" Kroh's gestures had gone cockeyed. Sitnell had the thought that he needed his portfolio for balance. "You should all know. I came here *bareass!* Here, you think I'm lying all the time, take a look at—"

Kroh had just about got the wallet out of his jacket's inside pocket when the businessman jumped him. No doubt everyone had expected a gun. As it was, Kroh could only flip the empty billfold away short-armed; the first of the mill workers in knocked Sitnell sideways, and so he could see it flop open and fall among the well drinks. He hadn't needed to see it was empty. Sitnell already felt so sorry for Jimmy Kroh that what he wanted most just now was somehow to get the man out of there and maybe share some coffee in a quiet place. But the rest of the crowd were in too fast. One guy actually stiff-armed Sitnell. The shot to the chest made him aware of his age, all loose skin and fragile bones, and he couldn't catch his breath as he stumbled back. Though he knew they wouldn't chase an old man, he couldn't run. He could only keep staring. The businessman's girl had disappeared. Kroh was throwing elbows and hopeless jabs, screaming—"You think I'm *lying?* You think I'm *kidding?*" —as he circled from man to man. Or rather, as he and one other man circled each other. Not the businessman; he'd backed off almost as far as Sitnell. But though everyone there had gotten a piece of Kroh in the first moment or two, so that one leather sleeve was coming off at the armpit and his lapel hung torn, now the artist appeared to have squared off inside a loud and obscene ring of the others with the biggest cowboy in the place. Red-cap type. Extra studs on his belt, real liquor in his look.

Sitnell couldn't say where he sat. He found he'd started shivering, but he couldn't do a thing with his reversible. The zipper itself seemed like too much for him, a black V of teeth made into a triangle by his own aching head. When the first punch landed, he swore he could hear a bone crack.

Could this have been what he'd wanted, coming here? Maybe it was like his wife had said when, two months shy of forty, she'd told him she was pregnant again. She'd said then that Sitnell just didn't believe in things till they hurt him. Sitnell just kept moving on—"like a goddamn *pioneer*," she'd said—till something hurt him. Of course he'd played it cool, he'd pointed out what a comfortable life they had. But he'd gone on wondering. And no question, this book had shaken him worst. He'd started out wanting simply to cheer on the brave men he'd fought with, to celebrate their time together, the way he'd sat here and cheered the night the bartenders had nailed Maurice Lucas's sneakers to the wall. But in order to write he'd put himself through it all again, even that sham picture of his wife he'd used to get himself running towards the enemy line. So in the end it seemed he'd done the opposite of what he'd wanted to. It seemed he'd proven that he and his company had been miserable. They'd rushed to their death out of a blind crush of silly notions and baby-talk, seeking elbow room, seeking a minute or two more of comfort and a good cigarette, and instead they'd come up hard against the nightmare.

He was finding it easier to think, there wasn't so much noise. Had the fight ended already? A man was crying, anyway.

"Hey you!" the barmaid shouted. "*You!*"

He turned to the window, needing a minute. But Mt. Hood was gone, and under the rain the neighborhood had turned black and white.

Minimum Bid

BY THE NIGHT of the art auction Kath had achieved the look she wanted, the wallop of a freethinking woman in her fifties. Endless sessions at the Fitness Center had honed her for the role (that, plus the calcium pills), a New Year's resolution made a fact by mid-autumn. For the auction she chose a black pantaloon one-piece, a romper with a tank top, showing off flat and burnished pectorals. Round her waist she knotted a thong strung with native medallions, gargoyle faces, and she pegged on witty earrings. She was Katherine Wick, divorced and remade. If people wanted to talk about her, if they wanted to whisper and glance sidelong—then she might as well be the talk of the night.

And Kath's biggest coup was to arrive at the event with one of the artists. She paid the ticket for a prodigy, a pretty girl young enough to be her daughter.

Kath introduced the girl, Dory, as "my date for the evening." When someone asked, she made it clear that Dory was a housemate. Might as well be the talk of the night.

Kath wouldn't cling to the youngster, either. In the three years since she'd at last gotten out of her marriage, she'd made a few runs at this crowd, the money crowd, and she'd learned who she could count on for the least hypocritical reception. She introduced the girl to a few of those—heteros, but not entirely tongue-tied in Kath's presence. Then, alone, Kath found a table beneath the auctioneer's podium. She set down her bidding paddle and made it over to the art work up for auction. Local stuff, varied in size and splash, it was strung like a Miracle Mile halfway round the function room. Only after she'd checked the first several pieces against the descriptions in her program did the woman allow herself a look back at Dory.

The girl was as much an eyecatcher as Kath. Dory's skirt was carhop-retro, a cherry electricity well above the knee. She'd topped that off with a rockabilly shirt, a spangled tornado across its back; plus, God knows why, she'd torn away the sleeves. Did she want to call attention to her skin? That indoor skin, white, chilly? Kath suffered the chill; she dropped her chin.

Oh, Kath. Oh, didn't she get off on teasing the heteros, throwing around a word like *housemate*. The fact was, she'd never touched the girl. Kath had never come closer than sitting in a heap outside the youngster's bedroom door, buzzing with insomnia.

By this time she'd even come up with tricks to help through the worst of the infatuation, the mania; an old woman has her tricks. Now, raising her eyes once more, she forced herself to picture how Dory would lose her looks. The girl had a mill worker's thick trunk, and those upper arms were already as much pudge as muscle. Tonight's event generally brought out a more hammered shapeliness.

Tonight was a fundraiser, a benefit for a proposed performance center in downtown Corvallis. The small Oregon city had one sizable hotel, the hotel had donated its largest basement room, and the space looked nearly filled to capacity. Clusters of auction-goers sidled past each other, exchanging smiles over their shoulders, while champagne stewards in starched coats circled outward from the rollaway bar. Nonetheless there was almost no one with a beer belly, no one with saddlebags over the hips.

In the Willamette Valley, the money crowd stayed in shape. Kath had seen more than a few of these people at the Fitness Center. She'd seen them hesitate between the Nautilus machines, heaving, doubtful, and then press on, no match for the social pressure. What other means of proving they'd made it did these people have? In the Valley, what wasn't farmland was suburb, suburb without a city attached, without a place for the more oddball glitter. You wouldn't find a colored face at the auction (other than in Dory's piece, a portrait), none of the Asian or African or Middle Eastern influence that supposedly carried weight in the faster-moving markets. The Valley was high-tech pastoral. Dory's getup had the women fiddling with their shoulder pads. And if a man found himself near the girl, he preened, cocking a knuckle at one hip and showing off a belt line crunch-trim. For a moment the people around her were nothing but a bunch of performing dwarves.

Kath downed some champagne, hiding in the cup. She had to watch it on these mean thoughts.

She turned back to the display, while others fell in beside her. The work was hung salon-style, crowded between the hinges of the room's unfolded partition. Nonetheless whoever stood next to Kath would concentrate on their program, keeping their elbows to themselves. She would have thought it impossible to move around in a sardine-tin like this and not at least bump a few elbows. No wonder she had mean thoughts. Only once did someone say hello, one of her so-called friends from the Clinic, and the man immediately asked about her children.

He flexed his mouth, but you couldn't call that a smile. Kath lifted her chin, showing off her shoulders and pecs.

"Oh," she told him, "I keep the kids at Christmas-card distance." She was divorced and remade.

Then came Dory's piece, in the corner. Kath couldn't bid on it; the girl had made that a condition of coming. Dory had wound up sleeping with her subject, a married man, a father. God knows he must have seemed fascinating, a surgeon born in Morocco. Plus Dory had worked in pastels, which required repeated sittings, long hours together. Even tonight Kath had to admire the layered effect, like a winepress in which the grapes bulged yet froze, forever just at the point of bursting.

The back wall held more, making sixty items all together. Dory's piece however had left Kath distracted, frowning.

"Who does these *landscapes*, anyway?" This was a stage voice, practically in her ear. "Do they have cars?"

Kath turned, frowning. But this was Leo Farragut, one of her patients, one of the terminal cases. He sounded more rheumy since last time.

"I'm asking, Mizz Wick. Do they have cars?"

Her face relaxed. "I believe most of our artists can afford cars, Leo."

"Oh yeah? Real cars? *American* cars?"

She opened her stance, the gargoyles clinking at her waist. "You're saying you find our offerings a tad precious? A tad, oh—out of touch with the hurly-burly?"

"I hear the Japs now'll sell you a car like this one." Leo raised a discolored finger towards a lithograph, a beige heron taking off over swoozy reeds. Every curve in the picture was a Coca-Cola wave. "They got a car that just floats out there."

"Not really."

"I'm telling you. The thing's *made* for a painting like this, it never touches the ground at all."

"We live in an amazing country, Leo."

"Yeah," he said. "Japan."

She chuckled, her cup to her naked breastbone. Above the man's ears, his grinning, his shaved head wrinkled. Cases like Leo had come her way a few times before. While she filled out the prescription forms they would stand around hitching their belts, loudly up front about their dying. Gal, let me tell you about bad. Gal, it's got me nailed to the *wall*. This when Kath had to work in a cubbyhole—the Clinic didn't allow much room for a physician's assistant. Nonetheless whenever Leo or one of her other terminals went into their act, playing cowboy past the graveyard, Kath found herself cheering them along. She let them strut all over her cubbyhole. Now she made a fuss over the man's hat, a stiff and short-brimmed black fedora.

"It's a rapper's hat," he said. "All the little black kids wear 'em."

"Looks like Bo Diddley to me," she said. "Bad to the bone."

The couples within earshot smiled wanly, not quite risking eye contact.

"Bo . . . Diddley?" Leo asked. "Where'd someone like you ever hear about him?"

"You remember my friend." Kath kept her tone sprightly. "The singer."

Of course he remembered. Kath's story had all but made the headlines—*Mother Of Two Dating Feminist Folksinger*. Her husband had actually found someone to serve her with papers at one of the woman's concerts. Kath was using a little stage savvy of her own, here: Leo, let me tell *you* about bad. The old man, give him credit, said nothing stupid. His nod and his grin remained decent.

"Say, Leo," she said then, "have you got a table yet?"

The two of them had to circle the room to pick up his bidding paddle, and then they slowed down for hors d'oeuvres. But Kath didn't mind the additional averted faces and uptight elbows. She enjoyed—though appropriately jaundiced about what she was doing here, her debutante's ball for one—a mounting excitement. Under the stage lights, the auctioneer appeared enlarged, a Rockwell centerpiece in bow tie and suspenders. Around him the volunteers running the show fretted over clipboards and wads of champagne scrip.

Once she and Leo were seated, he asked if she were alone. Kath turned, pointing. Against the bar, the dark service entrance, Dory's arms and legs appeared to glow.

Kath hid in her purse, the stink of rain on leather.

Wonder Woman, she recalled, used to change costumes simply by whirling in place. Too sudden for the naked eye. But Kath lacked the power, especially after fifteen or twenty minutes polishing a different act. Since her last look at Dory, she'd been working the crowd, conventioneering, and it took effort to switch to a more intimate brand of theater. Yes, these three months sharing the house had been continual theater, more smoke and blue lights than Kath would have thought she had in her. She'd even learned to poke fun at the girl's determination to get back to art school. What Dory was really studying to be, Kath would claim loudly, was a martyr. And yet how many nights had she ended up outside the girl's door, buzzing with insomnia? How many times had she replayed her fantasies, imaginings by now as brown and worked-over as her showy new pecs and abdominals?

Even here at the auction, Kath realized, she might have some seduction scheme going. Kath might have a back-of-the-mind notion that Leo here, old Heparin-dosed Leo, would somehow make her interesting. Oh, Kath. Please. These days Dory found no one in Corvallis interesting.

She'd begun writing to New York, to Dr. Ossaba, the surgeon in her pastel portrait. Dory would vanish upstairs as soon as she saw the man's postmark; Kath knew only that the last two letters had been finger-thick. What could they have to say to each other? No question, the girl had wanted the doctor's picture out of the house. Kath had needed every trick in the book just to get Dory to come watch the item get sold.

The gavel sounded, *rick-kity wick.*

Everyone else sat heads-up. Earrings appeared elongated, under slant working-woman haircuts, and the men ate carefully, using both hands. Then Dory hurried over, a head-clearing tang of soap and baby powder. At first she wouldn't sit.

"Hey there, gal," said Leo. "You look like you've seen a ghost."

"You won't believe who's here," Dory said.

At the time of his portrait, Ossaba had been the hottest new arrival at the Clinic. He'd come to town as a transfer from Harlem Hospital, with a smart-mouthed two-year-old and a wife who taught a section of French at Oregon State. The one thing that none of the gossips seemed to know was just how he and Dory had met. Now the girl came to Kath and Leo with the news that the wife—the ex-wife—was at the auction.

"Mrs. Glynde," she kept saying. "Mrs. Glynde."

Did she feel safer using the woman's new name? Kath looked in the direction of Dory's nod. The French instructor preferred what used to be called a Jean Seberg cut, the only woman here besides Kath with such short hair.

"I see," Kath said.

The ex-wife lifted her champagne, oblivious. But then why should anyone watch her? What sort of fuss was Kath supposed to make, with Leo at the table? The man had tipped back his bowler, and his look carried the obvious question. Who is this girl? Kath fumbled ahead with the introductions ("Number twenty-three in your program, folks"), meantime trying to catch Dory's eye. But the youngster only made a face: I do *not* want to be here. She chose the chair beside the old man, across from Kath.

"Dorr," Kath tried, "in this town, you were bound to run into her sooner or later."

The girl stared away, showing her spangled back. Around them the bidding began, the paddles going up. Kath thought of flamenco dancers raising fans, hiding their heat.

"So," Leo said, "you're one of the artists."

"Well, I was." Now all of a sudden, Dory was smiling. "The money ran out before I finished sophomore year."

"Then tell me something, gal. Do you own a car?"

The girl allowed herself maybe two seconds of looking confused. Then she snatched Leo's paddle from the table, she jabbed him in the chest. Typical: Dory had him sheepish, explaining himself, and when a boy came by with champagne, Leo said he'd buy her a second glass. Another minute and he and Dory were playing tug of war. They gripped opposite ends of the paddle's wooden spine, almost giggling, and Kath took more of the bulk-order champagne herself. She got a mouthful, an eyeball-tickling belt.

"What's the *big deal* about the doctor's wife?" she asked.

The girl broke off the game, blinking.

"Dorr, you were bound to run into her." Levelly Kath reminded her that the woman's new husband—"Mr. Glynde"—was a vice president at the university. "Look, that's why they have the fundraiser in November. Most of the OSU people haven't had a decent paycheck since June."

Dory's mouth had gone square.

"Listen," Kath went on, "I used to think my husband was sentimental about November. It was the only time he ever took me to a restaurant."

"Oh, Katherine," Dory said. "Common-sense Katherine."

Kath fought an impulse to lift her drink again. "Common-sense?" she managed. She pinched up one strap of her top and with the other hand gestured at herself.

The girl refused to smile, she turned toward the stage. That left Leo. Kath kept her hand at her top-strap, making a fist. Tell me, Leo—you've never met our Dory? You didn't know our Dory won an undergraduate award?

The man's face wrinkled in new places, twitching.

"You didn't see the notice in the paper? You've never *heard* of our Dory?"

Leo wiped his lips; he licked them again. Kath had another question but lost it somehow in the man's doddering gesture, his undone flesh. One of those moments when her Master's of Health flickered in her mid's eye. She let go of her top. Dory's look was no fun either: like the girl had just come out of her Friday-night shift at the Video Circle. Kath checked out the stage. A volunteer beside the podium held up a miniature, a square piece that fit in one hand.

In her program Kath had marked this item a Maybe. A doll-sized robe, vaguely Oriental, it had hems and borders the yellow of split wood. From her seat Kath could see the sequins glimmer. Leo went on twitching, redoing his lips, and with that in the corner of one eye Kath put in the first bid, the minimum asked in the program. Twenty dollars more and the thing was hers. By the time someone brought the receipt the old man's face had better color. His finger steady, he pointed out a woman at the next table.

"That gal made the thing," Leo said.

The artist looked to be about forty, with an enjoyable swank in her grin. Her husband was dressed out-of-season, a canary shirt. Hello, Kath grinned back. Welcome to the party—the Desperate Debutante's ball.

Then came the heron over the reeds, the swoozy beige floater. A couple of rich men started a bidding war. Five-dollar increases went back and forth between Mr. Glynde from the university and, let's see, who was Dory looking at this time . . . of course. Another administrator wanted the print for his office. One of the muckety-mucks at the Clinic, his bidding sloppy with alcohol. Kath bent over her miniature; a runner had brought it to the table. But the fluorescents above her were reflected in the tiny robe, painful in its Chinese glitter. Behind her, some flunky loudly egged both bidders on: "Great piece! *Terrific* piece!"

The auctioneer socked his gavel against the podium. Applause rippled briefly through the underground room.

Dory was leaning into Leo. "I don't even want to know who got that one."

Kath lifted her head. "Don't be mean," she said. "It's for a good cause."

The girl turned. Her look might have been a quick hazel tree-dweller, stilled at a sound it didn't understand.

"Don't be *mean*," Kath said. "I've got to live with these people."

"With what people?"

Leo broke in, extending one thin arm. A stage whisper: "Not now, ladies. This one's the best thing here." And Dory played to him again, her face reanimated: "Oh yeah, oh really. Check out the scumbling."

What? Dory and Leo were talking about a wall-size oil, a stretch of Peoria Road in winter, roughed out in descending swaths. Rain, road, scrub. Midway up the closest foreground there jetted an orange flare, some New-Year's blossom, which made it look as if the murmurous view might split down the middle. Was that "scumbling?"

But the artist had set too high a minimum, six hundred dollars. Nobody lifted a paddle.

"This is humiliating," Dory said. "It's like a ritual slaughter."

"You know," Leo said, "you really should be more generous. You heard our Mizz Wick."

"What, about living with people?" Dory faced her; it felt like too soon after last time. "Kath, I don't get it. You're a grownup. You don't have to live with anybody."

"Well . . ."

"I mean, the only people you really *have* to live with—right?—are your lovers."

Unexpectedly Kath found herself laughing. Her chin dropped, her hand felt its way across her loosening mouth—and what, had she *forgotten* about laughing? About giving herself a *break*? The auction program on the table before her for once looked nothing like an actor's promptbook; its print had turned to feathers, to bugs.

"What's so funny?" Dory asked. "There's your lover, like whatever you have with him. And then there's everyone else."

Kath's diaphragm rippled, and along her waistline the gargoyles winked. Yes, laugh, Kath. Just laugh.

"Mizz Wick?" Leo asked.

"Hey, I mean it," Dory said. "There's your lover and then there's everyone else."

After all, Kath reminded herself, it wasn't going to get any easier tonight. The item after next was Dory's. And God knows Kath could make herself crazy with that face up beside the podium. That proud glare: *Hey, Wick—I had her and you didn't.*

"Come on, Kath," Dory said. "At least get it together while they sell off my piece."

Kath fought for a breath, she reached for the champagne. With that she noticed the faces nearby. The woman who'd made the miniature was watching again, with her Broadway grin. When Kath caught her eye the woman nodded, and meantime the artist's husband, eyebrows up and grinning himself, tapped a thumb against his canary'd chest. Well, well. The acoustics in the hotel basement had protected her. The wrangling with Dory had gone unheard; all that had come across was an interesting threesome having themselves a time. Kath checked left-right, she knew how laughter freshened her look, and she was met with honest eye contact. One or two of the men licked hors-d'oeuvrey fingers, but that was better than the rigged faces she was used to. Well. The only meanness she could find belonged to Dory's Moroccan doctor, up beside the podium.

No doubt as Dory had laid on the pastels, she'd fallen into a recapitulation of her father. The family lived in Unity, in the high desert country, and the hint of home gave her sheeny layers a baleful depth. Now bidding was brisk. No surprise to Kath, after the team spirit she'd read in these faces. The closing offer came from Mrs. Glynde.

"I . . . can't . . . *believe* it," Dory whispered.

When the girl had no expression—other than those puzzled eyes—you saw the baby fat in her cheeks. She leaned across the table, closer to Kath than she'd been all night. "I mean, what's going on?"

Didn't Dory notice these faces? Suddenly the girl was everyone's favorite. They tipped their heads, congratulations, attaway, and a man at the next table, a circuit-trainer Kath recognized from the Fitness Center, sent a runner their way with still more champagne. Kath kept her own look party-hearty.

"Well Dorr," she said, "the woman came out a winner. Nowadays she's got too much money to have hard feelings."

Behind the girl, across the room, the Jean Seberg cut bobbed beside the boy who'd brought the receipt.

"Oh, Kath." Dory's mouth had gone square again. "Would you for once stop thinking about money?"

"Hey," Leo put in. "What is it with this Glynde woman? What's going on?"

"Hush now," Kath said, "both of you. This next is mine."

Actually she'd marked this a "Maybe." She'd found it agreeably weird, a collage that combined shredded IBM discs with a straw doll dressed as the Flying Nun. But the design was like calendar blocks and it had a ponderous title: *The Woman's Point of View*. Plus anything by this artist would cost. She was well connected, a Hewlett-Packard wife. The men at the collagist's table were the most in-shape at the auction, and they settled back as the bidding began, sharps at the ball game.

Kath worked her paddle hotly. The auctioneer lead the crowd, pitch and yaw. She wound up ninety dollars over the minimum, duking it out with one of the wives at the artist's table. When the thing was gaveled sold—"To the lady in black!"—the room burst into applause.

Dory kept her hands in her lap. She sat stiffly, and Kath could see every stud on her rodeo shirt.

"That's what all this is about," she said, "isn't it?"

The kid with the receipt stood at Kath's elbow, but Dory felt closer. "Hey, I mean," she went on, "let's give the little lady a big hand. That's the whole point, right?"

"That's enough, Dorr." Kath tried to make it like Mother Knows Best. "We all know you don't want to be here."

"Oh, excuse me. I have some emotions, excuse me."

Behind the girl, the miniaturist wore a dandy smirk, worth a wink in reply. Hi, again; hi. But then that woman and her husband once more faced the stage.

"I should have realized," Dory said, "we have to forget all about *my* emotions. This is the Wicked Wick Show."

At the edges of the girl's sleeves, the torn threads were blue thorns. Kath was struggling for a comeback when Leo hooked her housemate by the elbow. The wine had threaded his cheeks but his eyes were purposeful. Did Dory have any idea, Leo asked, what Kath had been through when her marriage broke up?

"It was like a cyclone hit," he said.

"Don't give me that," Dory said. "She had money. She had a place."

Kath had more or less forgotten the old man was at the table. But he was wearing the girl down already; her cowboy buttons disappeared beneath her crossed arms. "Oh Do-ro-thy," Leo chided, "oh now, I certainly don't feel used." Kath let him take over, reopening her checkbook. That Flying-Nun piece had busted her balance down so far that anything else would have to go on plastic. Meantime Leo's tone grew warmer, more among-pals, and Kath understood that Dory didn't want a scene either. The gray nap on these walls, this plastic-wood furniture—it must have reminded the girl of the whispering rooms at the clinic. Now Dory was the one with a hand at her mouth.

"Leo, you don't know the whole story either. You're part of her hocus pocus too."

"Oh, what's the harm done?" he asked. "Why shouldn't the old gal go home with a few new friends?"

Dory shrank between them, her chin doubling against her collar, her looks briefly spoiled. Around their table erupted new laughter, the crowd was sensing success, and Kath brought up her head, open-mouthed. Oh, see. Numbers meant mercy. Besides her own, more than fifteen thousand homes had been mortgaged here, between the river and I-5, and given those numbers she was bound to find a few at least with whom she might laugh. Leo kept his eyes on the girl, his jowls limp. Not until the hubbub died did he reach for his paddle.

His paddle; right. After all, he'd come here looking to buy. Kath was watching Leo bid, his withered fingers ropy on the handle, when Dory angled towards her again.

"You know," Dory said, "Ossaba can get me into art school in New York."

The girl cleared out the night's commotion. She was a portrait and the rest was wall.

"He'll co-sign the papers for financial aid," she said. "He's already put down a deposit on a dorm room."

"He *told* you this?" Kath asked.

"In his latest letter, he told me." Thorns at her shoulders, studs across her chest. "I can move in the first of the year."

"Well—well, Dory—he'd have all the money."

"I'd have my own room, Kath. My own room, my own door."

"But it would still be his turf. His world, Dory. And you didn't even want the man's picture around."

"Oh, the picture. I mean, totally amateur work."

Leo was motioning for his receipt. Somebody made a crack, *Why don't they just keep a runner at your table?* Kath's own two pink forms however seemed suddenly flimsy, way too few. "Dory," she asked, "don't you understand?" But she was head-down, talking to her receipts; in this noise she might as well have been speaking another language.

"The picture's a separate question," Dory said.

At the Clinic, Kath recalled, the girl's story wasn't so special. An affair during the first year of a residency was a natural hazard. Ossaba's real problem had been that he lacked the necessary powerful insider to quiet the gossip. The man was black and Muslim, after all. But other doctors had seduced the occasional co-ed. In most cases the marriage survived, the rupture bridged with jewelry and trips abroad. Most households had the strength for only so much dislocation. Kath herself, just tonight, had lost a good half the wallop she'd come in with. It cost her to avoid Dory's stare, she felt it in the neck, and she couldn't believe the effort it took to finger together her receipts and weight them in place with the miniature. On an evening like this—cold and late in the year—

that doll's robe itself mocked her, more substantial than her whole rattling getup. At least the little gilded coverall didn't pretend to be anything other than a toy, an Emperor's new clothes.

"I can be out of here the first of the year," Dory said.

What was the next item? A work in bright fiber, a picket fence and a peacock beyond . . . but what difference did it make? She'd given nothing here more than a Maybe anyway. Kath slung her paddle up in front of her face.

Afterwards, Leo offered to drive Dory home. Just as well; Kath couldn't even see the girl. Once the last item was in the books (the only piece left not taken was the ominous view of Peoria Road), ten or a dozen in the audience closed around Kath, picking at their sweat-stuck clothes. The husband of the miniaturist settled behind her, his hands on her shoulders, his fingers greasy with chicken. Volunteers brought the credit-card machine to the table, and she punctuated her conversation with the clack of each imprint.

"What *happened*?" Kath asked, grinning. "At the bank they're going to think a bomb hit."

At last Leo eased through the knot around her chair, quieting the crowd. His smile had paled again.

"The gal would like to go," he said.

Kath couldn't see her. She tried to catch a glimpse through the pack of aging bodies, and found herself thinking: I had a family, I had a man who loved me—and now the girl wants to go? The girl too? Kath's contact lenses couldn't hold a focus. They needed a soak.

"These lenses," Kath said, "are going to get a soak."

And then, finding the old man's face: "My hero."

Her looks wouldn't hold up much longer either. Just getting the receipts in her purse left her blinking, and it felt like her mascara had loosened. Her long coat, whew.

Outside in the parking lot, the black and white leaden with rain, Kath almost walked right into the Glyndes.

Not that they noticed. In the farthest corner of the lot, half hidden behind a Volvo station wagon, the Glyndes were scuffling. Actually scuffling; Kath couldn't help but stare. The couple staggered back and forth, their arms locked upright above them. Somehow, together, they'd hefted overhead the portrait of Dory's surgeon. It was like a workout station at the Fitness Center, the extended straining arms, the ungainly square weight. Mrs. Glynde's open overcoat had been forced back under her armpits, revealing a Gothic label stitched in golden thread. Now a word that might have been *please* came through the drizzle, now a grunted obscenity. What was going on? Who was trying to hit who? Kath couldn't even see which of them had hold of the portrait. The art work jigged above the struggling husband and wife, neon exploding off its glass cover. And those colors sweeping that foreigner's face—could this be a trick of the glare? For a moment those colors looked to Kath like Dory, Dory the way she'd been tonight. Kath saw Dory's glimmering tornado, her up-a-tree staring and electric ruby skirt; she saw Dory's bruised pearl, scrap blues, profound whites: the whole wizard's wardrobe of the disappearing girl.

In the end she moved on without interfering, without lifting a finger. She kept to the hotel, the shadow. There the lights off the youngster's painting couldn't reach her.

Highway Trade

A SATURDAY MORNING when he came in, that alone made the guy look promising. Plus the day was so sunny for October that the taverns must have been slow all over the valley. Nellie saw no wedding ring. No signs of a real bender in progress either, bloody eyes or black veins. She shot Fitzie a look. Later on she more or less apologized: "I know you'd never mess with my game, Fitz." But the other waitress had to remember—for weeks now Nellie had been worrying about how she was going to make ends meet till New Year's.

He said he'd seen the satellite dish from the highway and he'd wanted to watch the Series. "It's always something like that," she told Fitzie later on. "Something a little herky-jerky-crazy that gets it started." She gave away the secret deliberately, needing some support herself by then.

But when he first came in, all the standard openers seemed to be working. They seemed to be *clicking.* Nellie pooh-poohed the dish, cheap and black; the guy came right back with, yeah, looks like an umbrella got caught in a hailstorm. You didn't usually get that kind of speed around the Drop By Cafe. She hung in—yeah, she said, and it's about that flimsy—but when Nellie discovered he was rooting for the East Coast team she wasn't surprised. She went for something fancier, she adjusted the dish so they could watch the World Series in Japanese. He loved it. He said he wanted to leave here knowing the Japanese for "foul ball." Plenty of time, she said, on a Saturday morning.

"He told me he only got divorced this past summer," she told Fitzie later. "So I think that would have kept it from getting complicated, between us. Also they never had kids. So I figured with my Wade, the disability, that gave me some leverage."

Though of course when she told the story she came out tougher than she'd actually felt. Nellie Nails: she didn't want anything to throw off the situation established between her and Fitzie. At the time, though, she'd found the man a rare one. When he shot her back a dime on the second draft, she'd noticed that even Ernie's hands were the kind you thought of when you thought of New York. Interesting quick small hands. His lips were better still, when he grinned it was like he'd lost fifteen years. And he had his cagey side. She never picked up where he worked, though the hours made it sound like something over at Oregon State. In fact she found herself getting defensive. Never mind how slow the place looked now, she lied; most weeks she made as much as most of the girls over at the university.

Then she got to the point. Ernie was starting on his burger, he'd said he might as well make a day of it. But when he made some crack about the ballplayers' uniforms she took the opportunity— with gestures, lip-action, the whole bit—to call attention to the tight red tops she and Fitzie had to wear. She added that some days she was in such a rush that she couldn't be bothered with a bra. After that she just let him look. She enjoyed the way her breathing made the leotard shift, and she knew that in this light the smoker's triangle round her mouth wasn't so pronounced. Why wait? She was the fast one at the Drop By. Behind her the Japanese announcers were having a fit, strange words so short and yappy that they sounded like Nellie's dog. And she became aware of the entire outsized room as well, bikini-beer ads up on one wall and the cigarette machine against the other, all of it falling into place around this one stretch of eye contact, altogether cool of course and yet sinking its weights through both of them, while she kept the rest of her face set in something a little mouthier than a smile. Fitzie minded her own business down by the grill. A few old lodge types had taken the tables with the best view of the TV. Looks like the game's a lock, the old guys were saying. No way New York's going to come back from this.

Except then the satellite hookup shorted out and the wiring caught fire. "I could just strangle that Richter," she told Fitzie, ten or a dozen times over the next couple weeks. "Getting his brother-in-law to do the wiring. He saves a few bucks, and I just may have lost my one chance to give Wade a half-decent Christmas."

The screen went static, the sound turned to a shriek. Ernie wound up with ketchup in his eyes. The old-timers dropped from their chairs and backtracked gingerly, covering their ears, while Nellie opened the fridge and ducked behind the door. She heard the set pop, but it was a good several seconds more before she noticed the smell. By then the burning plastic overwhelmed even the fridge-stink. She came out of her crouch cupping her face. The old-timers were stumbling over each other at the door, shit no *way*, lemme *out* a here. The sunlight was painful off their wind-breakers and rain gear—though Nellie didn't blink, she didn't shade her eyes. The pain came out of nowhere so far as she could tell. A spasm, a pang. Something else stung her about all that flimsy look-alike gear, shiny and stitched with the names of factory teams, clubs and schools. *Engine Co. #5, Elks, Sisters High*. But what was she doing standing blinking at the ones who were already gone? "Help, Nellie for God's sake *help!*" Fitzie was shouting. "The damn *menu's* on fire!"

"He was nice about it," she reminded Fitzie later. "At least he didn't just duck and run with the herd."

Much later: by now the fire was three weeks past. And Nellie didn't like the way the other waitress nodded, tonight. It made her worry that she'd been talking too much. Granted, the man was a lost opportunity. He'd never returned. But guys like that had blown through her life before, more than once, more than a couple times. Plus this was after hours. When Nellie got this tired, she couldn't be sure how she was coming across.

"Calling the fire department," Fitzie said, "that was really very nice of him." But she sipped her liquor flat-faced. "Though of course they already knew about it. I mean the guys from number five were sitting right behind him."

Nellie tried to look like she was checking the place out. Not much to it: the busier ads had been switched off, the jukebox was dark.

"Didn't that plastic stink, though?" Fitzie said. "Those little letters and numbers. I must've fitted them in that menu a thousand times, I never would have believed they'd stink so bad."

"I could just *strangle* Richter. That guy was just what I needed."

"Oh." Nellie didn't like the way Fitzie turned to look at her, either. "Forget him, would you? From where I sat he looked like a married man anyway. I know, I know." Fitzie waved her cigarette. "He said he was divorced, I know. But you still can have that look, even if you're divorced."

Nellie waited till her whiskey was at her lips before she spoke. "Signing the papers don't complete the deal." She drained the rest of the shot.

"Right. Exactly. So what're you getting all bent out of shape about, Nell? Social Security gave you that extension, didn't they?"

"Two more weeks. Two weeks, and then they're probably going to send someone out to the place to make sure I conform to all their piddly little regulations."

"Can't Wade help?"

"Fitzie. Wade isn't even fourteen yet. This whole goddamn— this whole reevaluation bullshit only came up in the first place because he's just started *high* school." She got off her stool and went for the Johnny Walker. "No, what I need's a goddamn professor. Somebody over at the university, he would have been perfect for them. He would have written them something on the fucking *letterhead*."

Fitzie laughed. Nellie felt the payoff herself, familiar by now, a rush in her chest and a bite in her grin.

"Only thing better than a professor would be if I got myself a man in the state legislature." She was twisting the pourer out of the scotch, working against the bind at the leotard's armpits. "I mean, that's what politics is all *about*, right? Just start messing round with some lightweight up in fucking Salem. Rig the whole damn game in my favor."

The pourer came free and she drank from the bottle. Fitzie slapped a hand to her mouth, she loved it.

"Nellie Nails," she said.

Nellie understood what the other waitress got out of the deal. Fitzie's Jack was one of the few married men she'd known that long who'd never made a play for her. Nellie to them was the local exotica. She kept them feeling hip, a little bad themselves. Oh, Jack might try and tease Nellie. He might recite her two rules for handling men. One, if you're sleeping with a guy never lie to him, and two, be sure to let him know from the start exactly what sort of a project he is. But when Jack had finished reciting his grin would be soft, impressed. Whoa *Nellie*, he'd say. It's like you've got different muscles from the rest of us. She'd only shrug. Her main thing was simple after all: just, never let a guy feel like he's settled in. If a guy's a rehab case, tell him he's a rehab case, and he'll stay a case till he's re-habbed enough to walk away on his own. If he's a little boy who needs to do some growing up, tell him so even if he happens to be sitting with the gang from high school. That way—though this part of the system, she wasn't so clear on—before the men moved on they always left her with something practical.

She wasn't so clear on just why. But it had gone on since Wade had first been accurately diagnosed. The first going-away present had been drugs, speed fresh from the lab. Of course the boy had expected Nellie to use it herself, eating your own was the party line. But she'd already sworn off the hard stuff by then and she'd needed the money more. Since that time, she'd received parting gifts of everything from carpentry around the trailer to free service at the Bug Works. She'd even picked up the occasional sale appliance. It was as if the guys couldn't wave goodbye till their fingers were bruised from splitting wood or stained with axle grease. Everything from rails on either side of the toilet to a cable hookup for the trailer. Why on earth—? Not that Nellie was complaining, no way Jose. But the strictness of the give-and-take had caused her aggravation. Lately especially, it had led to rough stuff. Not that anyone had actually laid a hand on her, nobody had done that since before Wade was born. But there'd been trouble nonetheless, strange and private trouble, the kind of thing she didn't care to let a drinking companion hear about.

Wade's father for instance still came through Philomath now and again, selling office supplies, and lately even he'd made it hard on her. This past summer, they'd wound up going halfsies on a new wheelchair. And beforehand she'd laid it down plain as newsprint that the project this time would be Memory Lane. She plucked the gray hairs from his mustache and called him good old Rustyroo. She reminisced about the blues crowd they'd run with, the record contract he'd been forever on the verge of signing. "How many girls'd you score with that record contract?" But at the end, as they headed up to Salem to get the chair, he turned desperate. He insisted they stop at a motel off I-5. Red-flecked wallpaper straight out of *The Wild, Wild West*, neon that growled so loudly she couldn't concentrate. And yet the sex wasn't the thing for him. The sex was incidental. The whole time there all the father could talk about was following her home after the trip in order to help set the chair up in the trailer.

She was well over the speed limit the rest of the way. When she parked she propped the checkbook on the steering wheel and wrote out one for her half. As she hustled across the lot the *screek* of passing carts made the perfect soundtrack. Then once he arrived she wouldn't let him in the store, he had to hear it right there on the entrance ramp. Take a hike, *Russell.*

"Lighten up, Nellie. Please." By now he was pathetic, looking for help up and down the nearby rows of cars. It only made her realize that this was another thing she hated about Salem. What kind of a state capital was it, when even in the middle of the city you never heard shouting in public?

"Wade wasn't any part of the deal, mister. Now just take your money and go."

"Nellie, Nellie . . . I realize I've always played the bad guy, okay? It went over big with the sorority girls, you know what I mean. But now, please. I haven't seen the boy in five years."

"Why don't you send him your *record?*" she said.

No, people like Jack and Fitzie didn't have the whole story. Nellie suffered complications. She suffered breakdowns; she was getting nowhere fast with the Social Security. Her lawyer, forget it. The man at least had finally left his wife. But the next time he and Nellie had gotten together, she'd had to back him off with something almost as mean as what she'd told Rusty. Now whenever she called his office, the secretary said he was out. The last straw came when the girl tried to tell her he was over in Corvallis, watching the Beavers.

Nellie checked the kitchen clock. Not quite 10:30.

"I don't mean he's actually watching them play," the secretary went on. But Nellie wasn't interested, all she could think was: Basketball already? No more World Series?

"No no, of course he's not watching the team play. He's talking with the men in charge over there. He's—"

Nellie hung up. The men in charge.

Four days remained before the reevaluation. She figured she could swear off the booze that long. She did a thorough fall housecleaning, even raking her turnoff (the trailer park was never more than half-full anyway; she'd taken an isolated lot in the back) and dumping her leaves in the woods. She bought Elmer's and reglued the maple-colored stickum where it had peeled from the kitchen plywood, the cupboard-doors under the sink especially. And she crocheted. She'd never been able to take daytime TV, the soaps made her sneer and the game shows got her angry. Instead there'd been afghans, dress mesh tops, or magnet-holders like the anvils and cherries that held the calendar to the refrigerator door. There'd been the liner for the dog's basket, designed so the section that lapped outside the opening bore his name, Lurid Romance. Now she started a new bedspread for Wade. She kept the stitching tight, so his fingers wouldn't catch in the eyes. Of course it made her think of Christmas, a bedspread wasn't much of a present, but then the dog got interested, that was fun. The animal would study her hands as they worked the hook and needle. Finally he'd lay one paw on her knee, heavily.

"Try my Mom, Lurid," Nellie would say. "I think my Mom would let the *cows* play with the yarn, if they wanted."

Still the day of the appointment she woke before five, and she couldn't stand the mirror. Looked like she'd spent the night trying to fit her face in a vise. She decided to drop Wade at school herself, swapping a few one-liners with the boy always steadied her nerves. But he hadn't slept well either. His eyes—Nellie recalled the doctor's word, *canthus*. Another nitpick bastard. So after that first look she couldn't seem to take the boy in, entirely. As if he'd grown bigger overnight. She saw how the coffee made him tremble, but she took his word for it when he said it was just that he'd never taken it black before.

Once they were out on Route 20, never mind that they had to

keep his chair strapped to the wall behind the driver's seat, Wade held up his end of the deal. Never mind, also, that he didn't quite know the difference yet between the locker-room gonzo and the man of the house. He made sure she could see him in the rearview. He worked up some pretty good faces, Bozo to Godzilla. Nellie however couldn't think of a decent comeback. She couldn't even be sure of her smile.

"Mom, come on," he said at last. "Look on the bright side. In five years we'll all be overrun by the Sandinistas anyway."

But when he said "Sandinista" it was obvious that his throat muscles were giving him trouble again, it sounded to her like "son hysteria." Even after she'd returned to the trailer, the winter mung in the floorboards reminded her too much of Wade in the bus. The chill had her aching for a drink. She lit a joint and poured coffee. She wound up out on the back stoop, staring up warily at the coastal hills.

This time of year you had fog every morning. It made the forest black at the horizon, roadless. After a few minutes, she recalled the guy who'd given her the dope. The guy had sketched directions to his place, grinning fiercely as the map took shape, grinning and telling her that every night was party night up in the hills. Every night, girl. After all the troopers might come rapping at your door any time, that's why you kept the keys in the truck and the Dobermans hungry. Nellie discovered that she was murmuring the stuff's name. "Red-haired Indica," tongue-full words, they had her retasting her coffee. Strange that the landscape looked black but what they grew there was red. But her laughter sounded papery, her perspective was off. The hills had grown bigger at the peak than at the bottom. She tried repeating different words: my home, my comfort. There was a throb like a bus engine.

Then Nellie had gotten no farther than bending over the yarn bag when the knock came at the door. So soon? Her hands were still cold, the dog still outside. When she found out it was in fact the Social Security, she could only go for her purse, her compact and brush.

"I'm sorry I'm early, I don't know the roads yet." The man's voice was tin, behind the shut door. "I expected it would take longer, everybody said the place was so far out."

"Far out? What does that mean, far out?"

"At the office. The people there all—"

"Oh the office, the office!" Now she was starting to catch up. Her lips and mouth looked so young and hot, it made her remember that the compact mirror bulged a little, it made her realize how furious she was. "That's all you people care about, is the office."

"Wait a minute, Miss Therow. Please. If you'd just open the door—"

"The office and your goddamn regulations." Next the hair, why not? Get one thing right this morning at least. "I mean you come out here with your regulations, and meantime I'm on this side doing what I can, on my own—but neither of us is really what this is all *about*, are we? Really, this is about Wade."

"Uhh. Well he's who the money's intended for, yes."

"So what are you doing here, then? What are you poking around in my private life for?" Her wave was coming out the way she liked, airy and full over her right ear. "Listen, my son has athetosic cerebral palsy. His muscle control come and goes. Sometimes it looks like he could almost go out for the Babe Ruth League, sometimes he has one of his seizures. It's a birth defect, it happened when I was carrying him. Now what the hell else do you need to *know*? Honestly. What the hell brings all you people barging in on me all the time?"

"Miss Therow, come on. One thing for sure, I'm not here to blame you."

"Blame me? Blame me?" Obviously the guy had it in for her. "Listen, brother. You ought to be here when Wade has one of his seizures. I'd like to see what you'd do when it gets that real. I'd like to see if you'd get so picky about dotting every 'i' and crossing every 't' *then*."

Wetting a fingertip, she did a last adjustment at the edges of her blush-on. If this joker was going to make her go to court to get her money, she was at least going to get the satisfaction of making him ache for what he couldn't have.

"Now I *ask* you." She whipped open the door. "Compared to Wade, what does, does either of us . . ."

The heat in her face changed. She'd come out shaking her fist, the one with the compact in it; now her hand dropped so limply that when the dog rushed in, the plastic grip was knocked away.

"Ernie?" she asked. "From over at the Drop By?"

He still had that great teenage smile. "I saw the name on the form. I had to come out here, see if it was really what I thought."

University hours: he said he could stay through lunch if she wanted. "When you work for the state," he said, "you can always give the apparatus a little fine-tuning." And there it was, the other university thing about him, talk as slick as a game of Frisbee. A line like that in fact made the guy seem a little spooky. She took him on a tour of the trailer, stick to business, sure. She got the folder of Wade's medical reports from the file in the bedroom closet. But though Ernie gabbed the whole way, it was all one-liners, nothing she could get a hold of. When they got back to the kitchen, he actually seemed more interested in the dog. She joked back, part red spaniel and part cannonball, but she figured that if they were going to get anywhere it was up to her. As she got out the butter cookies she brought up their last meeting, how long had it been. She tried to keep them headed in the right direction.

"Ahh, Nellie. I guess I might as well 'fess up. The night after I met you, she called me."

"Still something there, huh?"

"Something—something won't give, yeah. Oh it's all on my side, whatever it is, I know that much. I know on her side, she's just being nice to me."

"Oh? You just have a birthday or something?"

That got him grinning differently. And the wheels were turning on her end as well, the hangup about his ex might come in handy some time, with Fitzie if not with the guy himself. But then: "Don't try to be funny, Nellie. I'm the funny guy here. I practically get paid to be funny."

And with that he was off on a riff about his work, explaining how the job had been part of the trouble between him and his wife. Not that he wasn't sending other signals at the same time.

Whenever he paused, he'd stroke his chest, slowly. She still noticed his belly, that old-folkie turtleneck didn't fool her. But she played along, hooking an arm over the back of her chair and keeping her chin high. Look me over. And yet she couldn't be sure that was really what they had going here. Talking about the job and the wife was a way to get intimate, sure. But since when did a guy on the make ever come on so soft and nervous?

"Believe me, Nellie, I'm so sorry my wife never heard what I was trying to tell her." Shrug, stroke the chest. "See, what other people would call being selfless? I would say that was all just part of my job. I mean just sticking to the rules of my job, I have to be selfless." At the Drop By she'd liked his hands; now they seemed faggy. "That's politics, right? According to the rules, you have to be this very nice, funny guy." This was the second time Nellie had noticed him whipping round his wrist, snap snap, trying to spin his watch back face-up.

"And someone like my wife, she kept expecting that one day I'd break down and start screaming. Like I really hated welfare mothers or something. I swear to God, she *wanted* me to start screaming at the end."

Welfare mothers? By the time the conversation shifted to Nellie's job, she wasn't sure how to play it. He'd started working his lips, smiling then pouting, but by now the sex question seemed like the last thing she should be worrying about. A parent couldn't take home much above zero if they wanted to get the Supplemental. She told him the truth, she didn't make anything near those girls at the university.

"Most weeks," she said, "I carry my keys in my pocket just so I can feel a little *weight* in there." But the joke did nothing for her, her chin had dropped. Here was the hard part. Laying out how little she had and how much she needed—her grin had gone mean, smoke-sour—it threw her so much that at first she missed what Ernie was saying.

"So, Nellie, you don't even have to worry about that part of it."

"What?" Though she believed she understood already, her head had come up again. "Ernie, are you saying what I think you're saying?"

160

"Well actually, by the time you finished showing me around I'd made my decision on that part. I'll sign the approvals before, ah, before we're through here."

"S.S.I.?"

"You'll continue to receive the full amount. Sure."

Nellie got a little careless. She grinned so wide and happily that it gave him something on her, this was supposed to be business. Her hands wandered too. She was patting his forearm, total turnaround from fifteen seconds ago, while she fumbled her thanks. "Well well, Ernie, well hey. . . ." Though of course the man didn't have the kind of reactions you'd expect. It all just seemed to make him nervous. "Nellie, come on, I only wanted to get that part behind us." That part? "Oh yeah?" she asked. "Well what'd you have in mind for the *next* part?" Why not, after the rest had been so herky-jerky-crazy? Ernie started wringing his watch into place again. "Ahh, I mean I just wanted to put your mind at rest, so far as the state's concerned—"

At which the dog got into it. Lurid couldn't take it any longer: Ernie held a cookie in his watch-hand. The mutt sprang and got one of the saucers as well. A blur of hair and teeth, a *splatch* of plastic, and then Ernie was out of his chair with his fingers curled at his neck and coffee seeping down his thighs.

"I know you weren't expecting me," he said.

And she was giggling, making it worse. She wouldn't have had the strength to haul the animal to the door if the place hadn't been so small.

"Lurid," she managed, "*Lurid!* Get out of here." Ernie trailed behind her, so close that when she shut the door on the dog she hardly had room to stand.

"You have a dog named Lourdes?" he asked. "Like the place in France, Lourdes?"

The real laughter, too much for an answer. She needed to hang on his neck a moment, a long moment, maybe an entire minute or so regaining her breath while in the contact from neck to knee she made clear to him that before he left today they were going to have to see this thing through. Too fast? She didn't want to hear it, they weren't in high school. She could put the impulse in its place— Red-haired Indica, sure sure—and likewise Ernie insisted that they sign the forms first. He even came out with this incredibly formal black pen. She had to ask, "Richard Nixon ever own one of these?" He laughed so wildly she was afraid he'd break her hash-pipe. She went back with that thing, pretty little Moroccan cherry wood. But as he choked down his next hit she believed she had her project for the man: "Who's the funny guy here, Ernie? You think you're the smart mouth? Well we'll just see, we'll just see." The wimps who nitpicked about moving too fast, they thought control could mean only one thing. They didn't realize how far a person could go.

He charmed their pants off at the Drop By. Some nights it might be just her and Fitzie and a couple of the lodge types, the kind of men who didn't even bother to unbutton their jackets, and still as soon as Ernie hit the scene he'd make it seem like a party. The game everyone liked best was New York vs. Out West.

"Black *bars*, Ernie? You sayin' you actually walked right into bars that had nothin' but black people in 'em?"

"It's all right. I had my welfare checks to protect me."

"Ernie . . . are you tellin' me people actually talk when they eat a meal, back there? They actually sit around the dinner table and *talk?*"

"That's right, guys. Sometimes when I'm in a restaurant out here I start looking around for the sign. You know, the sign. 'Quiet Please. People Eating.'"

Yes, it appeared to be happening just the way she'd set it up. A thing of one-liners, breezing along on the culture shock. The word Nellie used was *assimilation*. "When he realizes he's not the only smart mouth to make it across the Great Divide," she told Fitzie, "then he'll move on." In this way too she could justify him buddying up to Wade. Now and again Ernie picked up the boy at school, and after dinner they sat talking basketball. The two of them had even established a running argument. Ernie claimed that pro ball was the only kind that mattered, and of course the only organizations that really knew what they were doing were Boston and Philadelphia (though she was over the sink pretending not to listen, Nellie had to grin; God she could see his lines coming so clearly sometimes). Wade meantime pumped for the college game. And if Ernie insisted on talking the pros, hey, how about those *Lakers?* Assimilation. Ernie bought himself a decent pair of hiking boots and replaced his over-the-shoulder bag with a Beaver orange backpack. "The man's sure getting with the program," Fitzie said. "Zip, zip."

Nonetheless all of this left Nellie once more with trouble she didn't know how to talk about. Zip, zip was the *problem*. She'd been sleeping with the man how long now, three weeks? And already he was out buying a new outfit. He was playing Papa, he was asking to meet her friends. In fact when it became clear that Nellie didn't have the kind of friends he was after—no one so close; no one who'd drop over and stay late—the result was something like a fight. Something like. What else should she call it when, after a couple nights of it, she was left combing all these quips and turns of phrase out of her overworked nerves? But when you were actually talking to the guy, it seemed he'd hardly laid a hand on you. Just, suddenly she would realize that he'd worked her job into every conversation. Her "so-called job." But this had gotten started at the Drop By after all; if he was so upset about her working he could have reported it the first time her name came across his desk. Instead, he came hinting and fluttering around. "If someone back at the office wanted to kick up a fuss, about your so-called job. . . ." Eyebrows up, significant pout. The first time Nellie fully understood what he was saying, she went straight for the heavy artillery.

"What if *this* got out?" she shouted.

She'd been bent over, lighting the incense candle; now she gestured round the bedroom with it, agitated enough to put out the flame. "What about that, hey Ernie? Think they'd like to know you've been popping one of your cases?"

She should have known. Ernie laughed. He took the matches from her and stood unnecessarily close, getting one of his own hands around the squat red candle as he relit it.

"Popping?" he said. "Last woman I did this with, we were consummating our marriage. Now it's just, popping?"

Admit it: she hadn't known too many like him. Most guys she'd been with, the first time they argued, that was the death knell. In fact most guys she'd been with couldn't argue. Their emotional baggage was too much, kick over just one piece and next thing you know the guy would be stamping off to his truck. Nellie would watch them from her stoop, still mouthing their sawed-off insults after the ignition had roared on. But Ernie now, watching him argue was like watching him eat. Only the good leaf lettuce, see Nellie, and God not *that* mustard; try some Nance's. Or: see taste the *beef*, Nellie, you don't have to have money to eat decent Chinese. You've just got to start the marinade the night before. She'd told him that Wade was the reason they could never meet at his place, when in fact what stopped her was this, his absolute killer instinct for quibbling. Sifting the facts through his active fingers and turning up yes partly this, but also partly that. Yes just a so-called job, but also maybe some serious trouble over in the Albany office. Quips and turns of phrase. On his turf, Nellie figured she'd be overwhelmed.

Even the way he'd wriggled out of the shouting match over the candle, the wisecrack comparing his ex to Nellie—that too started pitching around uncomfortably. Not till afterwards of course, when she stood by the sink trying to keep it quiet, using a washcloth rather than taking a shower. Then she started to think: on the one hand consummating a marriage, on the other hand merely popping. Who *was* this guy? Since when was that their only choice? Even her lawyer hadn't gotten in such subtle digs and irks.

Not that Nellie was completely in the dark about him. She'd seen some things like this before. "I mean," she told Fitzie, "it is so obvious that he's just gotten a divorce. It's like a goddamn billboard. He has to keep punching your buttons because otherwise he feels helpless."

After hours again, Johnny Walker Red, Fitzie nodded but kept on setting up tomorrow's menu, slipping letters into the new board.

"He just feels—totally helpless," Nellie said. "That's what makes divorced guys such a *drag*."

Fitzie only snorted. She'd moved on to the numbers, and Nellie found the red digits aggravating somehow, a reminder of the night before. Ernie had inadvertently put a foot through one of the sliding cupboard doors at the head of the bed. The trailer panelling was nothing but pressed cardboard, cheap and lightweight as the Drop By menu, and the bedroom walls were warped to boot. Though last night, none of that had bothered her any. On the contrary, Nellie had gone ahead and kicked in the other door. Howling with laughter, forgetting even Wade for a moment.

"You know, I think about his ex sometimes," she said. "That poor woman." Her sneer felt natural, Fitzie's snort was more satisfying.

"Because I mean, he hasn't really sprung her on me yet. Oh I've got the basics, everybody feels guilty. Sure. But I'd like to really— I'd like to get my hands on where the real breakdown was. Then I'd know something."

"I don't see how it'll ever get that far."

Fitzie had gone back to the other box. Fingering up black letters, it took her a while to realize Nellie was staring. "Well I just don't see it, Nellie. You already got what you wanted."

Nellie got both arms up on the bar. "Did I ask him to put the papers through on me?"

"Nellie, come on. Everybody knows—"

"Did I *ask* him to? Did I?"

"What are you getting so upset about? I'm just saying you already got what you were in it for."

"Fitzie, the last time I asked a man for money was when Wade was born. And that's the last time I'm going to."

"So? So that's just what I'm saying. This whole thing started because you needed some way to get through Christmas. And now that you got it, if you're not going to ask for anything else I don't see how you're ever going to find out about his ex-wife. Not Nellie Nails."

"Oh, so now you're going to tell me what I should do. You. Fitzie Faithful."

Fitzie's look shortened. She tongued her front teeth, *thit*, and returned to the toy-like letters and prices.

Still it was another week at least, three or four more times with the incense candle going and Ernie leaving his curls all over her neck and chest, before Wade gave her the kick she needed in order to make a move. Wade, as always. Before she'd started tending bar, same thing, she'd needed his go-ahead. Mom I'm *old enough*. This time, Ernie offered to take the boy Christmas shopping in Portland, and Wade just couldn't handle it. He'd already taken on managing the basketball JV's, something that had come out of all that sports-talk with the man.

"And Christmas shopping on top of that?" she told Fitzie. "In Portland? I mean, I shouldn't even have waited till they brought Wade home from that exhibition game. As soon as Ernie sprang that one on us I should have said no, this was getting much too serious. Too serious on Ernie's end I mean."

At least tonight Fitzie wasn't diddling around with the menu board. Nellie had let her know to begin with that it was some heavy-duty news, and the other waitress hardly broke eye contact to light a cigarette.

"But I blame myself, Fitzie. I blame myself. They had to bring Wade home, first basketball game of the year and he's like totally stressed out—he had to go through that before I realized the kind of pressure we were under."

The worst was how the boy tried to giggle his way through it. M-Mom, I'm afraid there's been an accident. This, when she could see he'd had to borrow one of the team's sweat pants for the ride home. Of course for months he'd been warning her that he wasn't going to haul around that stupid waste bag all the time any more. In front of the coach, Nellie had lifted Wade's chin, checked out his eyes. In fact she would have taken him off the team then and there, if it hadn't been for that coach.

"I mean Fitzie, who does that guy think he *is?* Big shot high-school junior varsity basketball coach." It made no difference that she'd suffered through his kind of thing before, all that smug I'm-so-sorry. You never got used to how people wanted to score points off the Bad Girl. "To hear him talk, you'd think he had a hotline to George Bush himself."

And Wade, well. This was all about him anyway, right? "The last thing he told me before he went to bed, the first thing he said when he got up—Wade really wants to stay on that team. So I figure I know the boy, it's worth the risk." But when it came to going out with Ernie, she'd laid down the law. No way.

166

"I mean I even called Ernie at the office to let him know. I even left a *message*, so the other people there would see it." She shook her head, crick-crick against the long night's ache.

"So that's your heavy-duty news? That's not so—"

"Hold on, hold on. It gets better." Fitzie was right, though; this wasn't coming out nearly hard enough. "I mean that man—I might as well be trying to stop a fucking bulldozer. Swear to God. The next time Ernie comes over, the very next time, he starts in trying to get around me." Ernie had suggested another kind of trip, all three of them together. "Some kind of benefit concert down in Eugene. I didn't get it all, something for the homeless." Still, that much had only left her worn down, worn and unsure; she hadn't gotten angry with the man till Wade had gone to bed. "See, once Wade's out of the way, the guy starts pulling all this *nostalgia* stuff on me. You know. Like, 'Some of your old crowd should be at the concert, Nellie.' Like, 'Some of the people you took drugs with, Nellie. They should be there.' I mean, he was asking for it after he said that."

Fitzie kept her look set, drawing smoke.

"Some of the people I took *drugs* with, Jesus Christ on a crutch. If there's one thing that really fries my ass . . ."

"What'd you pull on him, Nellie?"

"Oh." She fought down a shiver, pretending to shrug. "Wade's father came back through town a couple days ago. Him and me we went to the old motel. Then after that, you know me, Fitzie. I had to stick by my rules."

And she was able to look the other waitress in the face, another taste of Johnny Walker was all it took. The signs were good, just what Nellie had hoped for. Plainly the delay in getting to the point hadn't cost her, Fitzie was going through such changes. First she was shocked ("You told Ernie? You *told* him?"), then she was smart. The cigarette and the shot glass seemed suddenly much too delicate for such a big unstable body. Nellie got some of the old hardball payoff, especially after a fresh mouthful.

"Nellie Nellie girl. Sometimes you scare me."

"I can't out-talk the guy, Fitzie. I have to give him that, he's one guy I just can't out-talk."

Some of the old payoff, sure. But also the other woman's face sagged so badly by two in the morning. Had Nellie actually given her such a tumble, or was it just that Fitzie's eyes had gone pouchy, her neck was starting to flap? "Nellie Nellie," she was saying. "Whoa. Sometimes I think you should live up in those hills. I mean it. You should take Wade out of school before he gets too big to leave you, and you should go hide out up there with the growers. You know who I mean, the people up there who sell sensamilla. You went with Rusty to the *motel?*"

Nellie lowered her eyes but kept her grin fixed.

"How'd he take it, anyway?"

Through the red liquor, it looked as if her fingers were broken. Still the shrug came easy: "Ernie? You notice he didn't bring his act in here tonight." Then, drinking, she glared across the ungainly dim lounge and allowed herself to sink at last into the low-grade soreness that had nagged at her since she'd come in. Such a dud joint. Those lamp-cages along the ceiling, filthy with grease, the lamest kind of play for class. Especially combined with the cheesecake shots for Red Hook Ale, frat-house stuff. You'd think there'd be some decent highway trade at a place along Route 20. But it was over a year now since Richter had made them wear these damn tit-shakers, and the most interesting guy who'd stopped to talk—she admitted it, sank into it—was Ernie. How could she help but miss him? On her break tonight, when she'd called Wade, same thing. Tonight when he'd started in on his usual round of cracks about her boyfriends, it'd stung so much she couldn't even think to change the subject. High school had turned him into such a wise guy. And much as she needed that smart mouth sometimes, tonight as she'd listened she hadn't been able to think. She hadn't been able to tell the boy that Ernie most likely wouldn't be coming by any more. She'd sat with the phone at her neck, buffing her nails with a bar rag, working till the red polish was hot. Nellie didn't like to dwell on the sex in these things. She didn't like the idea that at the heart of all her machinations and teases there was nothing but a few soaked minutes of wildcat clutches and grunts. Kicking out the cupboard doors. More soreness just to think of it tonight. But then Nellie herself had been the one to keep a running tab on Ernie's performances, so regular that now she could probably remember every tumble. If you assigned a rating, it helped you maintain control.

So how was she supposed to handle it when the next morning, Sunday morning, Ernie showed up to make brunch? As if nothing had happened, sure. Except of course he'd come banging at the door before ten o'clock. While Nellie stumbled to get it she was fighting off paranoia, the FBI or a government crackdown. Ernie brushed past her and went into his setup like a pinball, so quick that at first she didn't notice how carefully he was checking the place out.

"Don't worry," she croaked. "Nobody else spent . . ."

But before she could finish Wade hauled himself out of his bedroom, skipping the wheelchair because he didn't want to miss anything. Nellie settled on a kitchen chair. She hardly glanced at the pack of Camels Ernie tossed onto her place-mat. Keep the priorities straight, check the boy out.

Like most of the c.p. victims she'd seen, Wade had a handsome head. She could read his eyes so well because they were so sensitive, with the kind of wide, slow lids that would be sexy on another man. His nose was large enough to give the rest a center, and while Wade hadn't stopped grinning since he'd seen that it was Ernie, his lips were so bright and defined that he didn't look goofy. When she'd finished her onceover—the strain told: the skin under one eye was twitching and that lid drooped—Nellie rose and got his juice and vitamins from the fridge. She took one of his unbreakable cups from the rack and fitted it into the boy's better hand; she made sure to slip the index and middle fingers inside the handle together.

Ernie kept up the hustle. The radio had gone on, some bang-the-can blues out of a college station somewhere, and he worked around Nellie and Wade as if the kitchen were house-sized. Even singeing a finger on the coffeepot didn't stop him. What sort of a person wakes up ready to rock? Wade made a crack about the burn throwing off his aim, and in another minute they were trading ball scores. Just *how* was Nellie supposed to handle it? She took a cup of Ernie's "earthquake bean"—Italian and Maxwell House, at least she'd had it before. The eggs were steaming spiky with dill in front of her and she was working up to them, nearly done with her first cigarette, when Nellie realized the conversation had gotten round to Mom.

"Wouldn't you like it if Mom here went back to college?" Ernie was saying. "Wouldn't you like to say, 'My Mom the bachelor?'"

Wearily she made a face. "Ernie, do we have to go through this?"

"Go through this? Gnarly girl, go through *this?*" God he was hungry for an argument. "How can you call this anything after what you've been through for the last ten years?"

"Ernie," the best she could manage was trying to be reasonable. "You just got finished with one catastrophe. What have you got to prove, that you have to go straight into another?"

"Mom," Wade said. "Come on, never mind that stuff now. Tell him about what happened with your comp teacher."

"I can imagine." Ernie opened the Sports, flat-faced.

Nellie had to laugh, the nasty thought starting to warm her up at last. "Oh Ernie. Honestly. You think I—"

"*Mo-om.* Come on. Tell him." Wade's robe-sleeve flopped over his hand when he tried to point. "And Ernie, you listen. Mom tells a great story when she gets into it."

Okay, made as much sense as anything else this morning. Nellie's comp teacher. "Talk about having something to prove. The guy wore a coat and tie and like, serious dress slacks in June. In June. I mean I know he can't be making more than 12 K a year." She noticed that while Ernie kept his eyes on the scores, he'd held one page so long that the butter on his burnt finger had started soaking into the print. "And then one day he starts telling the whole class about how he and his wife are trying to have a baby." That got his head up.

Wade was giggling. "Listen, Ernie. The best part is when she starts foaming at the mouth."

"Right in front of the whole class." Nellie liked that last crack herself; she figured she could risk a piece of bacon. "I had to wonder, was this Writing 121 or Sex Education?

"I mean, imagine if a guy like that walked into the Drop By. You'd see through him right away, right? But up there in front of the blackboard, dress slacks in June. The guy actually comes across like he's somebody who knows something. And he stands there, and he has the nerve to tell us that he and his wife have it all planned. I mean I'm sitting right there and he has the nerve to say that if they don't have a kid in the next year they're not going to have one at all, because it would increase the percentile risk of disability. Increase the *percentile risk!*"

Wade was laughing, Ernie grinning. He'd worked a hand up under his turtleneck, scratching for effect.

"Very next class I brought in Wade. Oh yeah, I hauled Wade in there front and center and I said, 'This is my son.'"

"It was *beautiful*," Wade crowed. "Really Ernie, I wish you could have seen it. Every time the guy tried to write on the blackboard he misspelled another word."

Now Ernie had begun laughing, Wade had got him into it. And she'd talked enough to blow off a little anger, so at last Nellie caught on to what the boy had been doing. Talking slick—"the guy." Setting up the rules for this part of the conversation and then following them through. Wade was even playing along with Ernie's touch-game, his better hand under his robe. Grinning smart and happy, father and son. And so here it came, a classic mybaby flash. Nellie never got used to them. Start with mybaby, mybaby and somehow in the same moment see him in the computer lab or behind the biggest desk at a government agency; start with picturing his disease as if the muscles drained from his arms and legs had to be dragged behind him in a sack, rotting and bleeding forever, but at the same time imagine a day when the c.p. might be nothing more than an offhand chuckle, a one-liner like "It was harder on my mother than it was on me." Grinning smart and happy.

Her eggs had gone cold, that helped. But after her second rubbery forkful Nellie realized that the two men were still at it: get Mom back to school. She needed another cigarette.

"No way Jose." But she hadn't meant to hit Ernie with the match, she'd been aiming for the sink.

Wade adjusted his lapel, his stalky fingers hooking the terrycloth expertly. "This isn't just you, Ernie. You should know that. The last couple Christmases, Mom was saying she was going to join the Communist Party."

"Ganging up on me only makes it worse. Look Wade, this guy is a *loser*."

"M-m-mom!" She felt his look in her spine. "All we're saying is, you did g-g-good that year you were in school. When you got that A in P-poly Sci, you p-put the exam up on the f-f-fridge."

She'd dropped her forehead onto her fists, but now the tabletop itself seemed to aggravate her. Jesus what clutter, a pepper mill and a jar of British jam. Wade had actually fallen for this?

"Tired of the same old grind?" Ernie said. "Of dead-end jobs that get you nowhere?" The rap was so-so at best, but Wade was laughing already. "Well have you ever considered a future in—"

The knock at the door saved him. Saved him, positively: she'd hooked her fingers under the coffeepot trivet. But the aggro was so zingy in her by then that when it turned out to be Wade's father on the stoop, thrusting roses in her hand and brassing his way through hello-may-I-come-in, Nellie could only stand and stare while the man kept going on whatever had brought him this far and brushed past her into the house. Wade's father, Rusty. His guitar-player's body still too rangy for a place this size. Plus he'd handed her these impossible cherry-red roses (fakes of course: paper was the best you could get on a Sunday), plus he carried three stacked, hefty presents for Wade. Somehow he made room for these on the kitchen table. Nellie couldn't really see, and she couldn't pick up what kind of excuses he was giving Wade and Ernie either. The back of the man's good London Fog or whatever blocked her view, and with the door open behind her the rain was too loud. Jesus God, had she *asked* for such a Sunday morning? The weather on her back was cold, as well; she had nothing but panties and a t-shirt under her robe.

At last the father turned, one hand nervous up and down his tie.

"You can call me all the nasty names you want," he said. "I'm not running scared any more."

Nellie couldn't trust herself. She lowered the flowers and tried to get the whole picture clear.

"I haven't seen the boy in five years, Nellie. And I was still a jerk back then."

But his smile was rickety. He didn't know how to play it except as the Gangster of Love, his old never-fails. Meantime Ernie had made himself unreadable, his eyes on Rusty's back and his hands steepled at his mouth. Wade however was nothing so predictable, a herky-jerk cut from a silent movie. No color in the boy's face at all. Lips and tongue and erratic fragments of teeth. Nellie didn't realize she'd begun to move towards him till the father flinched.

"Let me just talk to the boy, please Nel—" But the man had let her get too close. She had the knot of that tie up in his gullet, growling *get out of here get out of here.* No question she could push him around. The man's face had gone red and childish, all she felt of his chest was shirt and tie. She could turn him and drive him right back out into the rain. Except then Ernie was up, coming round the table playing peacemaker.

"Nellie, come on. Lighten up. The man is trying, here."

"You shut up too."

But she'd been distracted, the father'd had a moment to regroup. "Nellie, please." She felt his upper body against her forearm now, his fingers at her wrist. "There's the Scrooge movie over in Corval—"

"Shut *up!*" She saw Wade had begun to splutter. "Shut up and *let him speak!*"

So the dog erupted through the open door, the woman who fed him was in trouble. Nellie and Rusty weren't fast enough letting go of each other. They fell together against the table. The father's gift-wrapped presents, Ernie's Brunch Deluxe—Nellie went into a clench against the crash. She shouted, cracked her hip, and groaned. But the rest of the noise didn't seem like much, only plastic and the dying noise of flatware, buh-*dingle*, buh-dingle. Cardboard walls. Then she found herself wet, coffee grounds somewhere under the robe. But by now her muscles had relaxed and the only worry she had room for was that Wade hadn't used the wheelchair this morning. By the time she'd heaved herself over Lurid and the father (the animal was too much for a man with coat and tie in the way), the boy had already gone into a fit.

The nearest thing to hand was a newspaper. Wade sprawled across the kitchen, he'd kicked off the grill at the foot of the fridge and his head was almost in the opposite corner, bucking so raggedly that he'd flattened one of the paper roses. The hands trembled like a puppy doing Beg. Nellie fitted her knees against his shoulders, bracing his head between her folded legs. As she rolled the paper tight enough to gag him she noticed that it was scores and photos, the sports, and her thinking skipped to Ernie a moment. She realized he'd be doing something helpful like getting the dog out of the way. With that she was furious again. She put it into the effort of prying Wade's chin down, *who gives a fuck about Ernie*, till at last she jammed the scrolled newsprint between his teeth. As usual she couldn't bear to watch the boy's eyes. They became something different during a seizure, black somehow. Impossible color, it meant she made no difference, she fluttered useless and dithery over the surface of his need. Nellie tried concentrating instead on the gag. No better: spatters of blood off the lips were seeping already across the letters and numbers. Blood, another bottom line. It set off spasms of fright, actual shakes, even while she told herself to stop being paranoid. The ink had gotten into a cut. The scores from a damn ball game had poisoned him. And how could she have done this to him, *what a shit she was*; the blood was as hard on her as the dark in his eyes. Never mind that she actually helped the boy. Sweating so much her breasts itched, groaning with the effort of holding the gag—never mind. Nellie knew a fake when she saw one. She could spot a liar coming a mile down the road.

But now as she tried to find someplace else to focus, she saw that Wade's hands had settled onto his chest. The trembles were draining down his wrists, his neck, and she risked a look at his eyes. Flat and unconscious. His legs lay limp enough for Ernie to fold them away from one of the fallen chairs.

"Get away from him!" she screamed. "Don't you *touch* him!"

The rage surprised her as well. She dropped her chin, eased out the paper and saw that the boy's tongue was unhurt. But there was Rusty, arms spread against the stove front; just catching sight of him was all it took to set her off again.

"What're you staring at? What're you so *scared* of?"

He couldn't hide it. All those years of working indoors had left him so pasty that when he blushed it was like neon.

"This is what you're after, right?" She cradled Wade's head, still glaring at the father. "This is what you want to buy with your fucking roses."

"Nellie, it's over now." Ernie said. "It's over, okay? You just relax, lighten up now. I'll call the hospital."

"Yeah it's over. Yeah that's exactly *it*, that it's over." Revving like she hadn't felt since she'd given up amphetamines. She found Ernie tucked in the corner by the phone, but she hardly saw the breakfast wreckage, all she noticed was the stench. Wade's stench: of course a seizure meant you lost control of everything.

"If it's *over*, why are you calling the hospital? Hey Ernie? What the hell *difference* does it make, being such a nice guy? Oh you useless fucking phony. We know all about each other's games, don't we? I mean you're such a good committee member, you're filling in all the forms. Nice nice nice, pick pick pick! Except one day finally even your *wife* had to realize, it's a goddamn *act!*"

Forget the phone. Ernie was whipping his hand round, trying to wring his watch back into place.

"I mean, of course you wouldn't want to burden yourself with something like this." She was worried she would hurt Wade's head, she knotted her fists in her t-shirt. "Such a nice guy, you wouldn't have the *guts* to slow down for a minute and take on something like this." She nodded towards the space between her legs, but she was tearing up so fast that she couldn't be sure where she was pointing.

"Oh, you think we don't both know all about it? I know exactly how scared you are, you're scared shitless. I know every fucking one of your empty fucking *games*."

Then it was shirt to face, she didn't want her bawling to wake Wade. And who cared what the men saw? She was stained with coffee and egg anyway. It only bothered her to hear them talking, making decisions. The men in charge. But something had really given way now; it took all Nellie's strength just to back away from Wade, just to find a place against the nearest wall. When she heard the father leaving, the click and rustle of his London Fog, she couldn't lift her face. After that it was nothing but the radio for a while, some grindstone vocal, Well well well well wahwl. Tears spattered Nellie's lap and her aches made her think of her mother's arthritis.

Nobody touched her till the outburst was pretty much past. Nonetheless when she felt a hand at her shoulder, she scrunched up tighter still.

"Ernie," she gasped, "I chose to live this way. I wanted to live this way."

"It's me, Mom," Wade said. "And heh heh, I guess I got you all that time, hey? Hey? Ernie my man—whoo! Well I guess now you know the way it can happen."

Nellie sat up too fast, spots in her eyes. But she knew already what the boy was doing.

"I mean I'm sorry you had to see it, Ernie. My man. But hey, you know about those hormonal changes. Heh-heh-heh-heh. The doctor told me, he said the early teens are the worst."

Trying to breeze along, talking like it never touched him. Her head cleared, she saw the newsprint had left some bad stains and the front of his shirt was filthy with grape juice. But the boy's grin was strictly Elvis.

"Hey really, it's lightweight. It'll probably just, dry up and blow away by the time I get out of high school."

Nellie didn't have the strength. Yes this was the last straw, this was what it felt like. She got her first good look at the morning's ruin. The table's cast-iron base was upended, the frayed rubber mouth of the juice pitcher still dripping purple. The works at the bottom of the fridge were spattered with grounds, and the dog had left jam-prints everywhere. Now how dear God was she supposed to start with Wade? Someone like her, useless and dithery and fake, a fake—where was she going to get the energy? It must have been simple relief, then, that had Nellie smiling like such a Mongoloid a minute later.

Smiling so widely she tasted the morning's freshness: the door had stood open long enough to air the place out. Plus she was having the craziest thoughts. Nellie thought that now she'd like to have some breakfast, or how about if they let Wade open one of his presents early? Herky-jerky-crazy, it had to be relief. But though she believed she had a handle on it, Nellie couldn't stop, not even when it became obvious that a grin like hers was no help to Ernie.

The man was doing his best to hang in there, after all. He'd crossed
the room and cut off the radio. He'd found some paper towel and
squatted down to start the cleanup, bending under one of Wade's
arms, looking rather burly and heavyweight in contrast to the boy's
spidery pale reach. And Ernie's talk was quiet, serious. But there
she sat grooving away, fingering her robe together over her own
outstretched legs and settling more comfortably against the wall.
Not at all the kind of support he needed.

At the Drop By Cafe Christmas was another loss. Come New
Year's, Richter decided that the only way out was to have all the
girls wear something more revealing. His timing wasn't any good
either. The owner called everybody in late on a Monday, when
Wade needed a ride home from basketball and Nellie had already
agreed to run a special errand with Ernie. She worked it out. The
boy was taken care of and Ernie was with her in the bus. But then
she walked into the Drop By and found her boss tacking up a
poster of some cheerleaders.

The photo had been extensively retouched; the first thing she
thought of was the sheeny hard-rubber cars she used to buy for
Wade. These girls wore black skirts crotch-high. Plus, of course,
the same damn red leotards.

Yet with all the other shakeups going on that Monday, it was
Fitzie who got to her most. While Nellie stood gaping at the poster,
the other waitress was already redoing the buttons on her jacket—
pretty flashy stuff itself, since Jack had joined the Elks' over the
holidays.

"People," Fitzie said, "before I wear black and red like that,
somebody's going to be black and blue."

And she gave Nellie a look, and she walked. For a moment there
Nellie couldn't see past the word "Auxiliary" stitched across the
jacket's back: of course the Elks' was men-only.

It was all she could talk about when she got back out to the bus.
She didn't even make sure the other woman's car was gone. That
Fitzie was hard as *nails*, Ernie; she didn't care *who* she hurt. The
man pursed his lips. He waited till she'd stopped kicking the

floorboards and pounding the steering wheel. He went on waiting, tapping his fingertips against the window. But she couldn't pull out either. A VW this old needed a minute to idle during the rainy season.

Finally he asked if this was about the errand they'd planned for this afternoon. Was she really that anxious?

He whisked his spread hand side to side across the glass, clearing a sloppy crescent in the condensation. "I mean if the trip's such a problem for you, babe—if it's going to make you throw a fit—well hey." They could skip it. They could go pick up Wade instead. Or maybe she had a better idea: he showed her the old gym-class smile. When Nellie was slow responding, Ernie reminded her that the boy's father had left a message at the Social Security office. Rusty was only too glad to have some more time with Wade. He and the boy were cruising the music stores, looking for sheets Wade could use with the new synthesizer.

She geared up. "Fitzie's got nothing to do with today's deal," Nellie said. "And besides, when you've told a guy you're going to buy some of his sensamilla, you can't just not show up. The guy might be an outlaw, but he's an outlaw for keeps. For real, Ernie. If we wimp out on a deal like this, he's liable to sic the Dobermans on us."

Ernie wouldn't back off. On the first straightaway he lit a cigarette for her and took advantage of the eye contact. This woman shook you up pretty bad, babe? Nellie allowed her spine to sag. Okay, okay. Ernie *Hernia*. She explained that at one time it had looked as if she and Fitzie were really going to get close.

"I realize now that she's not like me. I mean, whatever I do with men, it'll always be a joke to her. 'The Lady in Red' or some such bullshit. She'll always think of me as the lady in red. When what I need is a person who can see the games for what they are."

"But you two nearly got close?"

Nellie's eyebrows came up slowly. "Ernie, I almost told her about the drugs I took when I was pregnant. Honestly, almost. I mean of course you're right about that, we can never know for certain. Even the amphetamines, we can never know. But Wade's sick, Ernie. Wade is very sick. I only got around to telling you about those drugs just last week."

Ernie nodded, spoke again. She didn't catch it because she was turning off the highway, fighting the transmission. The windshield quivered and the suspension was all chirps and squeaks. But Nellie got the message. She smiled when he patted her thigh. Nonetheless she wasn't prepared for how fast Ernie changed the subject. A minute later, not even a minute later, he seemed to be talking as if any feelings about Fitzie were way behind them. He was asking about her thing next week, up in Salem. Nellie wished she didn't have to keep her eyes on the road. She frowned and smiled, shook her head.

"Testifying for the Senate task force?" He was so loud that, for the first time in weeks, she noticed how much he still sounded like he came from New York.

"The disabled-children task force, next week Nellie? Up at the State House? You know if you actually go through with that, someone like Fitzie might not understand."

"Oh, I'm going to go *through* with it." Okay. He wasn't telling her to shrug anything off. "They think they can just go on the way they have, they think they can just drop by and tell me how to run my life? No way. I'm going to testify. From now on I'm going after them."

Ernie nodded so hard she could feel it in the seat-springs. "Yeah babe. Yeah, good." Nonetheless his look remained serious. "But see, Nellie, see. It's like you were saying earlier about games— politics can also seem like a game. Same as sex, exact same problem. And you're like already an outlaw to Fitzie about sex; just wait'll she sees you getting into politics. You think that won't be way too heavy for her? I mean when I give someone like Fitzie one of my contracts, I want to say, Look! This is for real! They've got your whole *life* right here between the black lines! But she just sits there trying to figure out what the trick is."

"Well I realize she's just trying to protect herself. I guess I can learn to handle that."

More nodding. "It's not like it doesn't make me crazy too, Nellie. I mean, we've gone from ocean to ocean here. We've shucked our whole former lives. We're outsiders, all of us. Outsiders. And still we all go on trying to play the same old pissant games inside the same old black lines."

She nodded, then shook her head more firmly. She hoped he understood. They were well off 20 now, out of the Valley now, rocketing up into the hills along an old logging road. Ridiculous trying to hold a conversation in such rough going. The bigger oaks and birches closed overhead, and this early after New Year's the sky was nothing but murk anyway. Murk, webbed here and there with darker clusters of dangling tattered moss. She may have glimpsed bright trillium fingertips, or the spastic knots of a dormant wild rose. But by and large roadside details were lost under a rain so fine and steady you noticed it only when the clay along the edges of the way ahead caved outward to fall among the undergrowth. Amazing, trying to do serious relationship work under such conditions. Ernie at least had lightened up. His face was a horror show, good and toothy. But Nellie could barely grin back, the ride was too hard on her breasts. She almost regretted turning in her leotard.

BIOGRAPHICAL NOTE:

John Domini has published fiction in *Paris Review*, *Ploughshares*, and elsewhere, as well as in anthologies. Three of his stories have made Honorable Mention for the Pushcart Prize, and his first collection *Bedlam*, was listed in *Library Journal* as one of the best books on a small press that year. He has placed non-fiction in *GQ*, the *New York Times*, and many other places, and is currently at work on both a novel and a non-fiction project. Grants have come from the National Endowment for the Arts and the Ingram-Merrill Foundation. He has taught at Harvard, Lewis & Clark, and elsewhere, and lives in Portland, Oregon.